'I cannot do what you expect of me.

'I hardly know you, my lord,' Eleanor said. 'I am beginning to admire and respect you, but... I—I would be your friend if you...'

'You would be my friend?' Suleiman's gaze narrowed and he appeared to be considering. 'Why should I need a friend, Eleanor? Do you not think I have many about me who would call themselves my friends?'

'Yes, my lord. Forgive me for my presumption. It was only that we share an interest in ancient manuscripts. I enjoyed our talk when you asked me to help you read them and I would like to do something that would be of use to you. There are other women more skilled in the arts of love. I think I would provide poor sport for you.'

Suleiman nodded, a faint smile curving his mouth. 'You argue convincingly, my lady. Yet I wonder...'

Anne Herries lives in Cambridge but spends part of the winter in Spain, where she and her husband stay in a pretty resort nestled amid the hills that run from Malaga to Gibraltar. Gazing over a sparkling blue ocean, watching the sunbeams dance like silver confetti on the restless waves, Anne loves to dream up her stories of laughter, tears and romantic lovers. She is the author of over thirty published novels.

Recent titles by the same author in Historical Romance®:

THE ABDUCTED BRIDE
ROSALYN AND THE SCOUNDREL

and in The Steepwood Scandal mini-series:

LORD RAVENSDEN'S MARRIAGE
COUNTERFEIT EARL

and in Medical Romance®:

A SPANISH PRACTICE
SARA'S SECRET

CAPTIVE OF THE HAREM

Anne Herries

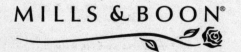

MILLS & BOON®

First published in Great Britain 2002
Harlequin Mills & Boon Limited,
Eton House, 18-24 Paradise Road, Richmond, Surrey TW9 1SR

© Anne Herries 2002

ISBN 0 263 83116 7

Set in Times Roman 10½ on 12 pt.
04-0402-86326

Printed and bound in Spain
by Litografia Rosés S.A., Barcelona

Chapter One

'I shall miss you, my teacher. The days will seem long without the benefit of your words of wisdom, Kasim.'

'I shall be sorry to leave you, Suleiman—the years we have had together have been truly a blessing for me, but the time has come for me to prepare to make my peace with God, my lord. I must go home to my own land to die...'

'Yes, I know. I would not hold you. Go then...and may Allah guide your footsteps to Paradise.'

Suleiman Bakhar felt the sting of the unmanly tears that would shame him as the old man left and he knew that it was for the last time; they would never meet again in this life.

He moved away to gaze down at the gardens of his apartments in his father's palace, his fierce, wild eyes lit by a silver flame in their depths. His expression for those who dared to look was at that moment much that of an untamed creature frustrated by the bars of its cage. The palace of Caliph Bakhar was a perfumed, luxuriously appointed cage—but nevertheless a prison to the man whose spirit wished to soar like the hawks he lavished with so much love and attention.

He was a strong, handsome man, though his features were at times harsh, his mouth capable of looking as cruel as the sharp beaks of his birds of prey. At other times his dark, mysterious eyes could be bright with laughter, and his mouth, slackened by desire, could look soft and deliciously sensuous—as was his voice when he chose to entertain the court with his singing. Now was not one of those times. He was bored, restless, and conscious of a growing anger inside himself that he did not understand. And he was losing the man who had been his teacher for many years, a man he revered and loved almost as a father. His life would be that much the poorer for the teacher's going.

Yet he would not have held Kasim for he loved him as dearly as he loved his own father. He must seek elsewhere to fill the emptiness the teacher's going would leave in his life.

Fluttering about the scented walks of the gardens below, the women of his harem twittered like brightly coloured birds in their scanty clothes as they paraded through sunlit walks. Here and there stone benches were placed in the shade, and the sound of tinkling water from fountains echoed the laughter of the women. They were all aware that Suleiman was watching them from his windows above. He was making his choice and one of them would be sent to his bed that night.

The favoured one would spend the afternoon being pampered by the other women. She would be washed in soft warm water in the baths of the harem, then perfumed lotions and creams would be massaged into her body and hair so that her skin would be smooth for the touch of her master, and finally she would be dressed in the finest silks…layer upon layer of diaphanous materials that he would either remove himself, or instruct her to remove as suited his whim.

It was an honour to be chosen by the Caliph's favourite son, and also a pleasure. Suleiman was young and virile, his body honed to masculine perfection by hours of training in the courtyards with the Janissaries. His love-making was legendary amongst the ladies of the harem, and word had spread to the other harems, some of which had less well-favoured masters, and there were many sighs as envious eyes peered at him from behind pierced screens. It was forbidden for the ladies of one harem to mix with those of another, of course, but it happened—as other forbidden things happened in secret places: things that could bring a swift beating or worse if they were discovered by the eunuchs.

Sometimes, the ladies of the Caliph's court were allowed to watch Suleiman at sport in the great courtyard of the palace. Suleiman delighted in trials of strength with the officers of the Janissaries, and it was very seldom that he lost his bouts.

'He will choose me. I know he will choose me,' Fatima said to Dinazade, who was her chief attendant. As Suleiman's favourite, Fatima had her own rooms and slaves to wait on her. 'He always chooses me.' She gave a satisfied smile as the chief eunuch beckoned to her. 'There, I told you so. Come with me, Dinazade. I must be beautiful to please my lord tonight.'

Suleiman moved back from the window as his chosen partner was led away. He had selected Fatima

again because there was fire in her. Most of the concubines had been given to him as gifts, either by his
father or merchants wishing to gain favour with the
Caliph, and were too obedient to please him. He had
dined too much on honey and wanted something with
more spice.

His features were set like iron, his mouth thinned
to a severe line. Sometimes he felt he would go mad
if he were confined to this idle life for many more
years. He could fight, ride out into the countryside
beyond Constantinople with his hawks or spend the
afternoon pouring over his manuscripts—but none of
these pleasures held any real appeal for him that day.
There was a hungry yearning in his soul—but for
what? Suleiman did not know, unless it was simply
to be free…to travel the world?

Such an idea was forbidden to him. His father had
refused to let him enter the Janissaries in case he
might be injured in a real battle—for his tussles with
the elite guard could only ever be play-acting. No one
would dare to inflict harm on the Caliph's son for fear
of the punishment that would certainly follow—not
from Suleiman, but from his father.

'Your place is here with me,' the Caliph had told
him when he had asked permission to leave and join
the Sultan's personal bodyguard. 'Together we are
strong. I am getting older, Suleiman. Soon you must
prepare to take over from me.'

Caliph Bakhar was known for his wisdom and fair-
ness throughout the empire. It was he who dispensed
justice and kept the common people in order in the
city for his royal master Suleiman the Magnificent.
The Sultan was the supreme ruler of the great
Ottoman Empire, and under his rule the empire had

reached new heights of power and splendour. Suleiman Bakhar had been named for him.

'Forgive me, my lord.' One of the eunuchs approached, his slippered feet making no sound on the marble floors. 'Your honoured father, the great Caliph Bakhar, requests your presence in his apartments.'

Suleiman's eyes were very hawkish as he let them sweep over the fleshy face of the eunuch. It was necessary to have such creatures to guard the women of the harem, but he did not like or trust them. They were sly, calculating creatures—especially this one.

'Very well,' he said curtly. 'I shall attend the Caliph.'

For a moment Suleiman thought he saw a flash of resentment in the eunuch's eyes. Abu was the child of one of his father's older concubines, and perhaps resented the fact that Suleiman and he shared the same blood but were treated in very different ways. Abu's mother had been a Nubian slave and of very little value, while Suleiman's mother had been the daughter of an English nobleman and the Caliph's favourite wife.

Taken from a shipwreck more dead than alive, Margaret Westbury had been presented as a gift to Caliph Bakhar. He had found her fascinating and taken her as his wife, but after she had given him a son he had offered to return her to her homeland. Margaret had preferred to stay on as his chief wife, and though she had been allowed little say in her son's upbringing, she had been allowed to see him twice a week in the gardens.

Yet another soft-footed eunuch with doe-like eyes conducted Suleiman into his father's presence. He fell on his knees before the Caliph as was the custom, but was immediately told to rise.

'The Caliph wished to see his unworthy son?'

'Suleiman is a most worthy son,' Caliph Bakhar replied after the ritual salute. 'I have a problem, Suleiman. The Sultan has made it clear that he is displeased over certain disorders in the city—there was a riot in the streets and the mob passed close to the palace walls.'

'The disturbance was swiftly quelled by the Janissaries.'

'But it should not have been allowed to happen so near the palace,' his father said. 'I have displeased our master, therefore, I must find gifts to regain favour in his eyes.'

'What does my father have in mind?'

'Something of rare beauty—an important piece of Venetian glass, perhaps?'

'Or a beautiful woman?'

'She would have to be an exceptional woman. The Sultan has many Kadins.'

The Kadins or Sultanas were women who had pleased their royal master and were given their own luxurious apartments—much as Fatima was favoured in Suleiman Bakhar's much smaller harem.

'Of course.' Suleiman frowned. 'Does my father wish me to visit the slave markets of Istanbul—or travel to Algiers?'

'You are not to leave our shores,' the Caliph said with a frown. 'We have too many enemies. Send word that we are looking for something special. She must be lovely beyond price and untouched.'

'It would be rare to find such a jewel,' Suleiman

replied. 'Perhaps I should look for some other treasure that would please the Sultan?'

'It would be wise,' the Caliph said, nodding. 'And now, my son—will you hunt with your father? I have a new hawk I would match against your champion.'

'None can match Scheherazade—she flies higher, swifter and her bravery puts all others to shame.' His pupils were lit from within by a silver flame as he spoke of his favourite hawk.

'She is truly a bird to prize above all others. Find a woman as beautiful, clever and brave as your hawk, Suleiman, and the Sultan will forgive me a hundred riots.'

'If such a woman exists, she would be a prize above all others,' Suleiman replied. 'I do not think we shall find this woman, my father—though we search all the markets in the Ottoman Empire!'

Eleanor stood at the top of the cliff gazing out towards the sea. The view was magnificent—sparkling blue water, gently wooded slopes and a dazzling variety of oleander and wisteria. The wisteria had spread from the gardens of the villa behind her, she thought, and inhaled its wonderful perfume.

Such a glorious day and yet her thoughts at that moment were of the house they had left behind five months earlier. It would be autumn in England now, the mists just beginning to curl in from the sea, swirling into the Manor gardens. The Manor was the home she had shared with her father and brother for the first eighteen years of her life, and she doubted she would ever see it again.

'Why so sad, Madonna? Does the view not please you?'

Eleanor turned to look at the man who had spoken, her deep azure eyes seeming to reflect the blue of the Mediterranean sky. Beneath the severe French hood she wore, her hair was long and thick, the colour of ripe corn in sunlight. She kept it well hidden, even though she had thought herself safe from being observed here, but wisps had escaped to tangle betrayingly about her face. She could do nothing to disguise the loveliness of her classic features, though she chose dark colours that did nothing to enhance her beauty.

'I was thinking of my home,' she replied, unable to hide a wistful note in her voice. 'It will be misty now and the fires will be lit in the library.'

'You cannot prefer the cold damp climate of your country to Italy?' His eyebrows arched in disbelief. 'But perhaps there was a lover...a young man who holds your heart in his hand?'

For a moment Eleanor was tempted to invent a handsome fiancé, but she was an honest girl and did not wish to lie.

'No, sir. I was thinking of my books. We were unable to bring many with us. As my father has told you, we were forced to leave in a hurry.'

Count Giovani Salvadore nodded, his expression sympathetic. He was a man of moderate height, not fat but well built with rather loose features. His hair and small beard were dark brown, his eyes grey and serious. Eleanor supposed he would be considered attractive, and his wealth made him an important man in the banking circles of Italy.

'It was an unpleasant experience for you,' the Count replied. 'Fortunately, your father had already placed much of his fortune with the House of Salvadore for safe keeping.'

'Yes, that was very fortunate,' Eleanor agreed, hiding her smile behind her fan. He was so pompous, so sure of himself! Yet she should not be ungrateful. He had generously made his villa available to her family until they should find somewhere they wished to settle. Sir William Nash had spoken of this part of Italy as being *pleasant* but Eleanor knew that he meant to travel on to Cyprus very soon. He had friends there: an English merchant who had settled on the island some years earlier and had offered both a home and an opportunity for Sir William to join him in business.

'Shall we go in?' The Count offered Eleanor his arm. 'Your skin may suffer in this heat if you stand in it too long.'

Eleanor had come out to be alone for a while. The Count's mother and sister chattered like magpies all day long, and they did not speak much English. She had hoped to escape for a while, so that she could have a little time to herself—but he had pursued her.

As she had feared, the Count was too interested in her for comfort. At home in the west of England, she had been allowed to do much as she pleased, and it pleased her to keep her distance from any gentleman she had considered a threat to her peaceful existence.

Eleanor had no wish to marry. She had become the mistress of her father's home when her mother died. She had been fourteen then, already a pretty girl but inclined to solitary walks and study. Lady Nash had spoken often of her lovely daughter's future marriage, but after her death it had been forgotten. Eleanor liked it that way.

To be a wife meant servitude. As a much-loved and indulged daughter, Eleanor had a freedom she might lose if she married. Sir William was an enlightened

man. He had taught his daughter to enjoy study for
its own sake, and her intelligence delighted him. She
spoke French fluently, a little Italian, and could read
some Arabic and Latin, of course. Her main interest
was ancient history, which she could discuss at a level
above most men of equal rank, and she had thought
that when the time came for them to leave England,
she would enjoy seeing the places of which she had
only read.

Indeed, she had enjoyed her visits to Venice and
Rome, drinking in the beauty of old palaces and wonderful scenery. It was only since they had come to
the villa that she had begun to feel restless.

Count Giovani Salvadore was too attentive! He
made Eleanor feel as if he were trying to smother her
with his generosity and his compliments caused her
to be uneasy. She was afraid he meant to ask for her
hand in marriage. Eleanor was almost sure Sir
William would consult her in the matter, but she
could not be certain. She would not feel comfortable
until they were on the ship taking them to Cyprus!

'There you are, Eleanor! Father sent me to find
you.'

Eleanor saw her brother coming towards them and
went forward eagerly to meet him. At fifteen, he was
slight and fair, a merry, happy boy—and she loved
him dearly.

'I am sorry if I worried you, Dickon.'

'Father wants to talk to you,' Richard said, his
smile shy and engaging. 'He has something to show
you—an illuminated manuscript. He wants you to
help him decipher it.'

At last! Eleanor felt her spirits lift. She had missed
working with her beloved father on his collection of

old manuscripts. He was beginning to build them up again. When they had their own house, everything would be as it always had been. Sir William would not force her to marry. He cared for her too much!

She glanced at the Count and smiled. 'Forgive me, *signor*. I must go. My father waits for me.'

'Oh, Father!' Eleanor cried as she saw the manuscript for the first time. 'I do not think I have ever seen anything quite as lovely.'

The manuscript was tiny, and when rolled could be stored in a space no larger than the handle of a woman's fan. Its container was made of pure gold and inlaid with emeralds and pearls, and there was a loop to suspend it from a chain or a ribbon so that it could be worn on the person.

'It is writ in Arabic,' Sir William said. 'But my eyes are not good enough to make out the words.'

The script was very small, though the decoration of gold leaf, rich crimson and deep blue was as clear and bright as the day it had been painstakingly inscribed.

'It is a part of the Qur'an,' Eleanor said. 'Or the Koran, as the Western world would name the Muslim's holy script. But there is an introduction…it praises the goodness of Allah, and asks for his blessing…' She paused. 'I think it says for the Abbey of the Far Cross…surely that cannot be, Father? I do not understand—would an Islamic prayer ask for Allah's blessing on a monastery?'

'Yes, that it is correct,' her father said and she saw the gleam of excitement in his eyes. 'It is the work of Abbot Gregorio. He was a very learned man who lived at an Abbey on an isolated island in Greek waters some three centuries ago. The monks were a silent order, but they had many secrets and there were legends of their fabulous wealth—though where it came from no one knew. According to the story, the Abbot believed that all religions stemmed from the same source and it is said that he was very interested in Islam—but his great wisdom did him little good. Not long after this manuscript would have been created, the Abbey was burned to the ground by Saracens and all the monks were slaughtered. No one knew what had happened to the treasures of the Abbey. They were thought lost...' Sir William's excitement was intense. 'This was discovered in an iron pot in the ground on Cyprus—on our land, Eleanor. Who knows what more we may find hidden away?'

'No, indeed, if the story be true—we might find untold treasures.' Eleanor caught her father's excitement. 'It is very intriguing,' she said and smiled at him. 'This must be worth a great deal in itself. Did Sir John send this to you?'

'He writes that it was discovered when the gardeners were working near to the house he purchased in my name. Knowing of my interest in such things, he sent it with his warm wishes for our speedy arrival.'

'Does that mean that we are to leave Italy soon?'

'Yes. It pleases you that we are to leave this house?' Sir William's eyes were a faded blue, his hair silvered by age but showing traces of the gold it had once been. 'Have you not been happy here, daughter? The Count has been kind...'

'Very kind, Father—but I shall be happier when we are in our own home and may begin to gather our things about us again.'

'My poor daughter,' Sir William said, tenderness

in his eyes. 'You miss your books, I dare say. It was a pity we could not bring more of them with us.'

'We dare not seem to be packing everything,' Eleanor replied, a flicker of fear in her eyes as she recalled the way they had been forced to flee in the night. 'You were likely to be arrested at any time. Your life is more important than books—however precious.'

'England is a dangerous place for a man who was known to be a friend to Cranmer,' Sir William said. 'Queen Mary senses treachery in the actions of any man not of her own faith.'

'But you took no part in any plot against her.'

'No—yet I knew those who did,' Sir William said and shuddered. 'Several of my friends had been seized and put to the torture. I was warned that the same was planned for me. Had it been myself alone…but I had you and your brother to consider, Eleanor. Better a life in exile than a painful death. Fortunately, I have long traded with the merchants of Venice, and much of my fortune was safe in Italy. We have good friends here and in Venice—and Cyprus. But it is there that I believe we should settle. Sir John is brother to your mother and a good, kindly man. If anything should happen to me, he would take care of you and Richard.'

'Pray, Father—do not speak of such things,' Eleanor begged him. A chill wind had seemed to blow across her heart as he spoke and she was afraid, though she saw no reason for it. 'You are safe from those who would see you burned.'

She shuddered as she thought of the cruel deaths suffered by the Archbishop Cranmer and others—and all done in God's name. She did not believe that the

God she knew in her heart would demand such wickedness—for it was surely wicked to kill a man simply for worshipping in his own way. She thought that she quite liked the ideas of the Abbot, who had embraced both Christianity and Islam, though of course she would never dare to voice those opinions aloud. The question of religion had caused fierce fighting all over this region of the Mediterranean for centuries, Christian against Muslim, west against east—and, indeed, she could not condone the culture of the Eastern potentates!

'Yes, we are all safe, child,' Sir William said and smiled at her. 'So you do not wish to marry Count Salvadore? You know that he means to ask you before we leave?'

'Please do not allow it,' Eleanor pleaded. 'Tell him that you wish to settle in your own home before you consider the question of my marriage.'

'Very well, Eleanor.' He was not displeased by her decision, because there was no hurry for her to marry. Sir John had a son of twenty years. It was possible that the two might please each other. 'We leave the day after tomorrow. Sir John has sent his own ship to carry us to our new home. It is a stout vessel and will have a precious cargo of rare treasures. Sir John trades much with the ruler of the Ottoman Empire and he has spent some months collecting pieces he thinks will tempt the Sultan.'

'Surely my mother's brother would not trade with such a man? From what you have told me, the Turks are barbaric! To keep others as slaves for their benefit is a terrible sin, Father.'

'Yes, Eleanor. It is a terrible sin, but you must remember theirs is a different culture. These people are not all barbarians by any means, though the Corsairs that plague these waters most certainly are. I believe that amongst the ruling class there are extremely clever men—and they have wise teachers. The rich live in wonderful palaces; they are also advanced in many things…medicine, for instance.'

'Because they have Arab slaves,' Eleanor replied scornfully. 'You told me that it was the Arabs who had wonderful knowledge and skills in such things—not the Turks!'

'In the Ottoman Empire there are many races blended into a melting pot of talents and wisdom. These people have developed the Devisherme system, Eleanor. That means that slaves—and the children of slaves—who convert to the faith of Islam are accepted into their society and allowed to prosper from their various talents.'

'Yet they remain slaves, subservient to the whim of their master!'

'In theory, yes,' Sir William admitted, his eyes alight with amusement. Such debates with his daughter were the bread of life to him. He was more tolerant than Eleanor, who could lose her temper when passionate about something—as she was now. 'But I believe many of them rise to become powerful men—even Bey of a province.'

'But they are still bound to their master!'

'Every man, woman and child in the Empire is bound in some way to the Sultan,' her father replied. 'He could order the death of any subject who has displeased him—so the free men are no more at liberty to do as they please than the slaves.' His eyes twinkled at her. 'Are they so very different from us, Eleanor? We were forced to leave our home because of the whim of a Queen. I could have been seized, tortured and condemned for a crime I had not committed.'

'Yes, I know, Father.' She shuddered. 'I am aware that your life was in danger and I thank God we escaped unharmed. But at least in England they do not shut women in a harem all their lives.'

'No—but some Western women suffer as much as their Eastern sisters. Disobedient women have been sent to a nunnery against their will, Eleanor, which is perhaps an even more harsh life. I believe the Kadins are rather spoiled, pampered creatures.' He chuckled deep in his throat. 'If ever you find yourself in a harem, daughter, you must make yourself indispensable to your master—that is the way to an easy life.'

'Never! I would rather die. I wonder that you can even say such a thing, Father.'

'It was but a jest, my dear,' Sir William said. 'I pray that you never will find yourself in such a place. You are right. I should not have said anything of the kind. Please forgive me. Though I would rather you fought for your life, my child, always remember that whatever may be done to your body, your mind and soul remains your own. Be true to yourself and to God and nothing can harm you.' He touched her head as if in blessing.

Eleanor closed her eyes and whispered a prayer. She had felt that chill wind again, but her father's words comforted her. If she kept her faith and her pride, she could face anything.

Yet why should anything terrible happen? They had only a relatively short journey ahead of them, and were to travel on board a ship belonging to Sir

William's kinsman and friend. Surely they would arrive safely within a few days?

They had been sailing for twenty-four hours when the storm suddenly hit the ship. It came from nowhere, a great, swirling wind that whipped what had seemed to be a calm blue sea into huge waves. The merchant vessel was tossed about like a child's toy, lurching and rolling in the grip of the atrocious weather.

'You and your children must stay below,' the captain had warned Sir William. 'If you come on deck, I cannot be responsible for your safety.'

Eleanor had been forced to obey, though she would have preferred to be up on deck. It was terrifying to feel the ship shudder and buck, and she feared that they would all die.

She felt ill and was sick constantly, managing only to whisper a prayer between bouts of vomiting. Surely they would all drown!

It was a terrible end to their voyage of hope, and Eleanor touched the heavy silver cross and chain she wore around her neck, together with her father's precious manuscript, which she was wearing beneath her gown for safe keeping.

'Oh God, let us all live' she prayed. In her terror she reached out to whoever was listening. 'Whether you be Our Lord or Allah—let us live…'

All night the storm raged around them, but suddenly just before dawn it died and the silence was even stranger than the wind that had preceded it. The ship was not moving at all. It seemed that the god of the sea had worn itself out in its fury and was resting.

Their captain told Sir William that they were becalmed and could do nothing but drift until the wind
returned.

'How long before that happens?' Sir William
asked.

'Perhaps hours…or days.'

There was nothing anyone could do except wait for
a benevolent wind. At least the ship had survived the
wild night. The sailors would spend their time clear-
ing up the debris of a broken mast; the passengers
could do nothing but sleep and wait.

Eleanor was woken by the sound of shouting from
the deck above. Immediately, she sensed that something was wrong and struggled into her gown, which
fastened at the front to make it easy for travelling.
Although she had a maid, the girl was in the next
cabin and still terribly ill from the sickness she had
suffered during the storm. Eleanor did not know her
well, and felt that it would be better to manage alone
for the moment.

She paused, then took a few seconds to don her
ugly cap, tucking all her hair beneath the veil at the
back. She was already wearing her father's treasure,
but her cross and chain were lying on the chest beside
her. She was about to snatch them up when her
brother came rushing into the cabin.

'Forgive me,' he cried, clearly frightened. 'But
Father says you must come. We must all be together.
He means to bargain with them…'

'Bargain with whom?' Eleanor asked. 'I do not understand you, Dickon. What is happening?'

'Corsairs,' he said, his cheeks pale. 'They have a
fast galley and are bearing down on us hard. We

cannot move, Eleanor—which means they will board us.'

'May God have mercy!'

Eleanor knew what this meant. Every vessel feared an attack by the fearsome pirates who roamed these waters—but their ship was fast and powerful and would usually be capable of outrunning the pirates' galley. Not without a wind! They were helpless, caught in a trap!

Now Eleanor understood what her father meant about bargaining with the Corsairs. Their only chance was that the captain of the galley would be prepared to sell them to their friends—rather than either killing them or selling them in the slave markets of Algiers.

She was trembling inwardly as she went up on deck. Their lives were truly in the hands of a higher being now. They could be dead within minutes—or prisoners. She held her head erect as she went to join her father. He kissed her on both cheeks.

'Forgive me, child. When I jested with you, I never dreamed this would happen.'

'Your jest did not make it happen, Father,' she replied, refusing to show her fear. Her eyes flashed with anger. 'The storm brought us to this—and these barbarians take advantage of our plight. Now tell me they are civilized people, Father!'

The galley had drawn alongside as she spoke and she could see the grinning faces of the men who had begun to swarm up the sides of the ship. They were strange, fearsome faces and she felt close to fainting—but she would not give in to such weakness! She would stand up to these heathen devils if she died for it.

The screaming and killing had begun as the sailors

prepared to defend themselves from the invaders.
They knew their fate if they were taken, and many
preferred a swift death to being chained in a galley
until they were flogged to death or starved at the oars.
Eleanor watched the carnage about her, her face re-
markably unmoved—but inside she was shocked and
horrified by the cruelty of the invaders. They gave no
mercy…even when a cabin boy, who had at first tried
to fight, sank to his knees and begged to live.

Eleanor put her arm about Richard's shoulders. If
they were to die, then they would die together.

One of the Corsairs—a tall man with swarthy looks
and cruel eyes—had seen them. He appeared to be
the leader of these men and he pointed towards
Eleanor, giving what was obviously a command.

She lifted her head, meeting those cruel eyes
proudly, daring him to touch her. He grinned suddenly as if he recognized the challenge and said
something more to his men. Three of them were coming towards them, their manner purposeful.

'Do not be frightened,' she said to Richard. 'Be
true to your inner self whatever they do. Remember,
you are Richard Nash, and—'

The men had arrived and started to grab at her. She
pushed her brother behind her, trying to shield him,
but one of the men swooped on her, lifting her and
throwing her over his shoulder.

'Father!' she cried. 'I love you—I love Richard.'

She kicked and struggled for all she was worth, but
knew it was useless. The man carried her as though
she were a sack of straw. He was taking her towards
the side of the ship where she was lifted over into the
arms of their leader, who was waiting to receive her.
The pirates were gathering what they could now and

retreating to their galley. Eleanor looked back and saw her father. He was trying to talk to one of the pirates, but the man struck him a blow to the side of the head and he fell to the deck, bleeding profusely.

'Father...' she cried despairingly. She saw that another of the pirates had her brother, who was kicking and struggling valiantly against his captor. 'Don't fight, Richard...try to live...' It was her father's instruction to her and she vowed that she would try. 'I love you, Father,' she murmured. 'I wish they had killed me too...but I shall try to do what you asked of me...'

She could hear the Corsairs shouting and pointing. Glancing out towards the sea, she saw another, larger, faster galley approaching them swiftly. It was a Spanish war galley—and the Spaniards were sworn enemies of the Corsairs.

'Oh, please God let them be in time,' Eleanor prayed. 'Let the Spanish captain of the galley wreak vengeance on these murdering devils. Let us be rescued...'

Tears were trickling down her cheeks as she was dumped on board the galley and then dragged off to what was clearly the cabin of the Corsairs' leader. She was thrust inside what was an airless hole and she fell to the ground, hitting her head against an iron chest as she did so.

Eleanor was claimed by the merciful blackness and did not know that the Spanish galley had chosen not to pursue their enemy. Its captain was even now climbing aboard the crippled merchant vessel, intent on rescuing the remaining crew of a Christian ship, unaware that the Corsairs had taken prisoners before they ran...

Chapter Two

Eleanor could not be sure how long she had lain in the stuffy, airless cabin. When she first came to herself, she had been aware of pain in her head and very little else. She lay in a state of semi-consciousness, drifting in and out of awareness. Hours passed before she felt her shoulder being roughly shaken and then found herself looking up into the bearded face of the man who had captured her. His fierce eyes snapped with what she thought was anger, sending a ripple of terror winging through her. She gave a moan of fear and shrank back, but instead of cruelly ravishing her as she half expected, he thrust a cup of water into her hand.

'Drink, woman,' he muttered in French.

'You speak French?' Eleanor asked in the same tongue. 'Please—tell me what has happened to my brother. Is Richard alive?'

'Be silent, woman. Drink now—food later.'

Eleanor sat up as the door of the officers' cabin closed behind him. She sipped the water gratefully. It was cool, fresh and sweet on her lips, taking the taste of ashes from her mouth. For the first time she was able to think clearly and began to wonder how long she had been on board the galley—was it merely hours or days?

Gingerly, she put a hand to the back of her head and found that her hood had been removed, and that there was a patch of dried blood in her hair. Someone must have taken the headdress off while she was unconscious, probably to see what had rendered her that way. It was the blow to the side of her head as she fell that had done the damage, but she ached all over and wondered if she had suffered some kind of a fever. Perhaps the effects of the storm combined with the terror of the pirates attack had… *Her father was dead!* The pain of knowledge returned likc the thrust of a sword in her breast.

Tears welled up in her eyes and fell in a hot cascade down her cheeks. She sobbed for several minutes as her grief overwhelmed her. It was hard to believe that the man she had loved so dearly was lost to her forever…but she had seen the blow that had felled him and believed he must have died of it.

What of her brother? Eleanor's eyes were becoming accustomed to the gloom of the cabin now, and she began to glance around her, trying to make out what the shapes were. There were no bunks or divans here, merely a collection of sea chests—one of which had caused her to have a nasty headache—and a table and stool pushed hard against one wall. Did these men never sleep? But there was a roll of blanket spread on the ground near her—perhaps that served as a bed on this war galley?

One thing was clear: she was alone. Her brother had not been thrown in here after her. Where was he? What had happened to him? Their captor had so far been gentle enough to her...but had Richard been treated differently? Was he still alive? The questions tortured her, increasing her own fear of what was to happen.

She tried to get up and found that she could stand, although her head was still spinning and she felt sick, but she kept upright and did not fall. After a moment or two she managed to walk towards the table on which were spread what she realised were charts and maps of the sea, also various instruments for calculating distance by the stars. Clearly the captain of this vessel was more educated than his appearance allowed, and with that knowledge came a lessening of her fear.

If he was intelligent she might be able to reason with him herself, to arrange for a ransom to be paid. Sir John often traded with the Sultan of the Ottoman Empire. A message could be sent to him...he would pay for her and Richard's release. Perhaps all was not yet lost.

She finished her water and sat down to look at the charts before her. The captain had clearly been plotting a chart—and seemed to be heading for the great city the Christians still called Constantinople, though it had been renamed Istanbul by its conquerors, which lay on the shores of the Bosphorus Straits. She was being taken there to be sold in the slave markets! She had imagined the galley's base would be Algiers, perhaps because the captain spoke French so well.

The French were more at home in these waters than most of the other Western countries. Some years earlier the Turks had signed an agreement that they would allow only the French flag to trade freely and safely in their waters, though of course there were other merchants who made individual agreements. There were also those who roamed where they would and took the consequences, as their kinsman's ship had—but only the French had the protection of the Sultan himself.

Her fate would be the same wherever she was taken!

Eleanor shivered as the realisation hit her. It was easy to make the decision to be bold and demand she be ransomed, but why should the Corsair captain listen? He could quite easily sell her—perhaps to the Grand Turk himself—and then she would disappear into a harem, never to be seen again. She shuddered at the thought of what her life would be like in such a place.

The idea of being a man's concubine appalled her. No! It must not happen. She would not let it happen. It was all a question of money. The Corsairs had taken prisoners to sell them in the slave market. What would her value be on the auction block? She had no way of knowing—but surely it could not be so very much? Her mother's cousin would pay twice as much to have her back.

Eleanor had no doubts that Sir John would do his utmost to recover both her and Richard. If he had heard of the fate of his ship, he might even now be trying to trace them. Her head lifted, her expression proud and determined. No matter what happened to her she would fight—she would live as her father had bid her—and perhaps one day she would be returned to her family.

But where was Richard?

Mohamed Ali Ben Ibn frowned as he thought about the woman they had captured; she had lain in a fever for several hours after they had taken flight from the Spanish war galley and at first he had thought she might die. That would have been a great loss.

He had seen her quality immediately and ordered her taken as his personal share of the plunder from the merchant ship. Unfortunately, they had not managed to snatch much else of value before they were forced to abandon their prize.

There was the boy, of course. His delicate features would appeal to certain men in the slave markets of Constantinople, and another woman. She was young but not beautiful and would fetch a moderate price—but his woman was more of a prize than he had imagined when he first spotted her.

That glorious hair! He had been shocked when he removed the hood that covered it to attend to her wound, and at first was elated by the value of his prize. But now there were rumblings amongst the crew because their prize was so small. He had been determined to bring the woman to Istanbul at once—and he knew exactly what he was going to do with her—but the crew was dissatisfied with their share.

He must make sure that none of them got near enough to her to see what a beauty she was. Not a hair of her head must be touched—and she must not be violated, for then her value would be lost. He would take her to a certain house on the shores of the Bosphorus where she would be safe from prying eyes—and then he would begin his bargaining.

In the meantime he must find a way of pacifying the crew. He took out the gold ornament he had discovered tucked beneath the girl's dress when he tried to loosen her bodice—Western women wore such ugly, restricting clothes it was a wonder any of them could breathe!

He saw that the little cylinder of gold was studded with precious stones, and noticed the stopper at the top. Opening what he had imagined was a scent flask, he discovered the tiny manuscript and drew it out. His face paled as he discovered what it was and he dropped it as though his fingers had been burned.

Mohamed Ali Ben Ibn was a Corsair by necessity, not birth. He had been educated in the best schools of his homeland before being captured by Spaniards, and forced to work in their galleys for long years before he had escaped, vowing revenge on the men he hated. Since then he had roamed the seas in search of prey—and he had been successful. He was now a wealthy man and owned a beautiful house, to which he would one day take a woman of his own beliefs, and make sons with her.

His brow furrowed as he looked at what he knew to be cursed. That manuscript was a part of the treasure of the Abbot of the Far Cross—and the legend was that anyone who sought to benefit from the sale of this treasure was doomed to a terrible death. The Saracens who had looted the Abbey and killed the monks had all died violently soon after and it was said that the treasure was scattered far and wide. How had the woman come by it? And why did she wear it around her neck like a talisman? Was she of the true faith and not a Christian as he had supposed?

He was a superstitious man. The treasure must be returned to the girl! Mohamed would find some other way of satisfying his crew. He would give them gold from his own coffers—and he would make sure he recouped his loss from the sale of the girl!

* * *

Eleanor was visited twice a day by the captain of the galley. He brought her food and water, and he returned her father's treasure to her. She had not noticed its loss at first, and was surprised when he gave it to her.

'Why have you returned this?' she asked. 'It is valuable. My family has money. My kinsman will pay a high ransom for me—twice my price in the slave market.'

He glowered at her. 'Drink and eat, woman.'

It was all he ever said to her

She had begun to wonder if she had overestimated his intelligence. Perhaps they were the only words of French he knew? The next time he came she spoke to him in English, then Italian and finally she spoke the only words she could think of that might reach him.

'*Insh'allah*...may the will of Allah prevail. And his blessings be upon you for your kindness...if you will ransom me and my brother to my family. My brother is Richard Nash...son of Sir William and—'

'You speak too much, woman,' Mohamed said harshly. 'A woman should have a still tongue if she does not wish to be beaten.'

'You are an educated man!' Eleanor cried. 'Why will you not listen to my requests? My family will make you a rich man if you ransom me to them. My uncle is Sir John Faversham of Cyprus—'

His look darkened to one of anger. 'I do not trade with infidels! I kill them. You are not to question me, woman. Be thankful that I do not give you to my men for their sport.'

Eleanor shrank back, the fear writ plain in her face. 'You would not...be so cruel?'

'Thank Allah that I am not the barbarian you think me,' Mohamed said. 'I have plans for you, woman— but I may still beat you if you do not still your clacking tongue.'

Somehow Eleanor did not believe him. If he had meant to harm her, he would have done it by now. It was clear that he did not like to be questioned by a woman, but she would not give up. If she kept talking about a ransom he was bound to at least think about it…

Suleiman Bakhar was laughing. He felt exhilarated by the sport he had just had with the man he knew was considered to be the champion of the Janissaries. It had been a fierce fight that could have gone either way, pressing each man to the limit—and he had won!

'Come, my friend,' he said, laying an arm about the shoulders of the man he had vanquished. 'We shall bathe, drink and eat together—and then I shall give you a woman for your pleasure.'

'You honour me, my lord.'

Suleiman nodded, accepting that he was being generous in victory, but he felt pleased with himself. His astronomer had that morning told him that he was about to enter a new cycle of his life—one that would bring him both torment and pleasure.

'You will gain your heart's desire,' the old man had told him after consulting various charts, 'but only if you are prepared to learn and to suffer.'

'To learn and to suffer?' Suleiman's expression had caused the astronomer's pulses to race for a moment. 'Explain your predictions.'

'All is not yet clear,' Ali Bakr told him. 'I see only

that a bright flame has moved into the heaven of your chart. This flame will burn you and yet it will eventually bring you all that you long for in the secret places of your heart.'

'You speak in riddles as always.' Suleiman dismissed the astronomer with a handful of silver. 'Come to me when I send for you—and give me a clearer reading next time.'

Suleiman had dismissed the old man's ramblings as a misguided attempt to please him. It had happened often enough in the past. Most of his kind were charlatans and liars, pretending to a knowledge they did not have—yet he had heard much good of this one.

Suleiman had trained and fought for most of the day, and now his body was free of the restless energy that so often plagued him. The afternoon would be spent eating and drinking the rich dark coffee he enjoyed, talking with the men he knew as friends. Then perhaps he would send for Fatima…and yet he had no real desire for her.

Perhaps he should visit some of the better slave merchants? The Circassian women were beautiful and much prized; if he were lucky, he might find one that tempted him.

It was as he was being massaged with perfumed, healing oils by one of the eunuchs that the news came.

'There is a message from Mohamed Ali Ben Ibn, my lord,' the slave said. 'He asks if you will grant him the favour of seeing him.'

Suleiman rose from the massage bench, wrapping a cloth around his waist. His back and shoulders glistened with the oil that had been rubbed into his skin, enhancing the honed beauty of his muscular torso. He had a presence, an air of power and confidence that kept others in awe of him, but also created a distance so that he had few true friends.

What could the Corsair want with him? Suleiman was aware of a tingling sensation at the nape of his neck and experienced the first prickles of a strange excitement. The Corsair's reputation was known to him, though they had never met.

'Ask him to come to my private room.' He glanced at the officers who were also enjoying the benefits of being massaged by Suleiman's slaves. 'Excuse me, my friends. This will not take long. Please, eat, drink—and the women will entertain you.'

He gave an order to the eunuchs for dancing girls to be brought as he retired to his inner chamber, where only a very few were ever permitted.

'Bring coffee and food,' he told one of the slaves, 'then leave us.'

Suleiman was seated on a silken divan, clad now in simple white trousers and a long white caftan belted at the waist, when the Corsair captain was shown into his presence. He fell on his knees but was immediately told to sit, which he did on the cushions provided.

'We are both men,' Suleiman said, his eyes narrowed and intent on the other's face. 'We shall speak as equals. You will take coffee with me?'

'You honour me, my lord.'

'You have something for me?'

Mohamed smiled. The Caliph's son wasted no time. 'I have been told you seek something rare and beautiful?'

'This is true. What have you to sell?' Suleiman frowned. It was said of this man that he had an eye for quality. When he had merchandise for sale it was always the best—always highly priced. Again he felt that tingling sensation in his spine and was conscious of excitement. 'Is it treasure—or a woman?'

'Some would say this woman is a treasure beyond price.'

'Why?' Suleiman's hard gaze intensified. 'There are already many beautiful women in my harem—what makes this one worthy of special attention?'

'Her hair is the colour of ripe corn in the sunlight and reaches to below her waist,' Mohamed said. 'Her body is perfect, her eyes are azure like a summer sky and—'

'And?' Suleiman was demanding, imperious, dismissive of such details. 'What else?'

'She is clever. She speaks three languages, and I believe she reads Arabic. She is the daughter of an English baronet—curse all unbelievers!'

The prickling at Suleiman's nape had become almost painful. He felt as if a thousand hot pins had been stuck into him, and it was all he could do to stop himself gasping. A feeling of intense excitement had come over him, but he had no intention of showing it.

'Her mind is of little account,' he said with a studied carelessness. 'If her body is perfect, I may be interested. Where did you find her?'

'I attacked the ship of a merchant of Cyprus,' Mohamed said. He was not in the least put off by Suleiman's apparent indifference. It was expected that they would bargain. 'The ship was damaged and becalmed after the storm, and we thought it ripe for plucking—but a Spanish war galley bore down on us.

We were able to take only the woman, her servant and a boy before escaping.'

'How do you know she is the daughter of an English noble?'

'She told me, my lord—in three languages. She insists her family would pay twice her price in the market for her return.'

'And yet you come to me?'

'I would not sell this woman in the market, my lord. Nor would I entrust her to the slave merchants, who might defile her. She is safe in a house I know of—and will stay there until I sell her.'

Suleiman nodded, his face expressionless. 'What is your price for this woman?'

'One thousand gold pieces, my lord.'

'For a woman?' Suleiman laughed scornfully. 'No woman is worth a third of such a sum.'

'Forgive me for wasting your time, my lord.' It was clearly the Corsair's intention to leave as he rose to his feet. Suleiman rose too, matching the Corsair for height and build. 'I was told you sought something rare, a treasure beyond price but—I see I was misinformed.'

'Stay!' Suleiman's face was very hawkish at that moment, his pupils more silver than black. 'We have not yet concluded our business.'

Mohamed Ali Ben Ibn smiled inwardly. He had not thought for one moment that he would be allowed to leave.

'She is truly beyond price, my lord. I would not have offered her to you if I had not thought the woman a rare prize. I swear you will not be disappointed in her.'

'Eight hundred if she is what you claim.'

'One thousand gold pieces—her family would pay more.'

'For a woman?' Suleiman scorned and yet he knew he would pay the price asked if she was all this man claimed. 'A thousand then, but I will take the boy you spoke of, too.'

'He has been sent to the slave market.'

'Get him back,' Suleiman commanded, determined that he must assert his authority in some way. The boy was of little importance, but a Corsair must not best the Caliph's son in business. 'One thousand for them both or you may send the woman to the market too.'

'Come with me, child,' the woman said to Eleanor in a soft, melodious voice. 'You must feel so dirty after being on the galley for so many days. Bathe and rest and you will feel better.'

'Who are you?' Eleanor asked. She had been too weary to notice much as she was brought to this house that morning, but she had been given a delicious meal of rice and vegetables in a sweet sauce, and allowed to rest in a room by herself and was feeling better. 'And where am I? What is going to happen to me—and where is my brother? Has he been brought here too?'

'So many questions! I cannot answer the half of them.' The woman laughed. 'I am called Roxana and I am what some people call a Morisco—but I have mixed blood. My father was a Moor but my mother was Spanish.'

'Are you a Muslim or a Christian?'

'I am of the true faith,' Roxana replied, but did not

meet her eyes as she spoke. 'Mohamed thought you might be of the Muslim persuasion—are you?'

Eleanor hesitated. She might be spared much if she was thought to be a Muslim, but she did not wish to lie to this woman, who had treated her kindly.

'No. I was raised as a Protestant—but I believe that everyone should have the right to worship as they please. How can any of us know that we alone are right in our religious beliefs?'

Roxana looked anxious. 'You should not speak so openly, child. Men are fanatical about such things— you could be put to death for those words. In Spain you would have been given to the Inquisition for questioning. Here too you could be punished for voicing such an opinion. It is always best for a woman to be silent.'

'But why?' Eleanor sighed. Was there no one left to whom she could open her mind? Now that her father was dead she would never be able to speak freely again. But Roxana was only speaking the truth. 'You are right, of course. But you have not answered my questions.'

'You are in my house,' Roxana said. 'I was given it by Mohamed Ali Ben Ibn for saving his life some years ago. I have some skill with herbs and I nursed him when he was close to death. He comes here sometimes and I live because he lives. If it were not for him, I would have to sell myself to a master— and I would prefer to die.'

'I do not think him a bad man. He was not unkind to me.'

'That is because you will fetch a good price,' Roxana told her. 'You are very beautiful. Your skin is soft and smooth, and your body is comely—though a little thin for perfection. Good food will soon cure that. Come, now, and cleanse yourself. Then we shall sit and talk until your master comes for you.'

'You are kind, Roxana.'

'I have known what it is like to be in your position. I was sold by my family to an old man. He was…not kind.' Roxana shuddered at the memory. 'But he died and I ran away before his possessions were sold. I lived in a hut by the river and it was there I nursed Mohamed…'

'You love him—don't you?'

'Yes.' Roxana smiled at her. 'My wish is only to serve him, but one day he will take a wife and go far away. Then I shall not see him again.'

'He will not marry you?'

Roxana shook her head. 'He will take a young girl of his own…class. He came from a good family. He has suffered much at the hands of the Spanish—in their galleys as a slave.'

Eleanor nodded. She had been terrified of her captor at first, but she was beginning to see that she had been lucky. Instead of being taken directly to the slave market, she had been brought here to this house to rest and refresh herself. It could have been so much worse, and her mind shied away from what might have happened to her. She was safe here for the moment with this kind woman.

Yet she would escape if she could! Her mind was frantically looking for a way of escaping as her hostess led her into a walled garden, which was planted with many bushes and flowers that gave out a heady perfume. They walked through little paths between the bushes and wooden trellises, up which scrambled flowering shrubs. At a sunlit spot in the middle of a very secluded area, they came upon a sunken bath.

'You may wash here,' Roxana told her. 'There is soap in the jars and towels to dry yourself when you have finished.'

'I have never bathed in the open air before,' Eleanor said, glancing round nervously.

'No one will disturb you.' Roxana smiled at her. 'I shall leave you to bathe in private—and bring clothes to you in a while.'

It was very warm as Eleanor removed her clothes. Her dress felt stiff with dirt and sweat and she was glad to be rid of it. The sun was warm on her skin as she stood naked at the edge of the pool, relishing the warmth on her skin. It was many years since she had swum naked in the river at her home, for when she assumed the duties of a woman she had left the pranks of childhood behind her—but it did feel so good to be free of her restricting gown for once.

She was of medium height and slender with slim hips and small, pert breasts, the nipples the colour of a dark pink rose. Her skin was a warm cream in colour, and seemed to have a slightly golden sheen in the sunlight. Seen in her naked glory she was truly magnificent, a goddess come to earth—or so it might seem to any who saw her thus.

She walked down the gently sloping steps into the water, which seemed to be perfumed and was cool to her skin. It felt delicious and she walked further into the shallow pool, dipping down into the water and splashing in it in sheer delight. She suddenly went right under, remembering that she had loved to swim beneath the water as a child. She was so dirty and her hair needed a good soaking to be rid of the filth of her imprisonment.

It was so good to relax here by herself. She would think about escape later. For the moment she was simply going to enjoy the luxury that had been granted her.

Suleiman caught his breath as he watched the woman bathing. She seemed to be content as she splashed and soaped her limbs, and then her hair. It *was* a wonderful colour. He did not think that he had ever seen such beautiful hair...so thick and wavy. Now that it was wet it had gone darker but he knew it would look even better once it was clean. It would be pleasurable to bury his face in hair like that, to stroke that skin and crush her to him.

He felt a stirring in his loins, and realised that she had affected him in a way no woman had for a long time. His breath caught in his throat, and for a moment he knew a fierce longing to take her there and then—but then his self-control asserted itself once more. He had not paid a thousand gold pieces for his own benefit. He needed something rare and beautiful to please the Grand Turk.

She was truly a gift fit for the Sultan, he thought as he continued to watch her. The money demanded for her price had been exorbitant, far more than he would normally have considered—but perhaps she was worth it. He frowned as she submerged beneath the water again, seeming to stay there longer than necessary.

Was she trying to drown herself? Such things were not unknown amongst infidel women—they did not always take kindly to the idea of becoming a slave.

He had heard of women killing themselves rather than being forced to submit to slavery.

He moved out from behind the pierced wooden screen, which had served as his hiding place, just as the woman surfaced once more. At first she did not seem to see him, then, when she became aware that she was no longer alone, she stared at him for a moment, screamed and ducked beneath the water again.

Suleiman cursed loudly and waded into the pool. The foolish woman *was* trying to kill herself. He saw her beneath the surface and bent down to grab her, but she shot out of his grasp, swimming beneath the water to the far side. Then she came up gasping for air. He caught a glimpse of her lovely breasts, the nipples a deep rose, peaked and tempting, and then she crossed her arms over herself, her eyes meeting his in a cold stare.

She was angry! Suleiman was also angry. He was wet and uncomfortable and he realised that she had no intention of drowning herself—which made what he had done seem foolish.

'Who are you?' Eleanor demanded as he waded up the steps of the bath. He had been wearing a long, heavily embroidered robe over loose white pants and the tunic dragged against him in the water. 'How dare you spy on me?'

'I thought you meant to drown yourself. I did not intend to frighten you.'

Eleanor realised that she had spoken in English and that he had replied in the same language, clearly as at home in her native tongue as she. She had not expected that somehow.

'Go away! You have no right to be here. Mohamed

Ali Ben Ibn owns me and he will kill you if he finds you here.'

'I do not think so.' Suleiman was amused by her show of defiance. Did she not realise that she was completely at his mercy? He could strip off his wet clothes and join her in the bath… The temptation to do so made him harden beneath his robes. He could feel his manhood burning and throbbing with a fierce need—a need he had not felt in a long time. 'Come out and dry yourself, woman.'

'Not while you're watching!'

'Foolish one! You have nothing to show that I have not already seen a thousand times.'

'I don't care how many concubines you have!' Eleanor retorted, stung by his mockery. How dare he speak to her so! 'I am not one of them and I am not coming out until you go away.'

'You will turn cold.' Suleiman sat down on a tiled bench, his eyes intent on her face, his mouth softened by amusement. 'I have no intention of leaving.'

'You are also wet.'

'But I shall dry in the sun.' He laughed huskily, the cruel mouth softened and suddenly appealing. 'What a fierce one you are, my little bird. You are truly worth the price asked. You will make a fine gift for the Sultan.'

Eleanor was chilled. So she was to be sold after all!

'Have you bought me?' He inclined his head, sending strange little sensations down her spine as she saw the brilliance of his eyes. 'Who—who are you?'

'My name is Suleiman Bakhar. I am the son of Caliph Bakhar—chief justice minister to the Sultan.'

Eleanor was silent, fighting her desire to weep. It

seemed that all her hopes were at an end. She had hoped so much that she would be able to persuade her captor to ransom her—but it was already too late. There was something masterful about this man, an air of arrogance that told her he would not easily give up what was his.

Suleiman relented as he saw her shiver. 'Come out, foolish woman. I shall turn my back.'

He stood up, turning away so that he could not see her. He heard her moving in the water and was tempted to turn as she left the bath, but resisted.

'You can look now.'

Suleiman turned. She had wrapped a towel around her body, leaving her shoulders and arms bare, and was clutching the cloth to her as if her life depended on it. He smiled, feeling oddly moved by her need for modesty. Most of the women were only too eager to show off their charms. He picked up the second towel.

'Come here. I shall dry your hair.'

She made no move to obey, simply staring at him with her head up and her eyes proud. No one disobeyed Suleiman! To do so could mean instant punishment—even death. He was stunned by her obstinacy. Was she mad or merely foolish? Had she no idea how important he was—or what he could do to her if he chose?

'You must obey me. I am your master.'

'You may have bought me, but that does not mean that you can make me your slave.'

Suleiman saw the pride and defiance in her eyes and felt a surge of excitement. She was like one of his hawks—when they were fresh from the wild and untamed to the touch of his hand. Most of the birds succumbed to gentle persuasion in time, but now and then one would attempt to tear out his eyes. If that happened the bird was returned to the wild. Some men would have ordered it killed, but Suleiman understood the wild spirit that could not be tamed—and respected it.

He had never met a truly spirited woman before. They were always trained in their duties by the eunuchs and older women long before they were presented to their master.

'What makes you say that? Do you not understand that I have absolute power over you? I can do with you as I will.'

'You can do as you will with my body,' Eleanor retorted, head high. She ought to be afraid of this man but she wasn't. 'But you cannot command my mind—or my soul.'

'Ah…' Suleiman nodded, enjoying this verbal tussle. 'Yes, I see. You think you can rise above the indignity of being a slave. I understand. But you do not. You are fortunate that I paid a great deal of money for you—or you might even now feel pain. I do not think you have ever experienced true pain, Eleanor.'

'Who gave you permission to use my name?' Her eyes flashed blue fire.

Suleiman moved towards her, towering above her, menacing her with the power of his strength and masculinity—yet she did not flinch. Her hair had begun to dry at the edges in the hot sun, little wisps curling about her face. He could imagine what it would look like properly dressed in its natural waves, cascading down to the small of her back. He was pleased with his purchase and inclined to indulge her for the moment.

'Here…' He put the second towel around her shoulders to protect her from the fierce heat. 'Go into the house and let Roxana help you to dress. We have a ride of some distance to my father's palace.'

Eleanor was torn between anger and caution. This man was a noble of his own country. A barbarian, of course, but better than many she might have been sold to. She was foolish to antagonise him. If she tried persuasion instead, he might ransom her to her family.

'I shall obey because I have no choice for the moment,' she said with dignity. 'But you do not understand either, sir. I am the daughter of an English baronet. I have powerful friends. They will look for me and they will pay a high price for my return—twice what you paid for me. You may name your own price, sir.'

'You do not know how much I paid…' A smile curved his mouth. 'Would your family give ten thousand in your English gold coin? I might sell you for such a sum.'

It was a king's ransom and her family could not pay anywhere near as much—and he knew it.

Eleanor paled from shock. 'That is impossible. You did not pay any such sum!'

Suleiman laughed, much amused by her reaction. She had not tried to lie, and that pleased him. 'No, I did not—but I am beginning to think I paid too much. You have too much to say for yourself, woman. Have you no respect for your betters? Do you not know that it becomes a woman to remain silent in the presence of her master—at least until she is given permission to speak?'

'When I am in company that deserves my respect I give it.' She felt a flash of temper. How dare this barbarian try to teach her manners? She was an English gentlewoman! 'Here, I see only barbarians.'

'Be careful, woman.' Suleiman's mouth hardened as he took a step towards her. 'My patience wears thin. Go to the house before I drag you back in the pool and drown you!'

'You wouldn't...' Eleanor began, but the look in those fierce eyes made her think he just might. She gave a little squeak of alarm, turned and fled.

Suleiman watched her flight, his eyes bright with laughter. He had won the first tussle—but what a fight she had put up. She was indeed a fine prize. A worthy gift for the Sultan...and yet perhaps she needed to be tamed a little first. She was too fiery, too defiant. From what he knew of the Sultan, her spirit would not be particularly appreciated.

Perhaps Suleiman would keep her for a while...

Chapter Three

'You are beautiful,' Roxana said as she brushed Eleanor's long hair. She sighed and looked at her with sympathy. 'It is a pity that you are destined for the Sultan's harem and not Suleiman Bakhar's own household.'

'Why?' Eleanor frowned at her.

'Suleiman Bakhar is young and strong—and they say that to be loved by him is like dying and going to paradise. Though perhaps this is only gossip brought by servant women to the markets.'

'I do not care if he is young and handsome,' Eleanor said, shivering as she remembered the look in those fierce eyes when he had threatened to drown her. For a moment she had truly believed he might do it. 'I do not want to be his concubine.'

'He might marry you—if you are clever. Until now he has taken only concubines. They say he must marry soon, because he must give the Caliph an heir…'

'I have no wish to be his wife!' Eleanor stared at her in horror. 'I can think of nothing worse.'

'That is because you do not know what it is like

to be the wife of an old man.' Something flickered in
the older woman's eyes. 'If you did, you would do
all you could to make Suleiman notice you and want
you for himself.'

'Was it very hard for you, Roxana?' Eleanor
looked at her with sympathy. It was easy to see that
the older woman had once been lovely—and that she
had suffered.

'Sometimes I prayed that I might die before night
came.'

'Is that why you left me alone in the garden? Did
you think I might escape? Were you trying to help
me?'

'It is not in my power. Had you tried to escape,
you could not have done so,' Roxana replied. 'The
walls are high and there are guards outside. Besides,
if you had got out you would have been noticed immediately. The clothes you were wearing marked you
as an infidel and an unbeliever. You would have been
chased and caught by the mob—then, when they saw
how beautiful you are, they would have begun to
quarrel over you. Unless Mohamed's men rescued
you, you might have been raped again and again...'

Eleanor turned pale. She held up her hands as if to
ward off the pictures Roxana's words had brought to
life in her mind.

'Enough! It is clearly useless to try and escape in
the city—but if I managed to slip away outside its
walls dressed like this...'

She was wearing a pair of drawers, very full, which
reached down to her ankles; they were of a fine green
material brocaded with gold. Over these, was a smock
of a paler green silk gauze, edged with pearls; it had
loose sleeves which covered as far as her elbows and

closed at the throat with a cluster of pearls. And to
Eleanor's disgust, her breasts were clearly visible
through it! The waistcoat fitted her close to her body
and had very long sleeves fringed with gold tassels,
and the buttons were again clusters of pearls. On top
of all these was what Roxana had called a caftan, and
that was a straight robe that covered her to the ankles.
A girdle of gold threads woven with what looked like
precious stones, but must surely be crystals, was fastened with a heavy clasp of gold, again set with jewels. If they were jewels. But Eleanor was certain they
must be false. On her feet she wore soft boots that
reached just to mid-thigh and were embroidered with
gold thread.

It all felt very strange and she protested when she
was told that she must put on a casacche before she
went out. Since this was a huge cloak that would en-
velop her in its folds, and she must also wear a veil
and a talpock to cover her head, she felt she would
suffocate.

'It is too much,' she said. 'I thought my own gowns
were restricting enough—but this cloak thing is ridiculous.'

'You will become accustomed to it,' Roxana said.
'When you are in the gardens of the harem you will
be able to dispense with some of these layers if you
choose. However, you will never be allowed to leave
the palace wearing less.'

'Shall I be allowed out? I thought that was forbidden—that once in a harem women disappeared forever.'

Roxana smiled. 'You Western people do not understand our culture. Men of good family guard their
women for their own protection. You would not be

allowed to leave at will, of course, but the Sultan grants his favourite wives certain indulgences. You may be taken on a shopping expedition—or to some grand ceremonial occasion.'

'But what of those women who do not have their master's favour? What is it really like in a harem?'

'You will discover that soon enough. Come, Eleanor, you must not keep your master waiting or he may become angry.' The look Eleanor gave Roxana at that moment was so full of despair that the older woman's heart was touched. She embraced her. 'It is not always so very terrible. Try to please Suleiman Bakhar. If he keeps you for himself, you will not regret it.'

Eleanor nodded but said no more. She knew that Roxana could not help her, that she was free but had no power, no way of earning her living other than by selling herself. She lived here because she pleased Mohamed Ali Ben Ibn, and was as much at his whim as Eleanor would be at her master's.

It was terribly unfair, but it was the way of the world. She had been spoiled, petted and indulged all her life—and now she had no loving father to protect her. She was completely alone. She did not even know if her dearest Richard was still alive, and her heart wrenched with pain at the thought of what might have happened to him. Richard might already be dead—but she would live and she would win her freedom one day.

She saw Suleiman Bakhar waiting for her in the courtyard, and her heart caught for one terrifying moment and then raced on. He was truly one of the most impressive men she had ever seen, and he looked…wild, an untamed creature and dangerous.

She should be afraid of him, and yet…there was something that drew her to him, some thin, invisible thread that seemed to bind her to him as surely as any cruel chains they might put upon her.

She lifted her head as she reached him, eyes bright and challenging. 'Am I to be chained?'

Suleiman's gaze narrowed. 'Should I chain you, Eleanor? Are you planning to try and escape?'

She had hoped there might be an opportunity to slip away from him and now realised that she had been foolish to put him on his guard. 'What would you do—if you were in my place?'

'I should kill my captors and run away,' Suleiman replied truthfully. He laughed deep in his throat, a soft husky sound that Eleanor discovered was very attractive. 'Foolish woman. I have never put chains on anything—beast or man—let alone a woman with skin as soft as yours.'

'What has the softness of my skin to do with it?' She gave him a haughty look.

'Chains would mark you and mean you were worth less,' he replied, his expression inscrutable.

'Of course—I should have known.' For a moment she had thought he was being compassionate. He was a barbarian and a savage—she should not expect anything from such a man. 'How am I supposed to ride in this ridiculous thing?'

Suleiman looked at the cloak that enfolded her. 'You could not ride like that. You will be carried in a litter. It is the usual mode of travel for a woman of class here. I did not know that you could ride.'

'I would prefer to ride.'

'Then perhaps I shall allow it one day,' Suleiman

replied. 'However, today you will be carried in the litter. Come, I am ready to leave.'

Eleanor looked round for Roxana, but she had slipped away as soon as she had delivered her charge. Besides, there was nothing the Morisco woman could have done to help her.

'Are you afraid?' Suleiman asked as he saw her hesitation. 'You have no need to be. You are being taken to my apartments for the moment. I have decided I shall let the older women of my father's household school you in the manners you need before you are fit to grace the harem of any man.'

At that Eleanor's head came up, eyes flashing with anger. 'Afraid—of you? Why should I be? You are merely a man…'

'Truly, this is so. Why should you be afraid of me? You have no need to be—if you please me.' Suleiman's smile flickered deep in the silver depths of his strange eyes. His remarks had had their desired effect. Her pride had leant her courage. 'Your escort awaits you, lady.'

She felt a tingle at the base of her spine. He had addressed her as a woman of quality at last, and he was behaving as though she were his equal instead of a slave he had bought. Perhaps she might yet persuade him it would be better to ransom her.

'Thank you, my lord,' she responded graciously. If he thought she needed to be taught manners, she would show him how an English gentlewoman behaved. 'Will you see that Roxana is rewarded for her kindness to me, please?'

'It has already been done.' Suleiman smiled. What a proud beauty she was! Already he was beginning to regret that his father had need of a gift for the

Sultan. 'We should leave before the sun begins to set. It can come suddenly in this land, and my father's house is outside the city…at times there are bands of lawless bandits who roam the countryside looking for unwary travellers to rob. We have guards to protect us, but I would not have you frightened by these rogues on your first night in your new country.'

'You are considerate, my lord,' she said and inclined her head. 'But this is not my country—it is merely a place I must live in until I can regain my freedom.'

Suleiman's gaze narrowed, but he refused to be drawn. She was like the hawks that fluttered desperately against the bars of their cage. When she had learned to be obedient to her master's voice, she would learn that she could fly high and free once more—provided that she returned to his hand when called.

Had he really made up his mind to keep her? It was a risk, for the Sultan might learn of Suleiman's treasure and be angry because it had not been given to him. If Suleiman kept this woman for himself, he must find another treasure for the Sultan—but not a woman. It would be an insult to give their lord an inferior treasure. Something else rare and precious must be found to take her place…

He was lost in his thoughts, and turned carelessly aside to speak to one of his men as they emerged into a street that was already beginning to fill with the shadows of night. Until one of his men gave a shout of alarm, he did not realise that Eleanor had dropped her casacche and started to run. What did she think she was doing? Foolish, foolish woman! Had she no idea of the dangers of this city? Alone and at night she would disappear into some stinking hovel and never be seen again.

'Eleanor! Come here at once!'

He began to run as he shouted, sprinting after her down the narrow alley. She was fast, but she could not outrun him and it was not long before he caught up to her. He grabbed her arm, but she struggled and wrenched away again; he lunged at her and brought her down into the dust of the street. She scratched his face, fighting and kicking as she fought to throw him off, but he held her as easily as he would a child, laughing down at her as she raged in frustration.

'You would make a fine Janissary, my little bird—but do not make me hurt you more than I already have.' His eyes gleamed with triumph as he gazed down at her and Eleanor experienced the oddest feeling deep down inside her—it was as if a tide of molten heat had begun to rise up in her. 'Come, defy me no more.'

'You have not hurt me!' she said defiantly, but it was a lie because the fall had hurt her shoulder and his weight had crushed the breath from her. 'I hate you! You are a barbarian and a savage!'

Yet even as she lay beneath him and gazed into his fierce eyes, she felt the pull of his power and charm. He was not what she had named him, for if he had been she would have been treated more harshly. Her breath caught in her throat and she experienced a strange longing—a desire to be held in his arms and comforted.

Comforted by this man! What foolish idea was that? Her wits must be addled!

'It was your own fault,' he said as he pulled her roughly to her feet. 'You were foolish to try and run from me—there are worse things than being in a harem. You would have been taken a dozen times before this night was out and worse…'

'Nothing could be worse!' She flung the words at him. 'You will never take me willingly. No man will take me willingly…I shall fight to my last breath.'

'Then you will suffer,' Suleiman replied, his features harsh and unforgiving. 'If I wanted you…and I do not think you worth the bother…I would soon have you eating from my hand like a dove.'

'Hawks kill doves for their food,' Eleanor retorted. 'And you are a hawk—wild and dangerous.'

Suleiman's anger faded as swiftly as it had flared. He considered her words a compliment rather than the insult she had intended and was amused. He smiled and took her arm, leading her firmly back to where the litter and horses were waiting.

'I'm not going to wear that thing,' Eleanor said as she saw that one of his men had picked up her cloak. 'And I am not going to be carried in that stupid litter.'

'Then you will ride with me,' Suleiman said, a glimmer of amusement in his eyes. 'And you have only yourself to blame for this, Eleanor.'

He picked her up and flung her over his saddle so that she lay face down, then mounted swiftly before she could attempt to wriggle free. His knees were pressed against her, the reins firmly gripped above her head and she knew she could not free herself.

'You devil! Let me down at once! You cannot treat me like this! I am a lady…if you know what that means.'

'Be careful, Eleanor,' he warned, but there was laughter in his voice. 'I may have to beat you if you continue to flaunt my orders. My men are watching and I cannot allow a woman to dictate to me. You will lie there quietly until I decide to let you up—or you will be sorry.'

As he kicked his horse into a sudden canter at the same time as he spoke these words, Eleanor was unable to do anything. She was fuming, but she was also very uncomfortable. How dare he do this to her? She was indignant.

'You are a brute,' she muttered into the blanket that lay beneath his leather saddle. 'I hate you. You are just like those murdering pirates who killed my father. I would have killed them if I could—I will kill you if I get the chance!'

'Speak louder, Eleanor,' Suleiman said. 'I cannot hear you.'

She could hear the mockery in his voice and knew that he was laughing at her. He did not believe she could touch him—because he was too arrogant and sure of himself. He was accustomed to being obeyed instantly, and thought himself all-powerful. Well, just let him wait! One of these days she would make him sorry!

They had left the city walls behind before Suleiman stopped and lifted her into a sitting position, his arm about her waist pressing her to him, as much his prisoner as before. She had seen nothing but a blur of stone walls and dirt streets, keeping her eyes closed most of the time because she had been afraid of falling if she did not concentrate.

'Is that better?' he asked softly against her hair. 'I am sorry, little bird. That was unkind of me—but you made me angry. Besides, I had to make sure you could not get away from me. Constantinople is a dangerous place for a woman—especially one as lovely as you.'

'I know…Roxana told me.' Eleanor was leaning back against him; she had been feeling dizzy when he raised her, but now the unpleasant sensation was beginning to fade and she was oddly comforted by the feel of his strong arms about her as they rode. 'I would not have run…but I was afraid.'

'You told me you were not.'

'How could I not be?' Eleanor turned her head to glance at his face. 'You are going to give me to the Sultan. I cannot bear to be the concubine of a man I do not know—a much older man…'

'Would you prefer to be my concubine?' Suleiman whispered huskily against her hair, his voice so soft and low that she was not sure she had heard him correctly.

'I—I do not—'

What she was about to say was lost, for one of Suleiman's men gave a warning shout and, looking over his shoulder, Suleiman cursed. A small group of black robed men were riding fast towards them.

'Bandits,' he said. 'Hold tight, Eleanor. If you are taken by these men, you will wish you had died…'

Suleiman kicked at his horse's flank and they set off at a tremendous pace across the open countryside. She could see the pinkish stone walls of a great sprawling palace looming up ahead of them in the gathering darkness. Behind her she heard shouting and screaming as Suleiman's men joined battle with the bandits to allow him to reach the palace in safety, and then, as they drew close to the huge wooden gates they opened and a small troupe of horsemen raced out to join the escort guards.

'You are safe now, little one,' Suleiman whispered in her ear. 'You must not be afraid. Do what the women tell you and no harm will come to you. I give you my word.'

'The word of a barbarian?'

'The word of Caliph Bakhar's son,' Suleiman replied. 'You will discover soon that that means more than you might imagine…'

Eleanor waited as he leapt down from his horse's back and lifted her to the ground. Men had come running, and also an older woman dressed all in black. At a command from her master, she took Eleanor's arm and led her away. Eleanor looked back and saw that Suleiman had mounted a fresh horse. He was going back outside the gates to fight with his men. She wanted to stop him, to beg him not to risk his life, but he would not have listened. She was nothing, merely a slave he had bought as a gift for another man.

'What is happening?' she asked the old woman, who was pulling at her arm. 'Is the palace being attacked? Why has Suleiman gone back out there?'

The woman shook her head, clearly not understanding a word she said. Eleanor tried the same question in French, but there was no response.

The woman began to talk to her in what was probably Arabic. Eleanor thought she recognised a few words, but was not certain—though it was obvious that the woman wanted Eleanor to go with her. There was no point in resisting any further for the moment; besides, all the fight had suddenly gone out of her. Oddly, her fears at this moment were more for the man who had brought her here than for herself.

He had told her she would not be harmed if she

did as the women told her and somehow she believed him. But what of him? It was obvious that those men who had followed them were armed and dangerous—would Suleiman be killed in the fighting? She suddenly discovered that the thought appalled her.

Nothing must happen to Suleiman Bakhar! He was her only chance of ever being allowed to return to her family. She had called him a savage and a barbarian, but in her heart she knew he was not that—though she did not know what kind of a man he really was. He looked fierce and proud, and undoubtedly he was—but she believed there was a softer side to him. If she could reach that inner core, then there might be a faint hope for her…nothing must happen to him.

'May Allah keep you safe,' she whispered. 'And may God be with you this night.'

Let her prayers be heard by his god or hers. It did not matter at this moment as long as he lived. For, despite her attempts to escape him, and her anger at the way she had been treated, something deep inside her told her that she had been fortunate to be bought by this man…

'Allah be praised!' Caliph Bakhar said when they brought him the news that Suleiman had returned to the palace triumphant with his prisoners, who would be speedily dispatched the next morning at dawn. 'These bandits have been a thorn in my side for too long. My son has done well.'

He had been furious that Suleiman had put his own life at risk, but now that he was safe and the bandits taken, the Caliph's pride knew no bounds. Suleiman was a worthy son!

'Ask my son to eat with me this evening,' Ahmed

Bakhar said to the chief eunuch. 'I wish to tell him of my pleasure in his victory.'

Suleiman was emerging from his bath as the request was brought to him. He frowned, wrapping himself in a large white towel and waving the slave away.

'Tell my honoured father that I will come soon,' he said. 'Ask him to forgive me that I do not come at once.'

Another eunuch was waiting to help him dress. He allowed the creature to help him on with a simple white tunic and trousers. He would put on his costly robes when he went to his father's apartments—but for the moment he must visit the injured. His men had fought bravely against the bandits and one had died. Suleiman must make arrangements for him to be given a funeral worthy of a hero, and for recompense to be sent to his family.

He would have liked to send for Eleanor this evening, to talk to her—for he understood how strange it must be for a Western woman to suddenly find herself cast into an alien world. His mother had spoken to him of her own feelings when she first entered his father's harem, and although she had been very different from Eleanor—a quietly spoken, gentle woman—she had feared what she did not understand.

'I had been told that all Turks were savages,' she had said to her son as they sat talking together during their privileged afternoons. 'I was afraid that my new master would rape and beat me—but your father was kind and considerate and very soon I came to love him.'

Before he went to see his men, he must make sure that Eleanor was being treated as a woman of her class was entitled to be, even in a harem. She ought to have her own rooms and a servant to wait on her. He believed there was an Englishwoman in the palace…an old crone who had long since been put to work in the kitchens. She must be fetched and told to wait on her new mistress, and the older women must take care of Eleanor…prepare her for her new life.

He was not yet sure what her new life was to be. If she was not to be given to the Sultan he must find another gift…something rare and unusual that would pacify their illustrious master. For the moment he had other things on his mind. She would come to no harm within the palace—and he would have her sent for when he was ready to decide what to do with her.

Eleanor looked round the large chamber, which was the main one used by the harem for relaxing, talking and, perhaps, in the case of those concubines who did not have their own rooms, sleeping. There were divans covered in silks and satins, and piled with cushions for taking one's ease, also little tables on which were placed what looked like dishes of nuts and sweetmeats, fountains that played into small pools and various chests or cabinets. One girl was strumming on a musical instrument, the music strange and sounding off key to Eleanor.

The women gathered in small groups, talking, whispering and looking at her curiously. None of them had as yet approached her though she had been sitting on a cushion since the old woman had brought her here and then vanished.

What was she supposed to do? After the terror of her capture and the drama of that ride to the palace, it all felt rather like an anti-climax, simply sitting here watching several lovely women idle the hours away.

One girl was brushing the hair of another and braiding it with flowers or ribbons, others were painting their toenails with some kind of a dye—and one was having her body painted with a pattern in some black stuff.

At the far end of the room, Eleanor could see there was a door leading out to what looked like pleasant gardens. Was she allowed to go out there? She had certainly had enough of sitting here by herself. Oh, well, if it was forbidden, someone would stop her. She got up and wandered towards the door, thinking that the floors of mosaic tiling were very beautiful, as were some of the pierced screens that were painted in bright colours of red, blue and gold.

No one shouted at her to stop, so she went out into the garden. It was evening now and quite dark, but there were lanterns hanging amongst the trees and she was able to find her way along a winding path towards the sound of water. She found a stone seat by a pretty pool and sat down, staring into the darkness. Was she really going to be forced to spend the rest of her life in a place like this? If she were reduced to living the way the other women did, she would go mad.

Tears came to her eyes as she thought of her father and brother, and the evenings they had spent playing games of skill together. Her poor father! Her throat closed with emotion. How could she bear to live without the two people she loved most in the world?

Where was Richard? She had not seen him since they were both captured and did not even know if he were still alive. His fate was probably far worse than hers! She thought that he might have been tortured or beaten. Poor, poor Richard! She prayed that he was not in pain or desperately afraid. He was only a youth, and he would have had no chance against his captors. Her head went up as she renewed her vow not to give way to self-pity or despair. She would fight to survive and somehow she would win her freedom one day.

'Are you there, my lady?'

The sound of a woman's voice speaking to her in English brought her head up. How could that be? The old woman that had first taken charge of Eleanor and then abandoned her had not understood when she had tried to talk to her.

'Who are you? Please come forward.'

A woman stepped out of the shadows and approached diffidently. She was obviously quite old, her face lined and her hair deeply streaked with grey.

'I am Morna, my lady. I came to the palace many years ago as a gift to the Caliph, but he was never interested in me as one of his concubines because I was not beautiful. I was sent to the kitchens and I have worked there ever since.'

'Morna?' Eleanor looked at her. 'I do not think I have ever heard that name before—it is pretty.'

'My mother was English, but my father came from the hills of Wales,' Morna replied. 'I think it is an ancient Celtic name, though I cannot be sure.' She smiled at Eleanor. 'I am sorry Shorah deserted you earlier. I do not think she knew what to do with you, so she left you with the other concubines—and they ignored you because they were not sure why you were there either. It is dangerous to form relationships in the harem unless you know the status of those you befriend.'

'Shorah—that is the old woman who took charge

of me? I think she could not understand what I said to her.'

'No, she understands only her native tongue,' Morna replied. 'When I was told you were here I was not sure I would remember how to speak English. It is so long since I have used our language—but as you see, it came back to me.'

'Have you been here many years?'

'Oh, yes, much of my life has been spent in this palace. But I am fortunate. I am not important, merely a servant—so I am allowed to come and go as I please. I visit the market to buy food and trinkets for the women sometimes. They repay me by giving me some of their food—so I live very well.'

'Can you help me to leave the palace?' Eleanor asked eagerly. 'Is there any way I could escape?'

'They would kill us both if you tried to leave,' Morna told her gravely. 'It seems that you have caught the eye of the Caliph's son. You are to be given your own rooms and I am to wait upon you—as befits a lady of your rank.'

'What does that mean?' Eleanor asked. 'Am I to stay here, then? I thought...' She let the words die unspoken. Roxana had told her she would be lucky if Suleiman Bakhar kept her for himself, and she was beginning to believe that that might be the case. Better a young, intelligent master who spoke her tongue and might just be persuaded to let her go home, than the Sultan who would scarcely notice her amongst his other women. 'No, it does not matter. You could not know what is in *his* mind. Please take me to my rooms. I am tired and I should like to sleep now.'

'Would you like me to bring you food from the

kitchens?' Morna asked, sounding eager. 'Surely you are hungry, my lady?'

Eleanor was about to reply that she had eaten earlier and was not hungry, but she realised that Morna might not get enough to eat and was hoping that some of her mistress's food might be left for her.

'Yes, bring me something,' she said. 'You can share it with me.'

'Thank you, my lady. You are generous.'

Eleanor nodded, but did not reply. She supposed there were probably hundreds of servants in this vast palace, which sprawled over a large area of land and consisted of a mass of different buildings. Many of the slaves were probably forced to live on the scraps left by others. The world was a cruel place, especially for slaves, and she was angry that people like the Caliph and his arrogant son believed they had the right to dispose of the lives of others as they chose.

'Where is the Caliph's son?' she asked. 'Has he returned to the palace?'

'Oh, yes, some time ago,' Morna replied. 'It is by his order that you have been given your own rooms.'

'He has not asked for me?'

'Our master's son has not chosen a woman this night,' Morna replied. 'They say he is with the physicians who tend the wounded—and that he has spoken to the family of the man who died. The Janissaries are all Suleiman Bakhar's friends. He trains with them every day. Sometimes there is much sport in the courtyard, and you may be allowed to watch him wrestling or fighting with the others if you are lucky.'

Eleanor was astonished. 'Why should I wish to watch that barbarian at sport?'

'Hush!' Morna glanced over her shoulder nervously. 'You should not say such things—ears may be listening. We are always watched in the harem. There are spies everywhere. Fatima will have heard that you have arrived by now and she will not be pleased that you have been given your own apartments.'

'Who is Fatima?'

'She is the lord Suleiman's favourite. She rules the harem and all the other women are afraid of her.'

'Why—what harm can she do them?'

'Many unpleasant things can happen in this place,' Morna warned. 'Fatima is jealous of any woman she thinks might take her place as Suleiman's chief concubine. She is hoping he will take her as his wife—but she has not yet given him a child, and they say he will not marry her unless she does.'

'I have no wish to lie in Suleiman Bakhar's bed,' Eleanor said. 'Besides, the other women will not understand what we say if we speak in English—will they?'

'Most will not,' Morna agreed, 'but there are those who do—some of the eunuchs understand English, French or Spanish as well as many other languages. It is the eunuchs who spy on the harem all the time. Some do it from idle curiosity, some to discover what they can for their masters—but others have their own reasons.'

'What do you mean?' Eleanor looked at her curiously. 'They…cannot desire a woman for themself, can they?'

'No—not a true eunuch,' Morna replied in a whisper. 'But sometimes…no, I dare not say. It is forbidden and would cause trouble if it were discovered.'

Eleanor saw that the old woman was frightened and
did not press her further, though she thought Morna
must be hinting that the women were not as protected
as their master imagined. It was clear that there were
many mysteries and intrigues in the harem, and that
life there was not quite as it had seemed as she'd
watched the women amusing themselves earlier

Morna had led her to a room that was slightly apart
from the main one that she had seen earlier. There
were actually three small interconnecting rooms. One
had a little pool for bathing and a place for relieving
the bodily functions, one for sleeping (with a couch
for her servant at the foot of her own divan) and one
for sitting. All of them were luxuriously tiled and
hung with silken drapes of pink and silver. There
were cabinets of dark wood inlaid with silver, mother
of pearl and small semi-precious stones, also stools
and little tables.

'The rooms are very nice,' Eleanor said. 'At least
I shall be able to be private sometimes—but what am
I supposed to do? What are my duties, Morna? Am I
to be given no work—no occupation?'

'The ladies of the harem are here to please their
master,' Morna replied. 'You simply amuse yourself
until you are called to the bedchamber and then...
well, then you do as you are told, and smile if you
do not wish to be beaten.'

A little shudder went through Eleanor. 'That is
truly a savage custom! I refuse to obey the whim of
a man simply because he paid another man money
for me.'

Morna shook her head at her sadly. 'You will learn
soon enough,' she said. 'I shall fetch food, my lady.
You should eat and rest—for tomorrow you will meet

the important women of the harem, and they will begin to school you for those duties you say you will
not accept…'

Eleanor stared in frustration as the servant left her.
She could not stay here! She would die of boredom.
How could all those women out there be content to
sit around and wait patiently until their master decided to send for them—and what if he never did?

What if she never saw Suleiman again? She would
not be able to win her freedom unless she could persuade him to ransom her…

Fatima glared at the woman who had brought her
the information that the new arrival had been given
rooms of her own. She gave a little scream of rage
and struck Shorah across the face, leaving a nasty red
mark.

'I told you to leave her with the other concubines.
I gave orders that she was to be ignored!'

'It was the order of Suleiman Bakhar himself,'
Shorah replied, her head bowed before the favourite,
hiding the gleam of resentment in her eyes. 'I had
nothing to do with it, mistress.'

Fatima swore beneath her breath. Word had been
brought to her that Suleiman had gone to the city to
see a beautiful woman and that he had paid a fabulous
price for her—but she had believed the woman was
to be a gift for the Sultan. Now it looked as though
Suleiman might be planning to keep her for himself.
He might even take her as his wife…and that was a
position Fatima wanted for herself. As a concubine
she could be sold or given away to another man, but
as the lord Suleiman's wife she would be safe and
ruler of the harem.

'Is she beautiful?' she demanded suddenly of the old woman. 'This new woman—more beautiful than me?'

'No one could be more beautiful than you, mistress.'

Fatima nodded. She knew that her dark hair was shiny from all the oils rubbed into it, and her skin was soft and smooth to the touch, exuding a heavy perfume that was guaranteed to drive men wild. And her lord had shown himself no different from others in that respect. She spent most of her time bathing and being prepared for the moment she would be sent for—but Suleiman had not sent for her that evening.

It was most unusual. He always sent for a woman after he had won one of his games of skill—and he was always in a good mood at these times—but he had not sent for Fatima that night. Her one consolation was that he had not sent for the new woman either, choosing to waste his time in comforting the family of the man who had died, and in visiting the wounded.

Yet she feared this woman she had not yet seen. It was said that she was an English gentlewoman—and therefore more dangerous than any of the other concubines. Suleiman's mother had been English, and Fatima knew that he had fond memories of his childhood.

Suleiman was hard to fathom. When he fought with the Janissaries, Fatima understood the excitement and his feelings of triumph when he won—and she knew that he was a skilled and passionate lover when he chose. However, he often spent his evenings talking, either with his teacher or his friends…they spoke of strange, intricate matters that Fatima would have found boring had she been allowed to listen. She was not, of course. Women were for pleasure, and when Suleiman sent for her she knew how to please him…except that he had not seemed pleased on the last few occasions he had sent for her.

Indeed, she had felt that he did not really want her, and that he would have preferred to be talking with his teacher. She had been glad when she learned the teacher had gone away, thinking that Suleiman would want her more often. Instead he had chosen to invite his friends from the Janissaries to eat and drink with him, and, though, he ordered the dancing girls to perform and he allowed his friends to take their pick of them, he had not sent for Fatima.

She had feared that her lord might have heard whispers concerning her and yet that could not be—he could suspect nothing, for her creature would have told her.

Fatima knew everything that went on in Suleiman's private apartments, because she held one of the eunuchs in the palm of her hand. He was her dog, less than dirt to her because he was not a proper man— but he was also useful. She held the power of life and death over him, could expose him as a traitor to his master if she chose—and so he reported everything that went on to Fatima.

She would soon know what Suleiman intended for his new woman—and she would make her own plans accordingly.

Chapter Four

Eleanor was roused by the sound of a disturbance. She had been dreaming happily of a certain misty morning in England, when she had ridden out with her father, and was startled by the noise of screeching voices. Waking suddenly to the unfamiliar surroundings, she had wondered where on earth she was. As realisation dawned on her she was swamped with a feeling of intense unhappiness; then, before she could gather her thoughts, a very beautiful, dark-haired woman, dressed in a rich red tunic and pants embroidered heavily with silver and pearls, rushed into the bedroom.

'How dare you tell your servant to keep me out?' she demanded in excellent French. 'No one tells me I may not enter anywhere within the harem!'

Eleanor stared at her as the mists of sleep began to clear, and she remembered what Morna had told her the previous night. This must obviously be Fatima, Suleiman Bakhar's favourite concubine—and she was clearly in a temper.

'I believe you would not appreciate a visit from me without some warning?' Eleanor replied in the same language Fatima had used. She lifted her head proudly and assumed the haughtiest manner she could. 'While you are always welcome in my apartments, Fatima, politeness shows good breeding.'

Fatima's mouth opened in surprise. No one addressed her in such a manner! Had they dared, she would have ordered Abu to flog them. For a moment she could not speak, then her dark brown eyes narrowed to suspicious splits, and she was tempted to order this woman beaten, but caution held her back. Suleiman had only recently bought her, and he might notice if her skin were accidentally marked.

'Who are you?' she demanded imperiously. 'And why are you here?'

'Because I was brought here much against my will,' Eleanor said, remaining calm despite her instant dislike of the other woman, 'I have no wish to be in this place and would leave this minute if I could. Believe me, I am no threat to you, Fatima—nor would I wish to be. My only desire is to be returned to my home. I am the daughter of an English baronet, and my family is wealthy—they will be searching for me even now.'

Fatima's dark eyes narrowed in suspicion, her lovely face still reflecting sullen anger. 'How do you know who I am?'

'I have been told of Suleiman Bakhar's beautiful favourite,' Eleanor said. 'Who else would you be?'

Fatima nodded. Put that way, it sounded like a compliment. She knew that the other women were afraid of her—and that the servant woman Morna was firmly on this upstart's side. Before long, the women of the harem would start to take sides, especially now that this Englishwoman had been given special status.

They would believe that Fatima had begun to lose Suleiman's favour, and once that happened they would not hesitate to follow a new leader. That could be dangerous for Fatima, for she had enemies who would use any chance to strike at her. Perhaps it would be wiser to get to know this woman better.

'Tell your servant not to bar my way in future— but do not punish her. She will be no use to you if she cannot work.' Fatima's expression changed subtly. 'I do not like to be thwarted, but if you truly mean that you do not wish to become Suleiman's favourite, we may be friends. You are more my equal than any of the other women here. I am the daughter of a French nobleman and an Arab dancing girl. Until my father was lost at sea we lived in a beautiful villa in Algiers, then my mother was cast out and she sold herself to a master so that we could live. I was trained all my life to give pleasure to the man who would one day own me…that is why Suleiman sends always for me. I am the only one who really knows how to please him. He will never put me aside for another.'

'I am very glad to hear it,' Eleanor said immediately. 'I have no wish to be bad friends with you, Fatima. Nor do I wish to be sent for in the way you speak of. Indeed, if you could help me to escape, I would leave the harem.'

'That is impossible,' Fatima said and frowned. 'We can none of us leave here unless Suleiman grants us freedom.'

'Does that ever happen?'

'Sometimes…' Fatima gave her a long hard look. 'The Caliph would have freed Suleiman's mother after she gave him a son, but she preferred to stay here

and became his favourite wife. They say he still
mourns her.'

'Tell me more about her, please?'

'Why do you want to know?' Fatima's mood altered once more. She would tell this woman nothing
that might help her to secure Suleiman's favour. 'I
have no time to talk with you. I came only to make
sure you understood your place here…'

Eleanor watched as the other woman left the room
abruptly. It was clear that Fatima still did not trust
her; she probably imagined Eleanor was scheming to
become Suleiman's wife.

'Forgive me,' Morna said as she came in after the
favourite had left. 'I could not stop her bursting in on
you. I told her you were sleeping, but she would not
listen to me.'

'It doesn't matter,' Eleanor replied. 'Do not risk her
temper again, Morna. Just ask her to wait one moment
while you wake me—but it was unusual for me to
sleep so deeply. What time is it? It feels as if half the
day has gone.'

'You were exhausted,' Morna replied. 'The refresh-
ing drink you enjoyed last night was a tisane I made
to help you pass a peaceful night. I knew that you
needed rest or you might have lain awake all night
thinking and weeping.'

'That was a kind thought,' Eleanor said, 'but do
not give me such a drink again unless I request it.'

Eleanor had been sitting up against a pile of silk
cushions, but now she put her feet to the floor, a feeling of hope and determination surging through her.
She had been at the edge of despair when Fatima
broke in on her so rudely, but for some reason the
other woman had aroused her fighting instincts. She

was not going to be put down by Fatima or anyone else! Nor did she wish to be lulled into a false sense of security by drugging drinks designed to dull her senses. She did not wish to be here and she would escape or win her freedom some other way if she could, but until then she would set herself to making what she could of her life.

'Is it possible to have writing materials brought to me, Morna?'

'Perhaps…but you would not be allowed to send a letter to anyone, my lady.'

'It is not for writing a letter,' Eleanor said. 'I must have something to occupy my mind or I shall go mad. I thought that perhaps you would teach me the language and customs you have learned. I could write the words down and practise them when I am alone.'

'I could bring you a slate and marker,' Morna said. 'We have them in the kitchens for noting down what is needed from the markets—but pen and paper would have to be authorised by the eunuchs.'

'And how do we ask them for things?'

'Fatima is usually the one to approach,' Morna said. 'But you have been given rooms and a servant of your own…you might be given other things if you ask.'

'Bring the slate for the moment,' Eleanor said. 'We can begin my lessons after I have bathed and eaten. What shall I wear? Surely I do not need all the garments I was made to wear yesterday?'

'Karin brought clothes for you earlier,' Morna said. 'She is the most important woman after Fatima…but much older. If Suleiman's mother still lived, she would rule over his harem until he took a chief wife, but Karin is one of the Caliph's older wives. She was visiting with relatives yesterday, but you will meet her later today. She will explain many things to you, much better than I could, my lady.'

'Very well.' Eleanor smiled at her. 'It was very fortunate for me that you were here, Morna. At least I feel that I have one friend in the palace—one person that I may trust.'

'I am happy to be your servant, my lady.'

'I would rather that we were friends,' Eleanor said and smiled. 'We must try to help each other, Morna. If there is something I can do for you—you must tell me.'

'I am always hungry,' the old woman replied. 'All I ask these days is food to eat and somewhere to sleep. To serve you, my lady, is much easier than the work I was put to in the kitchens.'

Eleanor nodded. 'Then I shall see that you share my food—and if ever I am able to leave here, I shall try to take you with me.'

'No, I do not wish to leave,' Morna replied. 'I have no life other than here. I am content to remain in the Caliph's household until I die…there is nowhere for me to go now. I am too old. I should be forced to beg on the streets for my food.'

Eleanor's eyes stung with tears as she turned away. How sad that this woman's life had been wasted in such a terrible way. Morna's hopelessness made Eleanor even more determined that whatever was forced upon her, she would not let herself become enslaved…

Suleiman spent the morning exercising with the Janissaries. After he had bathed and received a brisk massage from one of the eunuchs, he ate sparingly of dates and rice mixed with spiced lamb, then drank several cups of the rich dark coffee he enjoyed. The afternoon stretched emptily before him, and he felt the loss of his old teacher keenly. There must be other clever men, with whom he could share a pleasant afternoon, but Saidi Kasim had understood him so well, and they had been friends. There were few within the palace that Suleiman could truly call his friends—he could not even be sure of the loyalty of his half-brothers Bayezid and Hasan, for there was always rivalry between the sons of important men.

Suleiman's thoughts turned towards the woman he had brought to the palace the previous evening. She would have spent the morning with Karin, being taught how to behave in the harem, and what to expect of her new life. It was too soon to send for her if he expected her to please him as the other women did—and yet he wanted to speak with her.

All at once, Suleiman realised that he did not want her to be the same as the other women. He would send for her now and talk to her himself, explain that he would like to know her better before she became one of his concubines...no, perhaps his wife.

Suleiman must marry soon and give his father the grandsons the Caliph longed for, and Eleanor was the only woman he had so far found that he deemed fit to be the mother of those sons. She had spirit and intelligence, and she would surely accept her fate if it were properly explained to her. He would tell her that she was to be honoured above all the other women, and that he would give her time to adjust to her new life. She had accused him of being a barbarian, but he would show her that she was wrong.

He was pleased with himself as he summoned the eunuch and told him to send for Eleanor.

'She is to be brought to me at once,' he ordered. 'There is to be no ritual of the bath—no special pampering.'

The eunuch nodded and went away to execute his master's orders, which were most unusual. Indeed, no woman had ever been sent for in such a manner. Suleiman always made his choice early in the afternoon and the woman was prepared for him in the time-honoured way—to send for her so abruptly must mean that she was to be punished. Which would please Fatima, of course.

A little smile touched Abu's mouth. It would not suit him if Fatima were to be displaced by this new woman. Fatima was a bad-tempered, spoiled cat—but she suited Abu. She believed she held the power, and he allowed her to dictate to him while she kept his secrets. It was an arrangement that gave something to them both—and placed both in equal danger. For if Suleiman ever guessed what sometimes took place in the secret places of his father's palace, both Fatima and Abu would be put to death.

So Abu would help Fatima to overcome the challenge of this new woman—and Suleiman had unwittingly helped them by showing his displeasure in this way.

Eleanor was fascinated as she listened to Karin talk of life in her country, telling her of simple family life and the way the common folk lived, which was very different from the noble lords in their rich palaces.

The older woman had come to her after she had bathed, taking her into a secluded corner of the gardens so that they could talk in private. Speaking in French, which was the foreign language spoken most often in the harem, she had told Eleanor a little of the history of the Turkish Sultans and their Sultanas, and found her an apt pupil.

'I have been told that you speak three languages,' she said in her soft, musical voice. 'And that you may understand a little Arabic.'

'I can read it a little,' Eleanor said. 'But I do not understand the language the other women speak...'

'That is because they have so many different tongues and dialects and they have found their own way to communicate. The perfection of pure Arabic is only found in the written form, and that is what you have learned—but here you will soon begin to understand what is being said to you.'

'I have asked Morna to bring writing materials so that I can write down the words and learn them when I am alone.'

'But you must not spend all your time alone,' the older woman told her. 'You should learn to enjoy the pleasures offered you in this place, Eleanor. There are many more than you might imagine. Once you learn to relax you will enjoy having sweet oils massaged into your skin, and it is pleasant to bathe in the pools—there are large pools both in the garden and inside the palace. Also you may have music lessons and you may learn to dance if you choose; it is good exercise and a skill that may be helpful to you. The other women will be friendly towards you after I have spoken to them, and you may pass your time in playing games or helping each other to braid your hair.'

'But what of my mind?' Eleanor replied. 'I have

been used to study—is it possible for me to have books?'

Karin frowned. 'I am not sure if this would be permitted. I cannot grant you such a favour, Eleanor—you must wait until you are sent for—' She broke off as she saw the eunuch striding purposefully towards them. 'Perhaps you will not have to wait so very long…'

She rose to her feet as the eunuch approached. 'You wish to speak with me, Abu?'

'The woman is to come with me!'

'Now?' Karin was startled. This was unheard of! Suleiman never sent such a message—unless he was very displeased. He must be angry with Eleanor for some reason. 'Where are you taking her? Is she to be punished?'

'That is for Suleiman Bakhar to decide—he has sent for her.'

Abu grasped Eleanor's arm, pulling her roughly to her feet. She stared at him haughtily as she felt his fingers dig cruelly into her arm. Something in his eyes sent shivers through her and she knew that this man liked to punish others.

'How dare you?' she said. 'Take your hand from me, sir.'

Abu looked into her eyes, and for a moment he felt compelled to obey her, and then he recalled Suleiman's orders. 'You are to come with me at once!'

'Unless you take your hand from my arm, you will have to drag me there.'

'Disobey me, woman, and it will be the worse for you!'

'Go with him, Eleanor,' Karin told her, looking

anxious. 'Let go of her arm, Abu. It is not necessary. She will not try to run away—where could she go? Besides, if she resists you, you may bruise her skin, and that would not please your master.'

Abu's eyes narrowed. Most of the women obeyed him instantly. Indeed, they were all afraid of him— afraid of his power—but Karin was not under his jurisdiction, and he could not threaten her. Besides, he was not absolutely sure that this Englishwoman was to be punished.

He glared at Eleanor, but let her arm go. 'You are to come at once. My master wishes to see you now.'

'He wishes to talk with you, Eleanor,' Karin said, seeking to reassure her. 'You have not been prepared for him, nor received instruction—so there will be nothing else required of you today.'

Eleanor looked at the older woman and nodded, understanding what she was telling her. She was not to be taken to Suleiman's bed that afternoon. Perhaps he had decided to tell her what he intended to do with her—he might even have thought over what she had said to him the previous day and was perhaps prepared to sell her to her family. She lifted her head proudly as hope flowed anew.

'Very well, you may lead me to Suleiman Bakhar.'

Abu thought of the soft whips he used so skilfully that they left barely a mark on the skin of his victims, and of how much he would like to teach this woman a lesson she would not soon forget. He had been robbed of the pleasures that were his right as a man by the surgeon's knife, but he gained much pleasure in seeing women on their knees begging for mercy. One night he and Fatima would pay this haughty bitch a little visit...

Eleanor was aware of evil in the man who walked so softly just ahead of her, leading the way through the women's apartments to an even larger and more luxurious chamber which formed part of the harem, but was used by Suleiman and not entered by the women unless invited. This was furnished much as the harem, with richly patterned tiles on walls, floors and some ceilings, but also contained many items, which she knew had come from other lands. She was not allowed to linger and examine the curious items she saw placed in alcoves and on little tables, but she believed that some of them were scientific instruments for the study of astrology, and there were also several rather beautiful clocks.

Who used the astrological instruments? She had no time to wonder for they continued through this apartment into another, which was clearly used for sitting with soft cushions and divans placed here and there on gleaming marble floors. Her attention was drawn to the man who occupied the largest divan; he seemed to be interested in some object he was holding, which as they drew closer she saw was what appeared to be a fabulous clock. She thought it was made of gold and saw that it was shaped like a polygon, with intricate workings clearly visible at the top. Quite fascinating!

'On your knees, woman!' Abu hissed.

'No!' Suleiman countermanded the order instantly. 'You may remain standing, my lady.' He stood up and held out his hand to her. 'Come, sit with me.'

Suleiman drew her down to the divan beside him and, seeing that the object he had been looking at as she entered had caught her interest, smiled. 'It is a clock, you see,' he said. 'Made by the great French clockmaker Pierre de Fobis—it strikes the hour…'

'It is beautiful,' Eleanor said, marvelling at the beauty of the clock. 'Is the case of gold?'

'Yes—but it is the way the running mechanisms are arranged one over the other so intricately that is so fascinating. Do you see?'

She looked closer as he demonstrated the strike to her and nodded, thrilled by its wonders. 'It is truly magnificent, my lord. My father had a beautiful German clock at home in his study. Its case was of ebony, jasper, lapis lazuli and silver gilt—but the works were hidden and the clock was not as fascinating as this one. I have never seen anything to equal this. It must be very valuable? I noticed others as we came, and I think that you have quite a collection of them.'

Suleiman nodded, then, looking up, he saw that Abu was still standing there as though waiting for something, and he waved his hand impatiently to dismiss him.

'Do you think this clock a gift worthy of a Sultan?' he asked Eleanor when they were alone. 'I must give our master something rare and fine instead of the gift I had planned for him. To give him less than the best would be an insult—is this fine enough, do you think?'

'It is a gift any prince would appreciate,' Eleanor replied honestly. 'Such things are usually only found at the courts of rich and powerful rulers. I think it extremely fine and it must be rare. I dare say there is not such another anywhere in Christendom—or the Ottoman Empire either. You have a unique treasure, my lord.'

Suleiman nodded, his eyes moving over her with approval. She was as intelligent, as he had thought her at the start. The clock was the rarest of his own collection and he had prized it greatly—but he could offer nothing less to the Sultan since he had decided that he could not bring himself to part with Eleanor.

'Then it shall be given to him,' Suleiman said, a wicked gleam in his eyes. 'Which brings me to you— what shall I do with you, my lady? I fear you are too wilful and disobedient to make a gift for the Sultan, which means that I have paid a great deal too much for you.'

'Ransom me to my family,' she replied eagerly. She had seen the gleam but missed its significance, for she did not yet know him. 'I should be so grateful to you, my lord. I know they would pay much for my safe return.'

'But I have no need of money,' Suleiman pointed out. He was enjoying himself toying with her, watching the emotions play across her expressive face. She was beautiful, but there was much more to her, and he wanted to know all. 'My father is very rich and I shall one day inherit all that is his…so what can your family offer me?'

'My father had many rare books at home in England…' Suleiman dismissed the offer with a dismissive shrug. 'He has other treasures…and I have this…' Eleanor took the little trinket she wore about her neck, which had been hidden under her clothes, and handed it to him. 'It has a little stopper, my lord—open it and see what it contains.'

Suleiman stared at the gold trinket suspiciously, almost as though he imagined it might contain poison, she thought, then he removed the stopper and took out the tiny manuscript inside. He looked at it in silence for several minutes.

'What is this? And why do you carry it with you?' He looked at her with interest. 'Do you know what is written here?'

'Yes, my lord. It is a part of the Qur'an, and the work seems to have been executed by a Christian Abbot. It was my father's and he gave it to me for safe keeping before we left Italy,' Eleanor replied. 'It is believed to be part of the treasure of the Abbey of the Far Cross and was found buried on my father's land in Cyprus. There may be more…and I believe it to be very rare.'

'I have heard of this,' Suleiman said and frowned. He replaced the tiny manuscript in its holder and returned it to her. 'The story escapes me for the moment. Kasim told me once of the Abbot of the Far Cross, but I cannot call his words to mind for the present.'

'The Abbey was burned to the ground by Saracens,' Eleanor replied, 'and the treasure stolen, but I do not know any more of the legend. My father was researching it…' She gave a little sob of grief and Suleiman's gaze narrowed.

'What happened to him?'

'He was killed when the ship was attacked.' She raised her head, her eyes bright with the tears she refused to shed before him. 'He was trying to defend me.'

'Ah…I see,' he said and nodded, understanding the terrible grief in her face. He would feel thus if his own father were killed before his eyes. 'And you were fond of your father.'

'Yes. I loved him very much—and my brother. I do not know what happened to Richard…'

'You grieve for your loved ones,' Suleiman said. 'I understand, my lady. It is hard for you—to come to a world that must seem alien to you after losing all that was dear. You thought us all like the Corsairs who attacked your ship, but I hope that you have begun to see that this is not the case?'

Eleanor was silent for a moment, then she nodded. 'I was wrong to call you a barbarian,' she said, 'but your ways are strange to me. I find it very wrong that one man should keep another as his slave. And why must you keep your women imprisoned?'

'Are your customs so very different?' Suleiman's brows arched. 'Your servants are treated no better than our slaves. We do not pay them money for their service, but they are housed and fed as well as your servants—perhaps better. Those who deserve it can rise to positions of importance—and we have a system by which men who convert to Islam can become persons of wealth and standing, no matter what their beginnings.'

'The Devishirme system? Yes, my father told me of it,' Eleanor replied. 'But they are still bound to a master in most cases—and women are not given the same privileges.'

'Women cannot expect to live as men,' Suleiman said and frowned at her. 'But they are protected and cared for and most are happy to live within the harem. Some become influential in their own right. My mother was one such woman. My father always asked her advice on anything that troubled him. She was granted many privileges and might have returned to her homeland had she wished.'

'Then she was fortunate,' Eleanor replied, a flash of anger in her eyes. 'But what of those who are never allowed to leave the harem? What are they supposed to do with themselves? What am I supposed to do? I shall die of boredom if I am forced to live as the others do, idling the hours away in vain pursuits. I need to be able to study…to use my mind…to think for myself.'

Suleiman nodded and smiled. 'These things may be arranged in time. Would you like to see my scientific instruments, my lady? I think they might interest you—and I have many ancient manuscripts, which we might study together if they please you.'

'They would interest me very much,' Eleanor said, caught by his promises despite herself. 'But will you not consider returning me to my family, my lord?'

'That is out of the question. I wish to hear no more of it.' He frowned at her, his mood of indulgence gone. 'Have you listened to nothing I have said to you? I have been trying to show you that you have nothing to fear here—that if you please me, I may choose to honour you as my mother was honoured.'

Eleanor's head went up, her eyes proud as she looked at him. 'No matter what honour you choose to give me, I should still belong to you,' she said. 'I should be no different from your other women—a slave and kept here in the palace against my will. I can never consent to such an arrangement, my lord.'

'If you had married in your own world you would have belonged to your husband. A woman is no freer in your country than here,' Suleiman said, a glint of temper in his dark eyes. Why would she not listen to what he was saying? Did she still scorn him as the savage she had named him? 'Where is the difference?'

'My father would never have forced me to marry,' Eleanor replied, tears in her lovely eyes. 'I would only have done so if I loved—and in love a man does not own, or demand, he gives himself. The woman also gives of her own free will. Only in this manner can true happiness be achieved by either.'

'And how do you know this?' He looked at her hard, his mouth drawn into a thin line. 'Have you known love—the love between a man and his woman?'

Eleanor blushed as she saw the accusation in his eyes. 'If you are asking if I have known a man in…*that* way, the answer is no. I am insulted that you should need to ask! I know because I have observed others—and seen unhappy marriages, some amongst my own friends and relations.'

'Do not lie to me. I can have the women examine you to discover the truth. It will go hard with you if I learn that you have deceived me!'

She could see that he was angry, and though tempted to lie in the hope that he would no longer want to keep her, something held her back. She did not want him to think her a loose woman.

'I swear by my father's love and all that I hold sacred that I have not.'

'If I thought…I would send you to the slave market,' Suleiman said harshly. 'But, no, I believe you…you would not be so foolish as to defy me. You know that I could have you punished. I still might. If you defy me too often I might decide to have you disciplined, to teach you to respect your master.'

'You will not break my spirit that way!'

The sudden defiance in her eyes made him smile inwardly. 'Oh, I think I could find a way to break you if I chose, Eleanor. Do not tempt me, woman—or I might have you whipped. Did you know that there are whips made of leather so soft that they can inflict terrible pain without breaking the skin?'

Eleanor flinched as she saw the way his eyes had suddenly become as cruel and bright as a hawk's about to pounce on its prey. He was an intelligent man, perhaps even clever, but there *was* a streak of savagery in his character. It was a part of his birthright, and though he had learned discipline and respect for others, something warned her that it might be possible to push him too far.

'If you want me to beg you not to punish me, my lord, I shall not. I cannot pretend to feel other than I do. As yet, I have been shown only generosity at your hands. I know this—even though I cannot but resent the fact that you bought me as if I were a horse.'

'Not as if you were a horse,' he said and laughed deep in his throat. There was such fire in her! She burned him while she amused him—and he had not been amused this much in an age. 'I would never pay so much for a horse, my lady—however noble its breed.'

Eleanor felt the power of his smile, and it made her gasp. She felt that she was being mesmerised by something in those dark eyes as he leaned towards her. She could smell the cleanliness of his body, so different from the smells that attached to many men of her own race, and another more subtle perfume she could not name. The combination was intoxicating!

She was powerless to move as his eyes held hers in a compelling gaze, her throat catching with some strange emotion. His mouth touched hers softly and she felt herself swaying towards him, as if wanting his kiss to deepen and become something more, but she suddenly pulled herself back sharply, refusing to give into the wicked urgings of her sinful body. He would bend her to his will and then discard her.

'No! You shall not bewitch me, sir! I do not know what arts you would employ, but I shall not succumb to them.'

Suleiman's mouth twitched at the corners, releasing her as if her defiance amused him—and his amusement made her temper flare. Did he think himself too powerful to be resisted? She leapt to her feet, facing him defiantly.

'Please send me back to the harem—or to the kitchens. Since I am not to be returned to my family, I would prefer to work in the kitchens as Morna does.'

Suleiman's gaze narrowed. 'You do not know of what you speak, foolish woman. Is it that you would prefer to bed with one of the Janissaries? You would not long remain untouched in the kitchens—ask Morna if you do not believe me.'

'I wish only to be free!'

'My patience wears thin,' he replied. 'I have told you that you are to be honoured in a very special way—and yet you still refuse to be pacified. I could have you punished, woman. Shall I summon Abu?'

'Is that the eunuch who brought me here?' Eleanor shivered. 'I do not like him—he is evil.'

'What do you mean?' Her words echoed a feeling long held by Suleiman without truly knowing why. 'Explain yourself.'

'I—I do not know,' she confessed. 'It is only an

intuition—but I sense that he likes to punish others. I think him cruel and sly…'

'Yes, he is sly,' Suleiman agreed. 'I have known it before now. I confess I do not like the creature—but I shall not have him frighten you. He shall be given other duties.'

'Thank you…you are kind, my lord.'

'I would be much kinder to you if you would be as kind to me.'

The husky tone of Suleiman's voice made Eleanor tremble inside. She drew a deep breath, knowing that he had already indulged her beyond what was normal for a man in such a position as his. Even in her own land very few men would show as much patience as this one had.

'I would be your friend if you wished it,' she said after a moment's thought. 'If you wished for someone to help you decipher your manuscripts, I would copy them in a fair hand. And I often helped my father when he was researching some legend he wished to authenticate.'

'You can write a legible hand—one that others can read?'

'Yes, my lord.'

'My own writing is very small,' he replied. 'Kasim told me anyone else would need spectacles to read it—he could not read it himself. Are you able to decipher small lettering?'

'Yes, my lord. I can read Latin and Arabic, but I fear I have not yet mastered Greek. It was my hope to learn when we were settled in Cyprus.'

'I might teach you,' Suleiman said. 'If it pleased me—but you would have to please me, my lady.'

Eleanor raised her head, her face proud and haughty. 'I do not bargain for my honour, sir.'

'You are too proud and wilful,' he cried, a flash of temper in his eyes because she still defied him after all the concessions he had made her. 'Go back where you came from before I change my mind and send for Abu to punish you after all!'

Eleanor knew that she had angered him as he turned and went into the adjoining chamber, leaving her alone. She hesitated for a moment, then she too turned and walked back the way she had come.

What would he do next? He had said that he would never ransom her to her family, but perhaps if she could do him some service—but he was angry with her now. He had called her proud and wilful, and she knew that was true—it had ever been her way. Her father had indulged her, and she had always shown him her obedient face, for she'd had no reason to defy him. Perhaps she ought to have spoken more diplomatically to Suleiman Bakhar. He was clearly a reasonable man—though she had caught a glimpse of the other side of his nature just for a moment.

He was capable of anger, that she knew. How close had she come to being punished? She could not be sure. He had walked away from her after his threat, but supposing he changed his mind—supposing he had her beaten with the whips he had spoken of?

A shiver ran through Eleanor and she knew a moment of fear. Would she be as brave if her master had her beaten? Would she be able to face him so proudly in the future?

And yet there was a little voice in her head that told her Suleiman admired her spirit. She had seen his eyes gleam with inner amusement when she defied him. Why was that? He had absolute power over his harem. Why should he have tried to persuade her?

He could simply have had her prepared for his bed and then he could have forced her to become his concubine. Why had he not done so?

Eleanor sensed that he was a complicated man, that perhaps there was a battle going on inside him. He was, after all, the son of an English gentlewoman. Could it be that he was not completely at ease in the world in which he lived?

Was it possible that he saw the evil of slavery, but could not deny his heritage?

Suleiman was the Caliph's favourite son and his heir. To deny the very foundations of his life would be to throw all the benefits of rank and privilege away—to deny his very being. And yet she had sensed restlessness in him, a desire for something more than he had…yet what was there that a man like Suleiman Bakhar could not have with a snap of his fingers?

It was clear that the Caliph was extremely wealthy, and that his son was equally so—and yet she had sensed a need in him. Perhaps if he sent for her again she would try to reach that inner being…through talking of things that must interest him.

Eleanor knew much that might catch the attention of a man who wished to learn more of the world outside his own—but would he listen to a woman?

Women were considered so much less than men in this world to which she had been brought against her will. Even in her own world there were few men who were interested in a woman's thoughts—it was beauty that was prized and a sweet temper.

Her own father had been an exception, and she

should not look to find his like again, especially here. It was foolish to imagine that Suleiman Bakhar might respect her for her intelligence—might choose her company simply to study and talk.

Eleanor's heart was heavy as she recalled the times she had ridden and played with her brother when they were both much younger. In later years she had studied with Richard...where was he now? She felt tears sting her eyes. She had been lucky to be brought here and she could only pray that Richard had also found a master who would be kind to him.

She blinked back her tears, knowing she must not dwell on her brother's plight or the happiness they had known as children. She might never see Richard again, but perhaps she might find companionship with Suleiman. No, that was only a dream. She would be a fool to let herself be swayed by it.

If Suleiman sent for her again...it would be to force her to his bed.

And what would she do then?

Chapter Five

Eleanor was sitting in the gardens with three of the other women that evening when she saw Karin coming towards them. The older woman smiled and nodded approvingly.

'You are beginning to make friends,' she said as she reached them. 'That is good, Eleanor.'

'Yes, it is,' Eleanor said and smiled at the three women who had been brave enough to ignore Fatima's orders and approach her. 'Anastasia has been telling me of her life in Russia, and Elizabetta is from the north of Spain—and Rosamunde is Venetian. We have much in common, and since we all speak a little French and a little Italian there is no barrier.'

'That is fortunate,' Karin replied. 'I am glad you have taken my advice, Eleanor. You will need friends if you are to be happy living here—but I am pleased to tell you that your request has been granted.'

'My request?' Eleanor looked puzzled for a moment, then nodded as a feeling of excitement gripped her. 'I asked for pen and paper—have I permission for these items?'

'It is much better than that,' Karin replied with an indulgent look. 'Come with me and I shall show you. You may return to your friends later if you wish.'

Eleanor followed her obediently. Karin was in charge of the harem ladies, but she did not try to assert her authority in an unkind way, and Anastasia had told her that the older woman was very kind when any of the women were ill or distressed.

'She is our comforter,' Anastasia had told her. 'When I was brought here I wanted to die, but Karin showed me that life in this place can be good and now I am content. My lord has only sent for me once, and since then I have been left to live a life of ease. If I had remained in Russia I would have been servant to a lady of the nobility, and here I have a much better life.'

'But do you not miss your family?'

'They were all killed in the raid on our village,' Anastasia replied simply, with no sign of emotion. 'Only the young women and boys were spared to be taken as slaves.'

'Did that not make you hate the people who took you prisoner?'

'Yes—but they were pirates and thieves. Our master is a good man and we are treated fairly.' Anastasia sighed. 'I was a gift from a merchant to the Caliph, who gave me to his son—but I did not please Suleiman and he has no use for me. I content myself with helping the others—and Karin sends for me when anyone is ill, because I have a little skill in nursing. My life is full, for though I have no children of my own I sometimes see the children of others playing. I should have liked to give the lord Suleiman a son—he has two daughters, but no woman has yet given him a son.'

It was obvious that Anastasia was saddened that her master did not summon her to his bed, and Eleanor wondered at it. Why was it that most of the ladies seemed eager to please Suleiman Bakhar? They had told her that he often watched them from a window above their garden, and that they all paraded back and forth along that particular path in the hope that he would notice them and send for them that night.

For a moment Eleanor recalled the treachery of her own body as he had kissed her softly on the lips. The sweetness of that kiss had surprised her, and aroused a longing for something that she did not understand, robbing her of the will to resist him. She had felt as though he cast a magic spell over her by some sorcery—was it this that made so many of the harem women eager for his notice? It was certain that every woman in the harem would have felt honoured to be sent for by her master. Yet did they not feel the shame of being his concubine—did they not fret at being bound to him by slavery?

Eleanor's ponderings were brought to an abrupt end as she saw what had happened in her absence. An exquisite desk and chair of French design had been placed in her sitting room, and upon it lay a leather-bound journal with pristine pages of cream vellum, writing quills, ink in a pewter pot, and a large pile of papers with close writing upon them.

'What are these?' Eleanor cried, pouncing on them with glee. 'They are in Latin, I think—and the writing is very small.'

'Our master has sent these scripts for you to decipher and copy into a fair hand,' Karin told her. 'They are his own work, done some years ago when he was a student, and he can no longer make out the lettering. He asks that you transcribe them for him—into English or Latin, whichever pleases you.'

'Oh, what treasure,' Eleanor exclaimed joyfully clutching the papers. 'I wish to thank Suleiman Bakhar—how may I do so?'

'By doing what he has asked,' Karin replied, an odd smile on her lips. It had seemed a strange request to her, and even stranger that Suleiman should choose to answer it in this way—but now she saw that perhaps he had found a way to soften Eleanor's heart. 'I have been told by our new chief eunuch that it was not an order but a request.'

She sounded a little puzzled and Eleanor looked at her curiously. 'Is it usual for our lord to request such things?'

'He always asks respectfully when he wishes to speak to me,' Karin replied. 'But I am not of his own harem. It is more usual for Suleiman to order than ask…and there is another strange thing. Abu has been transferred from his duties in the harem to the Caliph's storehouses, where he is to be in charge of ordering supplies for the palace.'

'Is that a demotion to a less important position?' Eleanor asked, remembering the odd expression on Suleiman's face when she had said she did not like the eunuch.

'No—for it involves much responsibility, and a chance for Abu to better his standing. He might even become wealthy if he chooses to trade with the merchants on his own behalf.' Karin's eyes narrowed as she looked at Eleanor. 'I have long distrusted Abu and I would have had him removed from his duties here before this had I dared—but he is a dangerous enemy, Eleanor. If he believes that this change was due to interference from one of the women…she might have to watch her back very carefully in future. Especially if she should lose the favour of our lord, for then no one would care or notice if she disappeared.'

'I only said that I did not like him,' Eleanor replied. 'Our lord asked me what I meant, but I could not tell him—it was just a feeling that Abu liked to hurt others.'

'Yes, that is very true,' Karin replied. 'I have suspected him of inflicting punishment for his own pleasure in the past, but the victims were always too afraid to speak. If I had had proof I could have gone to Suleiman—but it seems you have achieved more in one hour than I in six years…'

'Oh, no…' Eleanor blushed and looked down. 'I am sure it was not a chance remark of mine that made Suleiman Bakhar change Abu's duties—he must have had it in mind to do so.'

'Yes, perhaps you are right,' Karin said. She knew that Suleiman had sent for Fatima that night, and that surely meant that Eleanor had not appealed to his sensual nature. He would not have moved his chief eunuch from the harem simply because a woman had voiced a dislike of him—or would he? The gift of writing materials was a very generous one, and Karin had never known it to happen before. 'I dare say it was as you say—and it would be best to mention nothing of what has passed between us here. I shall tell others that you have been ordered to do this work, because Suleiman has no other scribe fit to do it since his teacher left.'

'The lord Suleiman's teacher…was his name Kasim?'

'Yes. What do you know of him?'

'Suleiman mentioned his name, that is all,' Eleanor replied. 'I had the feeling that something had happened…something that made him sad.'

'Saidi Kasim is dying of an incurable disease,' Karin told her. 'He was in great pain and asked permission to go home. The lord Suleiman granted it to him—but he misses him, for they were great friends.'

'Was Saidi Kasim a slave?'

'In the beginning,' Karin replied. 'But he was a wise man and had much learning. Suleiman valued him and gave him great honours. Kasim was a humble man who did not wish for the riches of life, but he could have had whatever he wanted had he asked. They spent many hours together, I believe. He was closer to Suleiman than anyone—except the Caliph.'

'It is sad to lose such a friend,' Eleanor replied and, despite herself, felt that she would have liked to offer comfort to the man who had lost his best friend, though she knew he would not have wanted such words from her. 'But a man like Suleiman must have many others?'

'He has many friends amongst the Janissaries,' Karin replied. 'But so far he has not replaced Kasim. I do not think he can bear to do so…though he has summoned an astrologer on two occasions.'

'Ah, yes,' Eleanor replied. 'I saw the instruments such men use for reading the stars in his hall. They looked interesting.'

Karin nodded, and her expression was thoughtful.

'It is very rare for a woman to be appointed to the position of adviser,' she said. 'But it has been known. You might please our master in many ways if you do your work well, Eleanor. You should not despair that he has sent for Fatima and not you this evening.'

Eleanor stared at her. She was conscious of a very odd feeling; it was like a pain in her chest and she did not understand it, though she knew what had aroused it. Yet she could not be jealous because Suleiman had sent for his favourite! After all, she did not want him to send for her in that way... Even so, there was a feeling of disappointment that he should have summoned Fatima to his bed.

'It is good that he has sent for her,' Eleanor said when she could form the words. 'She was afraid that I might take her place and it made her spiteful—now she will be happy again.'

'And you—you are not disappointed that you did not please him?'

'No...' Eleanor knew that she was not telling the whole truth. 'I told him that I would never consent to be his concubine willingly.'

'You told the lord Suleiman that?' Karin stared in astonishment. She could scarcely believe that Eleanor had been so bold or so foolish. 'And he sent no word that you were to be punished? Instead, he grants your wish to have pen and paper...I do not understand this, Eleanor.'

'Perhaps it as you say,' Eleanor replied. 'I am useful in other ways.'

She did not tell Karin that Suleiman had promised to favour her above all others if she pleased him—or that she had defied him when he kissed her.

'In that case I must leave you to begin your work,'

Karin said, clearly still mystified. 'You may send for fresh lamps if you need them, but do not work too long into the night—or you will overtire yourself and lose your looks.' Her gaze narrowed thoughtfully. 'You are very lovely, Eleanor. I cannot believe that you do not stir Suleiman Bakhar. I do not know what is in his mind concerning you—but I think he may yet surprise us all…'

Suleiman watched as Fatima performed one of her dances for him. She was extremely graceful, and there was no other woman of his harem who was more skilled in the arts of pleasing a man—both with her dancing and in bed.

He had enjoyed her performance many times, and been roused to make love to her after the dance, but tonight it left him unmoved. He could still appreciate her skill, yet there was no burning in his loins, or any desire to lie with her.

'Come,' he invited as the music ended and she sank to a position of supplication before him, arms stretched out as if in entreaty. 'Sit on that cushion next to me and talk to me.'

Fatima obeyed, though she was puzzled by this odd request. Always before he had raised her up and taken her into his private room and made love to her. She had looked forward to it eagerly through all the ritual of the bath and preparation. It was her reason for living, for she was a passionate woman and relished the act of physical love. He had never asked her to talk to him before, and she did not know what to say.

'What would my lord have of me?' she asked. 'Would you have me sing to you?'

'No. I wish for conversation,' Suleiman replied and

frowned. 'Tell me what you do with your days, Fatima.'

'I wait for you to send for me, my lord. I bathe and perfume myself—and sometimes I dance so that I retain my skill for your pleasure.'

'But what do you like to do yourself?'

'I live to please you, my lord.'

Suleiman stared at her. Was her life so empty? And what of the other women in his harem—those he had not sent for in months? Some that he had never asked for in all the time they had been here—what did they do with their time?

'Have you no friends? Do you not laugh and talk— walk with them in the gardens or bathe together in the pools? Do they not gossip with you or tell stories?'

'I could not say what the others do,' Fatima replied with a look of disdain. 'I seldom bother with them— they are jealous of me because you send only for me.'

Suleiman saw the look of spiteful delight in her eyes and was disgusted. She was an empty vain woman—and he had created her. She was this way because he had taken his pleasures carelessly without thought for what he did, not loving her but using her to slake the physical urgings of his body.

He knew that he did not desire her, that he would probably never want her again. His first thought was that she should return to the harem at once, but he checked it before the words were spoken. If he sent her back so soon, the other women would know that she had not lain in his bed—and they would despise her for losing his favour. She did not deserve that, for she was as lovely and graceful as she had always been—the change was in him

'So…you wait all day for me…' He stood up and Fatima's heart raced. Surely now he would take her to his bed and she would make him forget this strange mood that troubled him. 'I do not want you to pleasure me this night, Fatima—but I shall not send you back to the harem. You may stay here in this room until the morning and return at your usual hour.'

'But, my lord…' Still on her knees, Fatima caught at the hem of his tunic as he would have passed her. 'What have I done to displease you?'

'You have not displeased me,' he replied coldly. 'Your dance was excellent—but I do not desire you in my bed. You will sleep here and leave in the morning as soon as it is light.'

'Forgive me…' Fatima threw herself to the floor at his feet, abasing herself before him. 'Whatever I have done I will make amends, my lord.'

'You displease me by this display of temper,' Suleiman said, guilt making his voice sharper than need be. 'If you persist, I shall send for the eunuch to take you back now.'

He walked on past her, leaving Fatima stretched out on the tiled floor, her body shaking with the tears she could not hold back despite his threat to send her back at once. She longed to follow him, to plead with him again, but she dared not for he would surely send her back to the harem in disgrace. And then the other women would laugh at her. She had flaunted herself over them and some of them would not lose their chance to make her suffer now that she had lost their master's favour.

Suleiman felt both guilt and pity for her as he looked down on her misery. He had not truly understood how empty were the lives of the women in his harem until…until one of them had asked him how she was to pass her life. He had sent her work to do since it seemed that this was what she required, but it would be useless to offer such a boon to Fatima, for she would neither appreciate nor be able to do such intricate work. He doubted that she could write, let alone read Latin…it was a rare thing in a woman. Even his own mother had not been able to read Latin, but Eleanor could.

He wondered what Eleanor was doing at that moment. He wished that he might send for her—but to do so would be to offer a grievous insult to the woman he had left sobbing on the floor of his outer chamber. He would not choose to be that cruel, even though it was only now that he had begun to realise his actions could be cruel…that he hurt those he did not send for by omission. It was a heavy burden, and one that must be given careful consideration.

Tomorrow must suffice for his own pleasure. He would sit and read some of his manuscripts, though of late he had noticed that it was something of a strain to decipher his own lettering. The scripts he had sent to Eleanor for transcribing were some he had written long ago and concerned matters of astrology that he wished to consult again, so that perhaps he might be able to interpret his own charts and not have to trust the words of the astrologer.

He took the scripts to a stool by a table where a lamp was burning and began to read the fair hand inscribed for him by his old teacher, sighing as he did so. He missed Kasim so much…and there was no one else he could talk to in the same way, for his father was not interested in ancient teachings and mysteries. The Caliph was a man much concerned with the daily administration of justice in the Sultan's capitol, and had no time for the kind of work that gave Suleiman so much pleasure.

The mysteries of the stars, of medicine and ancient knowledge, some handed down from empires now lost to mankind, held a special fascination for Suleiman Bakhar. He had many books, which came from the printing works of Germany, France and Venice, which were easy enough for him to read— but it was the ancient manuscripts that he found difficult to decipher these days. He was forced to hold them at a distance and that was uncomfortable, and sometimes made his eyes ache if he worked too long into the night.

For the moment he must content himself with the books that showed pictures of medical practice and were self-explanatory, depicting lumps and sores on various parts of the body. He had been visiting at the bedside of one of the Janissaries earlier; the unfortunate man had developed a lump on his side. And, after consulting with the physicians, Suleiman was trying to ascertain whether it would be best to cut the lump from the man's body or treat it with powders to try and burn it off.

The sobbing from the outer chamber had ceased at last. Suleiman forgot the woman as he read his medical books, his mind now fully concentrated on a cure for his friend.

Eleanor had spent many happy hours poring over the scripts sent to her and had begun her transcription into both English and Latin, copying a page of each at a time. She had slept afterwards and woke feeling so much happier than she had in an age. At least now she had some purpose to her life—and she could almost imagine herself back at home with her father.

The memory of Sir William's death lay heavy on her heart. She knew that she would never cease to grieve for him, and for her brother—who was as lost to her as her father. Yet perhaps if she asked Suleiman, he might be able to give her news of Richard... It would require some payment, of course.

Eleanor knew that she had already been granted a considerable favour. Why had Suleiman done so much for her? She had thought him angry when he sent her back to the harem...and yet he had granted her request for some occupation. She was very grateful to him, and she was being very careful in her copying so that he would be pleased with what she had done.

'Come into the garden,' Anastasia said from the threshold of her sitting room. 'It is a lovely day, Eleanor. Karin bid me tell you, you have worked enough for now. You must take a walk in the air.'

'I am glad to do so,' Eleanor said and rose with a smile. 'I do not wish to study all the time. It is good to have friends and I like to talk with you and the others.'

'Fatima is in a bad temper this morning,' Anastasia said. 'It is unusual for her to be so cross after spending the night with our master.'

'It does not matter about her,' Eleanor said linking arms with the other woman. 'Tell me about the dancing lessons, Anastasia. I think I should like to learn. I can play a harp and the virginals—but I do not know how to play the instrument you were using the other night.'

'It is a dombra, and comes from the province of

Kazakhstan.' Anastasia smiled at her. 'It is very like a lute in some ways, but the music it makes is different. I could show you how to play it if you wish?'

'Yes, I think that would be pleasant,' Eleanor replied. 'I am so glad that we are to be friends. I felt so alone the night I came to the harem—and no one spoke to me.'

'That was because Fatima forbade it,' Anastasia replied. 'The three of us decided the next day that we would disobey her—especially now that Abu is no longer in charge of the harem. He used to punish us for her if we did something that displeased her... He was cruel and it was his pleasure to whip us for some imagined slight of her.'

'Why did you not tell Karin?'

'Because she is not of the harem,' Anastasia replied. 'If we had told her, something might have happened while she was not here...women have disappeared without trace from the palace. I think Abu sold them to slave merchants.'

'But did no one notice they had gone?'

'Who would care?' Anastasia frowned. 'The Caliph hardly ever sends for a woman these days, and it would only be Karin or one of his other wives who have given him children—none of the concubines are ever requested. Unless the Caliph sent for someone who had disappeared he would never know—and then he would probably be told she had sickened and died of some mysterious ailment. No one could prove otherwise, for those who knew would not be asked.'

'That is terrible,' Eleanor said. 'Do you think Suleiman knows of this?'

'No—for who would dare to tell him? Abu was in charge of the harem and the only woman Suleiman sends for is Fatima—and I believe she knew what was going on. She helped Abu and he saw that she was obeyed in the harem… It was a strange partnership, but of mutual benefit.'

'Yes, I see,' Eleanor said. 'It is a happy thing for us that Abu has been sent to the stores.'

'Yes…' Anastasia nodded. 'And yet I think…' She shook her head. 'No, I cannot be sure and it is safer not to notice. I shall say no more and nor should you.'

Eleanor looked at her curiously but did not press her to continue. Karin had told her it was dangerous to speak too openly in the harem, and although some of the women had shown themselves willing to be friendly with Eleanor, others remained aloof.

As they entered the main hall, Eleanor saw Fatima seated on one of the divans. Several of the women were hovering about her, offering dishes of sweet-meats and fruits. It was clear that she was displeased about something and her eyes snapped with temper as she looked at Eleanor. However, before she could speak Karin came up to Eleanor.

'Suleiman has sent for you,' she said. 'You are to bring your journal. He wishes to see what you have done so far.'

'Yes, of course. I shall fetch the journal at once.'

Eleanor left Anastasia with a smile of regret and a promise that they would talk later. She collected the journal from her apartments, then hurried after Karin.

Just before they reached the first of Suleiman's halls, Karin stopped and turned to her with a worried expression.

'I have heard strange whispers,' she said. 'One of the women from the palace kitchens died horribly last night. They say she was beaten and then strangled;

there was no attempt to hide her body. I do not know why but this makes me afraid…for you.'

'But why?' Eleanor's eyes opened wide with surprise. 'You do not believe it was Abu…but, yes, you do!'

Karin nodded. 'I think it may have been anger or spite on his part, because he was stripped of his powers to punish. I may be wrong about this, but please be careful, Eleanor. I would not have anything unpleasant happen to you.'

'Yes, of course I shall take care. I thank you for your care of me, Karin.'

'I like you,' the older woman replied. 'And you are in my charge. I would not have you disappear or die mysteriously, as others have. Now you must go. Our master seems impatient to see you.'

Eleanor's heart was beating very fast as she continued on into the grand chamber, which contained all the cabinets and scientific instruments. Suleiman was not there and she ventured into the next room. She saw him at once. He was standing by a trestle and board, on which were spread several manuscripts and seemed intent on what he was doing.

'You sent for me, my lord?'

Suleiman swung round at her words, a flame of pure silver shooting up in his dark eyes as he saw her. Eleanor's heart caught and for a moment she could not breathe. How magnificent he was! He frightened her with his overpowering masculinity, yet she felt drawn to him against her will. He must not look at her so! As if he were pleased to see her, had awaited her coming eagerly. She could not bear it—it terrified her and excited her too, making her feel as if she had been running very fast.

'You brought the journal?' His gaze narrowed as she held it out to him wordlessly, unable to speak. He opened the first page and then turned to the next, his brow furrowing. 'You have translated into English and also given the original Latin transcription—why?'

'I thought it might please you,' Eleanor replied. 'In English the meaning becomes clearer—the Latin script was somewhat ambiguous. I gave it a literal interpretation…'

'Which makes it easier to understand how a chart should be drawn and understood…' His mouth curved into a smile that set her pulses pounding. 'Very clever…and exactly what I needed. How did you know that I wished to read my own horoscope?'

'You had made such detailed notes,' Eleanor replied. 'I saw the instruments used to take readings of the stars in your hall…a rather fine astrolobe and others I was not sure of. And I knew you had spoken recently with an astrologer.'

'Indeed? I suppose Karin told you that?'

'Yes, my lord.'

Suleiman nodded. 'I am pleased with your hand, my lady. It is easy for me to read. I find these difficult to decipher.' He waved his hand towards the scripts he had been studying. 'It was always my chief pleasure of an afternoon, but of late…' He shrugged and frowned. 'My eyes ache from trying to make out this lettering.'

'It is a medical treatise,' Eleanor said. 'Writ in Arabic. It tells of a bark that must be ground into a powder and mixed with wine. If used in the treatment of a bowel disorder it is promised most effective.'

'Then it is not the remedy I seek.' He sighed as if he were weary after many hours of study. 'I am looking for a treatment for a swelling of the body.' He squinted at the next script. 'I am sure it is here somewhere.'

'Would you like me to look for you?'

'If you will. I am sure there is a certain powder that may save my friend from the evil of having a lump cut out of his side by the surgeon's knife…'

'I think this may be what you are seeking, my lord.'

Eleanor had seen that the text he needed was just beneath the one he had been studying. She handed it to him and he held it out at arm's length, then nodded.

'Yes, the very one. I shall copy it and give it to the physician.'

'May I do that, my lord? Here is paper and ink. It will take but a moment.'

'As you wish.'

Eleanor sat on the stool and wrote the name of the bark used in the treatment of swelling and lumps, and the way in which it must be used, then handed it to Suleiman. He had been staring down at the various scripts and his difficulty was obvious.

'Perhaps you should wear spectacles for reading, my lord?'

'I have eyes like a hawk.' He glared at her indignantly. 'I can see small objects from a distance. My eyes are perfectly sound.'

'But you obviously cannot see to read properly. My father's eyes were much the same. He thought it was because he studied so much, but when he bought some magnifying lenses he discovered that it was much easier for him.'

'I am aware of these things…in the Arab world we have known of their properties for a long time. In your country they are far behind us. Besides, I do not need them. It is merely that my eyes are tired after too much work.'

'Yes, my lord. My father said the same until he tried them. And in China they have used these glasses since the tenth century. It is an old wisdom and not something you need to feel ashamed of using to your advantage.'

Suleiman gave her a hard stare, then, seeing the gentle smile on her mouth, he laughed. 'You think me too vain to use such aids? Well, I have been told before it would help me. Kasim advised the use of them, but I thought it a passing thing. It seems that I may have been wrong.'

'My father was sent his glasses by a Venetian friend, but I dare say he would not have bought them for himself.'

'Your father had a wise daughter.' Suleiman nodded, his eyes intent on her face. 'Are you pleased with the work I have sent you?'

'Yes, my lord. It was my habit to study with my brother at home.' She sighed as she thought about Richard, as she so often did in the privacy of her own rooms. 'We were very close…' She held back a sob, then lifted her head. 'We shall not speak of that—it was kind of you to send me the work, my lord.'

His gaze narrowed as he looked at her. Was it his eyesight or was she even more lovely than he had thought her? 'Karin tells me you have begun to make friends—is that true?'

'Yes, my lord. I have three friends in the harem. Anastasia, Elizabetta and Rosamunde.'

'What do you talk about with your friends? Come, sit with me. I have ordered sherbet and sweetmeats

for your pleasure. Drink and eat as we talk. I would
know more of how the women spend their time.'

Eleanor looked at him in surprise. Did he really not
know or was he merely testing her?

'I can tell you only of those women I have begun
to know, my lord. Anastasia plays the dombra, and I
thought the music very strange for it is different from
the music I play.'

'What instruments do you play?'

'At home I had a harp and the virginals that were
my mother's—but Anastasia has promised to teach
me to play the dombra.'

'And will that please you?'

'Oh, yes, my lord.' Her face lit up with eagerness.
'I could not bear to sit in idleness as some of the
women do, but I am to learn to dance—and to sing
in the manner of your own people…a kind of chanting, I understand. And then it is pleasant to hear about
the other women's homes and their lives before they
came here…'

'What of your land, Eleanor? Tell me of your
home—describe it to me in detail and the countryside
around it. Make me see it through your eyes.'

'Willingly, my lord.' She smiled at him. 'My father's house is timber framed and the upper level pro-
trudes out over the lower. The walls are of a grey
stone and panelled inside with English oak, the roof
deeply sloping and thatched with straw. It is not a
large house, though gracious and well built—but to
you it would seem very small. Your father's palace
is so huge…'

'Too large,' Suleiman said and frowned. 'It is impossible to know what goes on everywhere. But con-

tinue—tell me of the gardens and the landscape. What do you do when you are at home?'

Eleanor began to describe her home in detail, leaving out nothing that she thought might interest him. She spoke of woods and meadows and the creatures that inhabited them, of misty mornings and the beauty of the English countryside, of the autumn when the leaves began to change colour. She told him also of the winter when the snows came, filling the roads and ditches, and sometimes cutting them off for days. She described her father's collection of books, maps and manuscripts, and his other treasures that they had been forced to leave behind, her words eloquent and flowing like beautiful music.

Suleiman listened entranced, the sound of her voice holding him spellbound, and wishing that her tale might never end, but when she reached the part where they had been forced to flee England, he interrupted.

'You were unfortunate that your Queen has set her heart on Spain—those Catholic devils are without mercy.' Suleiman frowned. 'You called me a savage—but my people are no worse than the murderers of the Inquisition. Our justice is often harsh, but we can also be generous. We are neither savages nor barbarians, even though our customs are strange to you.'

'No, perhaps not.' Eleanor blushed. 'I was wrong to judge without knowing you, my lord. I thought you the same as the men who murdered my father and I hated you as I hate them.'

'And now?' His eyes seemed very bright and intent. 'Do you still hate me?'

'No…I do not hate you.' Eleanor took a deep breath. 'I know that you are not like the men who raided our ship. But I still ask that you will ransom me to my family.'

'No!' Suleiman got to his feet and reached down to pull her up to stand before him. 'You must learn to accept your fate, Eleanor. You can never leave here.'

'Then I shall hate you!' Her temper flared suddenly. 'Why will you not listen to me? Why can you not—?'

Before she could say more, Suleiman reached for her and crushed her against him in a powerful embrace. His mouth sought hers in a hungry, ravaging kiss that seemed almost to burn her. For a moment she was close to surrendering to the need she sensed in him, then she pushed against him with the flat of her hands, turning her head to one side. For a few terrifying seconds he held her and she sensed that he was close to losing all control, then he released her so abruptly that she felt she would fall. Daring to glance at him, she saw that his nostrils were flaring and he was breathing hard as though he laboured beneath some extreme emotion. She thought that he might be very angry—for what else could cause him to look like that?

'Why do you fight me?' he demanded. 'I have given you what you requested. What more can I give you? Do you want jewels? Silks…larger apartments?'

'No! How can you think these things would buy me?' she asked, her eyes bright with accusation. Her body felt as if it was on fire, and her limbs trembled with weakness. 'I am a woman of honour. To give myself to a man who was not my husband…' She stopped as she saw the gleam in his eyes. 'No! I do not ask for marriage, only that I might be free.'

'You ask too much!' His anger flared out of him now. 'I tell you that you shall never go from here. You belong to me and I shall never give you up.'

'Then you will never take me willingly.'

'Then I shall force you to succumb.' His eyes darkened, and she saw that his hands clenched at his sides as if he were struggling to control his temper. 'Next time I send for you, be prepared to obey your master, Eleanor. Now go before I lose all control and have you punished for your wilfulness.'

Eleanor gasped. His features might have been carved from granite. How foolish she was! As they talked, she had felt that he was inclined to be understanding of her feelings—but this was a different man. A more primitive, savage product of his culture and birthright—a man used to being obeyed.

'Forgive me,' she whispered, but he had turned back to his manuscripts and was ignoring her. She was not even sure he had heard her plea.

What had she done? Eleanor regretted her hasty words. They had seemed to be reaching a far better understanding before she had so foolishly defied him. Why had she not spoken more softly to this man who held the power of life and death over so many?

She was close to tears as she retraced her route towards the harem. Suleiman had been pleased with her when she read the ancient script for him. He had even accepted her advice about the matter of his eyesight—but she had rejected his embrace and now he was angry again.

When she walked into the main hall of the harem, she heard the excited chatter and laughter going on

and wondered what had happened to cause such a stir
in her absence.

'Oh, do come and look,' Elizabetta called to her.
'See what our lord has sent us!'

'What is it?' she asked. 'What has pleased you all
so much?'

'There is a parrot that talks,' the other woman
cried. 'And a monkey on a chain—and a cage of
pretty singing birds in the garden.'

'Oh, let me see,' Eleanor said, catching Elizabetta's
pleasure in the pets they had been given. 'Does the
monkey do tricks?'

'He is such a naughty little fellow,' Anastasia said,
coming up to them. 'He keeps stealing things, but he
is so sweet and pretty.'

'He seems to be causing quite a stir.'

Eleanor saw that most of the ladies were playing
with the monkey, who was clearly going to be spoiled
by them. Several of them were talking to the parrot—
which was swearing at the top of its voice. And in
English!

'Oh, dear,' Eleanor said and laughed. 'He is not a
very polite parrot, is he?'

'What is he saying?' Anastasia asked. 'No one understands him.'

'Perhaps that is just as well, for he is very rude. I
think he was brought up in the stables. We must teach
him better manners.'

Eleanor glanced around the room. She thought that
she had never seen the women so animated and
happy. The new additions to the harem were very
welcome, it seemed—and the thought to send them
was a kind one.

It had been Suleiman's idea, of course. He must

have given some considerable thought as to what might please and amuse the ladies. Eleanor wanted to thank him, but she doubted she would get much opportunity.

He had told her she must be prepared to submit to him the next time he sent for her—but when would that be?

'Are you pleased with your gifts?'

Karin had come up behind her. Eleanor turned to her with a frown.

'Surely the monkey and birds are for everyone to enjoy?'

'I was not speaking of them. Have you not been to your own apartments?'

'I have but now returned from Suleiman's halls.'

'You have been with him all this time?' Karin looked surprised. 'Have you eaten?'

'My lord provided sherbet and sweetmeats. I am not hungry, thank you.'

'Go and look at your gifts.' Karin smiled at her. 'We were wrong to think that you had not pleased Suleiman. Such gifts as he has sent you are usually reserved for a favourite wife.'

Eleanor felt hot and then cold. She trembled inwardly as she remembered Suleiman's words. In turn he had offered her both gifts and threats—if he believed the gifts had not tempted her, he might resort to punishment next. She had imagined he spoke of the journal and scripts he had given her.

She went to her own rooms, followed by a curious Anastasia and Elizabetta, who had both heard what Karin had to say. There, spread out over the divans, were robes of silk and cloth of gold. A large casket had been placed against a wall, inside which were other items of the finest materials she had ever seen. On her desk was a small wooden casket inlaid with ivory and agates. Morna handed her a small key, and when she opened the casket she found a rope of beautiful emeralds and pearls strung on gold wire. There was also a chain of emeralds for her wrist, and a huge emerald pendant suspended from a headband of pure gold.

'Oh…' Elizabetta breathed in awe as Eleanor lifted them out to examine them more closely. 'I have never seen such jewels. They are much finer than anything Fatima has.'

'No!' Eleanor was aware of a feeling of terror as she realised what the gift represented. 'I cannot accept these—they must be returned at once.'

'Do not be foolish,' Karin said from behind her. 'Suleiman has sent these things because he wishes to see you wearing them. He is obviously planning to send for you soon—which means there is no time to be lost. You will spend this evening with me. I shall explain to you exactly what will happen when Suleiman sends for you.'

'Please…do not,' Eleanor whispered her throat tight with fear. 'I cannot. I cannot be what you and he want me to be.'

'You must—for your own sake and ours,' Karin told her with what was a severe look for her. 'Suleiman has always been generous, but he is a man and men have a lurking beast in their nature. A clever woman knows how to subdue that beast, to have it tamely eating from her hand. You are the one Suleiman has chosen to be his wife…'

'His wife? How do you know?' Eleanor looked at

her with frightened eyes. 'Has he spoken of this to
you?'

'No, not yet—but I know. These jewels are price-
less. He would not give them to a mere concubine.
Suleiman will take you for his wife, Eleanor. You are
the most fortunate of women, for he will give you all
that your heart desires—even take you outside the
palace with him. Your life will be so much better than
it could ever have been as one of the concubines. You
must accept the inevitable. You have no choice.'

Chapter Six

Eleanor was forced to spend the evening with Karin in her apartments. She was treated kindly, and the food served to her was the most delicious she had tasted either here at the palace or elsewhere, but she was here for a purpose and there was no escaping the lessons Karin was determined she must learn.

Her cheeks grew warm for shame as the older woman described things that their master might ask her to do—and others he might do to her if he chose. It all seemed terribly wicked to Eleanor, and yet there was a very odd feeling in her lower abdomen as Karin described the pleasures Suleiman could give her. She found herself remembering the sensations his kiss had aroused in her and trembled. Surely such things were wrong—a woman was not supposed to take pleasure in what she had been taught was a sin unless sanctified by marriage.

'But I cannot allow...' She swallowed hard, unable to meet the other's eyes. 'I mean...it is not decent. Surely no respectable woman could do...all those things?'

Karin smiled gently. 'I know it must seem strange

to you, and perhaps sinful. You have not been taught these things as many of our women have by their mothers. Some have been trained for years simply to arouse a man's sexuality—some to give pleasure in other ways. But always to please, to obey without question.'

'I have thought…' Eleanor blushed. 'It was pleasant when he kissed me…'

'He has kissed you…nothing else? Nothing of which I have just spoken?'

'No! I would not allow it.' Eleanor was indignant! 'I pushed him away…and yet I did not truly want to stop him kissing me.'

Karin laughed at this confession. 'I believe I have been wasting my time, Eleanor. It seems you need no teacher. I suspect that Suleiman wishes to teach you himself. Yes…' She seemed struck by this thought and nodded to herself. 'Perhaps he grows tired of women who are skilled in these arts. Perhaps he looks for something different…'

'Perhaps you are wrong?' Eleanor looked at her anxiously. 'He may just forget me. Perhaps he will never send for me again.'

'No, I do not think so,' Karin replied. 'Fatima was angry when she returned to the harem this morning. I think Suleiman no longer favours her—he wants you. You must be careful of her, Eleanor. She will harm you if she can.'

'Surely not?' Eleanor frowned. 'I have done nothing to make our lord favour me above her. I believed he was angry with me. I know he was! He may yet send the eunuchs to take back his gifts.'

Karin shook her head at her. 'You foolish girl! Do not fight your fate, Eleanor. I think it was written in the stars that you should come here—and I think your destiny will affect all of us. Indeed, it has already begun to do so in small ways—but the choices you make may have far greater consequences for all of us.'

'What do you mean? Suleiman would not punish the others because he is angry with me—would he?' Eleanor stared at her in surprise. 'I had not thought him so unfair…'

'No, I did not mean that,' Karin replied. 'But my horoscope was cast some days ago and I was told that change was coming. Not just for me, but for others I cared for.'

Eleanor was silent. She knew that many people scoffed at such predictions, but her father had believed there was merit in them if honestly done. He had shown her how to read a chart, and she knew that predictions of a trend could be frighteningly accurate. She had known that her family would have to pass through a period of danger, and that they would be forced to leave their own land, long before it happened. There was more truth in the stars than any man knew.

'I pray that I do not bring bad fortune to you, Karin.'

'I believe that what happens here in the future is in your hands, Eleanor. You can bring good or evil…the outcome rests with you and you should think carefully before you reject your duty.'

It was a heavy burden to carry, and Eleanor was thoughtful as she returned to her own apartments later that evening. She found Morna working frantically to restore the rooms to order, and saw that some mischief had been done in her absence. Her clothes were on the floor, and ink had been spilled on some papers on her desk.

'What has happened here?' she asked, looking displeased at the confusion.

'Forgive me, my lady,' Morna begged. 'Fatima sent for me; when I returned, I found that naughty monkey making havoc amongst your things. I think nothing has been spoiled—except those papers. Are they very important?'

Eleanor looked at them anxiously, but to her relief the papers that had ink spilled on them were some she had already copied.

'I shall have to explain what happened to the lord Suleiman when I see him.' she said. 'It was not your fault, Morna. What did Fatima want of you?'

'She said she had not sent for me, that I must have been given the wrong message—but it was her servant Dinazade who summoned me.' Morna frowned. 'I think it was she who set the monkey loose in here, on Fatima's orders.'

'Yes, perhaps you are right,' Eleanor agreed. 'I shall ask Karin to order that the monkey be shut in its cage at night so that this does not happen again. Much precious work might have been lost had other papers than these been destroyed, and then the lord Suleiman would have been angry.'

'If you give the order it will be obeyed, my lady.'

'Why—what do you mean?'

'Everyone says you are to be Suleiman Bakhar's wife. You will then rule the harem. All the women will obey you.'

'What of Fatima?' Eleanor frowned. 'I do not think she will obey me.'

'Then you may have her punished. You could have

her beaten for this if you choose. I am sure the eunuchs would obey you.'

'I do not choose,' Eleanor replied. 'I believe that
Fatima may have caused this to be done—but it is
merely a spiteful prank. I would not have her beaten
for it. Besides, if it is true—if she is no longer our
lord's favourite—she is suffering enough. I believe
she truly cares for him in her way.'

'Fatima cares only for herself.'

Eleanor frowned. She knew that the other women
did not like Fatima, and she suspected that some of
the bolder ones might now try to punish her.

'Fatima may yet regain Suleiman's favour,' she
warned her servant. 'No one should assume that her
rule is over. I think it would go hard with those who
do if he should change his mind and send for her
again.'

Morna was regarding her thoughtfully, and Eleanor
knew that her words would be repeated in the harem.
It was all she could do to help Fatima, and perhaps
more than she deserved.

'Come into the garden,' Anastasia said persuasively. 'You work too much, Eleanor—and it is such
a lovely afternoon.'

'Yes, I shall stop now,' Eleanor replied. She sighed
and laid down her quill. 'I have finished all the work
Suleiman set for me. I shall give the journal to Karin
and ask her to deliver it.'

Standing up, she shrugged off a faint feeling of
tiredness. She had worked hard this past week—a
week during which Suleiman had been silent. No
one—not even Karin—had been sent for. Some said
that their master had been training even harder than

usual, some said that he had been out with his hawks every day—and others thought he had left the palace for a hunting trip with the Caliph.

Karin had told Eleanor that this last was not true. The Caliph had been working as always.

'He is a good and just man,' she said to Eleanor. 'I was fortunate—though I was only his second wife. He loved Suleiman's mother and no other.'

'Did you give the Caliph children?'

'Two daughters—both are married now,' Karin said a little sadly. 'They married into good families, but I never see them. I should like to visit them one day.'

'Would that be permitted?'

'If they lived in this city, yes,' Karin replied. 'My lord is generous. I am allowed to visit my brother's family sometimes—but my daughters live far away. I have my duties here for the moment, and cannot be spared—nor would I wish to leave while things remain as they are.'

'And if Suleiman had a wife?'

'Then I might be granted permission to leave for a while.'

'I see. You must hope that he will marry soon.'

'Only if he chooses the right woman. Fatima would make life intolerable for the others if I were not here to restrain her.' She frowned. 'I do not understand why Suleiman has not sent for you before this.'

'Perhaps he is still angry with me?'

Eleanor had wondered why she had heard nothing more from Suleiman Bakhar. Did he think her ungrateful for his gifts? She would have thanked him had she been given the chance. Indeed, she was anxious to do so.

'Listen to the birds calling,' Anastasia said, recalling her to the present. 'Someone has been cleaning their cage…'

Eleanor's attention was drawn towards the aviary of singing birds that Suleiman had sent to them. Her nerves tingled as she looked at the servant who had been tending them, and something about the slight figure who was now bending down to fasten the cage securely touched a chord in her.

'Richard!' she cried, her relief and pleasure in seeing her brother again leaping up in her. He was alive! Alive! Oh, God be praised! Her brother was alive and here in the palace. She forgot caution, and all that Karin and the others had taught her. 'Oh, Richard, my dearest!'

She was racing towards him as he turned and saw her. His face lit up with pleasure as he heard her call his name again and knew her for his sister. He moved towards her, his arms opening to receive her as she flung herself at him.

'Eleanor,' he choked, emotion welling over. 'My beloved sister. I have thought you dead long since. How are you—have these devils harmed you?' His eyes went over her and she saw understanding dawn as he realised how scantily she was dressed. 'You are one of our master's—' but she was pressing her fingers to his lips, kissing his cheek and hugging him, cutting off the terrible thoughts. 'It does not matter. Father would not think ill of you, Eleanor…he loved you too much. He would want you to live no matter what you were forced…'

'I am not yet…' she told him as soon as she could bear to stop kissing him. 'But I think Suleiman may soon take me as his wife…'

'Those murdering devils deserve to boil in oil for what they have done,' Richard said bitterly. 'I hate them all and would kill every last one of them if I could.'

'No, no, my dearest,' she choked. 'You must not say such things. Suleiman Bakhar is not like those men who…' The words died on her lips as she saw three of the eunuchs coming towards them. There was no mistaking their purpose, and Eleanor suddenly realised what she had done. 'Oh, no! It is forbidden for a man to be within these gardens. How did you come here? They have not altered you? You are not as they are?' Her fear was that he had been made less than a man, and given the work here, but he shook his head, denying it. Then, seeing the approaching eunuchs, he realised that he was in danger and she saw fear in his face. 'Who sent you here?' she asked, sensing some mischief.

'I think his name was Abu…he is chief eunuch of the harem…'

'No! No…no longer…'

It was the last thing either of them managed to say to each other before they were both seized. Eleanor's arm was taken in a firm grasp, though she was not roughly handled, but Richard resisted fiercely and was knocked to the ground and then dragged to his feet by the two eunuchs. She heard his stifled cry of pain and turned to her captor, begging him to save her brother.

'Please…he did no harm. He did not know where he was…he was sent here by…'

'Be quiet, woman! You will not speak until your master tells you!'

'You are taking us to Suleiman?'

Eleanor looked at his harsh face but there was nothing more to be gained from him. She glanced back at her brother and saw that he was fighting his captors, which meant that they were dragging him along the ground much of the time. She wanted to tell him not to fight, but knew that anything she said might result in him being struck again.

It was all her fault…all her fault. She ought to have remembered what Morna had told her on her first night in the harem—the women were always watched. By her impulsive action she had brought this trouble on them both, and she was very afraid for her brother. She might be beaten, but her brother—Richard could be put to death simply for being in the harem.

She held back a sob, praying that they would be taken to Suleiman. If the eunuchs decided to administer punishment themselves…but surely Suleiman would hear for himself what Eleanor had to say?

Suleiman watched from his window as the eunuchs laid hands on the woman and the man she had taken as her lover. He had never felt such a cold rage as that which possessed him now—that this woman who had resisted his embraces so fiercely should throw herself into the arms of another!

The man should die and she—she should learn to know the power of her master. His first reaction had been to order them brought to him, but now his anger was such that he was almost inclined to have them tossed into the darkest cell the palace possessed and left to rot. The man should die most horribly and Eleanor… Pain pierced through his rage as he thought of her being beaten with the cruel whips the eunuchs used to such terrible effect. How she would suffer…she might even die of such a beating.

Yet she deserved her punishment. His eyes were hard, his mouth set in a cruel line that told of the blood of his ancestors swirling in his heated brain. She must have known that what she did was forbidden, and yet she went unheeding to her lover's arms. Did she love him so much then that her life was nothing to her?

Suleiman was aware that his anger was turning to jealousy and pain—pain that she did not love him as she did this man, who looked to be a poor puny thing. She had rejected his embraces and yet went eagerly to this dog of an infidel. He was angry, but also curious to see what kind of man it was that had aroused such love in the woman he desired above all others.

They should be brought before him. He would let Eleanor see that he was capable of justice. If she begged for the man's life it might be spared—he could be sent to the galleys as a punishment and she… He would think of something more suitable for her punishment.

He heard the noise as they approached—the man was shouting and yelling defiance at his captors. He had spirit, then, despite his slight appearance. It would be interesting to see what kind of man Eleanor loved so much that she would spurn Suleiman for him.

His face was harsh as they were dragged before him, and sent roughly to their knees. He did not immediately give Eleanor permission to stand this time, for he wanted to make her suffer for her wilfulness.

'You have betrayed me with your lover,' Suleiman said coldly. 'What have you to say before I condemn you, woman?'

Eleanor looked up, gasping as she saw the rage in his eyes. She had never seen him like this! He was beside himself with anger and she thought that he might be capable of anything in this mood.

'He is not my lover…'

'Do not lie to me,' he said. 'I watched you embrace him. You ran to his arms as soon as you saw him—why? You must know the punishment for your actions. Did you wish to die? Are you so miserable that your life is nothing to you?'

'Please, my lord,' Eleanor said. She was terrified of this stranger, but she would not let him see her fear. 'I beg you to hear me…' He glared at her but did not tell her to be silent. 'Richard is my brother…I told you he was taken when the Corsairs attacked our ship. He is my only brother and he is a youth of fifteen, not a man.'

Suleiman's gaze narrowed suspiciously as he looked at her and then the man. Indeed, the youth could not be older than she claimed—and there was a faint likeness about the eyes. Her brother, then, in truth. His rage abated a little. He bent down, gripped Eleanor's arms and pulled her to her feet, propelling her roughly towards the inner chamber, and thrusting her towards the sleeping divan so that she fell against it and slipped to the floor.

'Stay there!' he commanded fiercely. 'Don't you dare to move!'

'What are you going to do to my brother?'

'Be quiet or you will feel the sting of the whip. I shall do what I please with both of you!'

'Have mercy, I beg you. Richard was sent to the gardens by Abu—it was a deliberate act on his part, meant, I believe, to cause trouble.'

Suleiman paused, eyes narrowed in suspicion. 'He told you it was Abu? You are sure of this?'

'Yes, my lord. Richard believed the man was chief eunuch of the harem. He did not know that it was forbidden for him to be there. He was merely obeying orders. How could he have been there if it was not so?'

'But you were aware that what you did was forbidden?'

'Yes, my lord. I forgot in my excitement at seeing him—but I knew.'

His eyes gleamed with some strange emotion she could not read, though she did not think it anger. 'Wait here, Eleanor, and prepare yourself for your punishment.'

She hung her head as he left her. What would he do to Richard? It no longer mattered what happened to her—but if Richard were made to suffer unspeakable torture because of her impulsive behaviour she would not be able to bear it. Then, indeed, she would rather die than continue to live here as a slave.

Her mind went back to the times she had Richard had played together as children in the gardens of their home, and of one particular day when he had dared her to climb the old apple tree and she had fallen and hurt her arm. Richard had been so contrite, so loving, as he picked her up, wiping her tears…and there was nothing she could do to help him now that he was in trouble. She felt so helpless, so guilty because there was nothing she could do for her beloved brother. He would be punished because she had kissed him.

She could hear only a low murmuring from the other room and knew that Suleiman must be questioning her brother about how he came to be in the harem gardens. He must have been sent there for a purpose—and he could not have gained access without the key to the gates, which were always kept locked. Eleanor believed she knew what was in Abu's mind. He blamed Eleanor for his removal from the harem, and must somehow have learned that Richard was her brother—or at least that they were captured together.

Yes, yes, that must be what had happened. Abu had gambled that she would know the youth captured with her, and that she would react to seeing him there. Richard had been sent to clean out the birds' cage in the hope that she would see him and do something unwise—and she had fallen straight into the trap that had been set for her. The eunuch's plan had succeeded better than he could have hoped. How could she have been so foolish?

What was going on out there? What would Suleiman do to her brother—and to her? Her fear was mainly for her brother, but she tried to control it. She thought that Suleiman seemed to be questioning Richard at length…but there was silence now. What had been decided? Oh, please God, let her brother not suffer for her folly. She feared the worst. Suleiman had been so very angry. Had he accepted her explanation—had it swayed him towards mercy?

She had been sitting on the edge of the divan as he had bid her, not daring to move less she anger him further, but as he came back into the room she rose to her feet and faced him proudly. She had begged for Richard, but she would not do so for herself.

'I see that you are ready to accept your fate, Eleanor.'

'Punish me as you wish, my lord—but spare my brother.'

'Your brother's fate is out of my hands now.'

Eleanor gasped, her face turning pale. 'What have you done to him? He is but a boy—an innocent child.'

'You wrong your brother, my lady. He told me he had a great desire to kill me and all my kind—those are a man's words, not a boy's.'

'He—he is bitter over our father's death. He does not know you. He thinks you as evil as those devils who captured him. I did not have time to ask him, but I believe he suffered at their hands far more than I...'

'Yes, I do realise that. I may be a savage, but I am not a fool.'

Eleanor bit her lip as she saw the way his mouth had gone hard, his eyes as bright as a hawk's before the kill. 'No, my lord. I have never thought you a fool.'

'No? That is good, because you will learn to respect me. I had hoped to spare you much, but it is time you accepted your position here. You are my property. I can dispose of you as I wish—have you beaten, sell you to the slave merchants.'

'I know that, my lord.'

'Do you, my lady? That is something. I had thought you incapable of accepting your fate. I hope you have learned your lesson today. I have perhaps indulged you more than I ought. You might do better with some discipline.'

'Yes, my lord. I have all my life been indulged. My father often told me that I must learn more humility, but—but he liked me as I am. What happened was my fault and mine alone. I accept the blame. Punish me as you wish—but spare my poor brother.'

'What—shall I not cut off his head with my scimitar? Or perhaps he should be roasted over a slow fire and the Janissaries may eat him for their supper. Or shall I be merciful and send him to the galleys?'

Eleanor stifled her gasp of horror. There was something in Suleiman's manner that alerted her. He was mocking her—deliberately baiting her to see her reaction.

'He is yours to do with as you will, my lord. I ask only for justice.'

'Ah…' A wicked light danced in his eyes. 'Now you change your tune, Eleanor. You ask for justice from a savage! Think you I am capable of justice?'

'If you are like your father, yes. I have heard that he is a truly great man and that his words are always wise. I believe that you will do none of these things you threaten for they are not just in this case.'

Suleiman tossed back his head and gave a shout of laughter, as his rage began to abate. 'I vow you are a sorceress, Eleanor. How did you read my mind?'

'There was a look in your eyes that gave you away, my lord.' She met his gaze with a proud stare as she began to realise that he was mocking her for sport, taunting her to punish her for her defiance. 'I think you would make game with me, sir. So, what would you consider just for my brother?'

'We have a school for the sons of the Janissaries in the palace. There the boys study and also learn the skills of war. If your brother wishes to kill his enemies, it is just that he should learn how it may be done—do you not think so?'

Eleanor could hardly believe her ears. He was

sending her brother to school! She had expected many things, but not this.

He was watching her expectantly. 'You do not speak, my lady. Has something happened to your tongue?'

'I was thinking that it was the judgement of Solomon.'

'Ah, yes…that is a story from the book of fables your people call the Bible, is it not?'

'Yes, my lord. It is a story from the Bible. Have you read a Christian Bible, my lord?'

'Such a thing would be forbidden to one of the Faithful,' Suleiman said. 'Another day you shall tell me the story of this wise judge you call Solomon— but now we have other things to discuss. Your brother was blameless and has been treated accordingly, but you have admitted your fault and stand convicted of your crime.'

Eleanor sensed that he was lying when he said he had not read the Bible or at least looked inside its covers, but her heart quickened as she saw the expression in his eyes.

'Yes, my lord. There is the matter of my punishment.'

Suleiman nodded, his eyes narrowed so that the thick dark lashes veiled his thoughts from her. 'What would you think a fitting punishment for a woman who betrayed her lord in the arms of another man?'

Eleanor gasped as she saw the expression on his face—which was clearly jealousy. Her heart pounded and she felt as if she could not breathe. 'He was my brother, my lord. It was but an innocent kiss. I meant no harm—nor disrespect to you.'

'Women have been executed for lying carnally

with their brother before this, Eleanor. In your case I believe it was innocent—but nevertheless such embraces are forbidden unless your lord is present and permits a decorous embrace. Yours was not restrained or decorous—indeed, so free was your passion that I think I can be forgiven for mistakenly believing he was your lover.'

Her cheeks were hot as she looked at him. 'Indeed, I have never kissed a man other than my brother or father—and if my kisses seemed passionate it was because I was so glad to see my brother alive and well. I had no intention of betraying you with any man, my lord. I beg you to believe me—I would not do that! I would not willingly lie with any man other than my husband.'

'Yet you spurned me when I said that I would honour you above my other women, that I would make you my wife—why was that, Eleanor? Am I an ignorant, cruel savage and not worthy of you?'

'No! No, of course not—I think you a good and generous man at heart and I have wanted to thank you for your kindness in sending the monkey and the birds…' Her voice faltered as he looked at her with narrowed eyes and she blushed. 'And the gifts you sent me…they were too generous, my lord. But I do thank you for them, and for treating my brother so fairly. Indeed, if I wished to marry any man…' She faltered and blushed as she realised what she had so nearly said, hoping he would not guess what had been in her mind, but she saw from the gleam in his eyes that he knew.

'So we make some progress,' Suleiman said, nodding to himself. 'I should end this nonsense now, Eleanor. You are a foolish child and do not know

yourself. I would swear there was passion in you…'
His eyes narrowed and glinted. 'Shall I show you how
foolish you are to fear the loss of your maidenhead?'

Eleanor shook her head wordlessly. How could she
explain that it was not fear of the physical act that
held her back from giving herself to him—but the
need to retain her freedom of spirit?

'I know you can take me here and now if you wish
it, my lord. I cannot fight you, for your generosity
prevents me. You make me your slave by your generosity, and if the price I must pay is to be your concubine then I shall accept as best I can…'

'But I must take for you will not give—is that it,
Eleanor?' He looked deep into her eyes and she trembled at the fire she saw burning within them. 'If I
force you to my bed, I shall never have you willingly—I shall never have that part you keep sacred
within you—that is what you are telling me, is it not?'

Eleanor hung her head, for there was something in
his manner at that moment that made her ashamed of
her churlishness. He had given her so much, both in
material gifts and understanding, and yet she had
made no move to understand him or give anything in
return.

'I—I hardly know you, my lord. I am beginning to
admire and respect you, but…I cannot do what you
expect of me…what Karin says I must do. I—I would
be your friend if you—'

'You would be my friend?' Suleiman's gaze narrowed and he appeared to be considering. 'Why
should I need a friend, Eleanor? Do you not think I
have many about me who would call themselves my
friends?'

'Yes, my lord. Forgive me for my presumption. It

was only that we share an interest in ancient manuscripts. I—I enjoyed our talk when you asked me to
help you read them and—and I have finished the work
you set me. I would like to do something that would
be of use to you. There are other women more skilled
in the arts of love. I think I would provide poor sport
for you, my lord.'

Suleiman nodded, a faint smile curving his mouth.
'You argue convincingly, my lady. Yet I wonder...'

Before she knew what he was about, he suddenly
thrust her back across the bed and lay down with her,
his body pressing hers into the softness of the divan.
Eleanor felt his weight crushing her and then his
mouth sought hers and he was kissing her...kissing
her with a savage hunger that took her breath away.
His tongue pushed inside her mouth, darting at the
soft inner flesh, arousing strange sensations in her so
that she felt her body beginning to melt in the heat
of his passion. Oh, what was happening to her? She
had never felt like this before, never experienced such
pleasure. She moved her head restlessly on the bed,
her breathing thick and fast as a little moan escaped
her and she felt herself drowning in this new and
wondrous feeling that was flooding through her. She
knew that she did not want him to stop kissing her,
that she wanted him to do all the things Karin had
told her he would do—and yet if he did he would
truly possess her. And she was afraid of that—afraid
to surrender herself to him completely.

'No! No...' She suddenly began to fight him. 'No!
I shall not let you...I shall not be your slave...'

'But supposing I refuse to release you?' His dark
eyes seemed to devour her. 'Supposing I take my fill
of you now? What then, my dove?'

'I—I cannot prevent you, but I beg you not to force me to submit like this…' She drew her breath sharply as he glared down at her and closed her eyes, knowing she could not fight him further. He would do as he wished with her.

Suddenly, Suleiman released her and stood up. She gazed up at him fearfully, expecting to find anger in his eyes, but instead she saw laughter. Why was he laughing? She had defied him yet again. Surely he ought to be angry? He held out his hand to her and when she took it, pulled her to her feet. The grasp of his hand made her tremble inwardly and she could not look into his eyes.

'That was just a little reminder, my lady,' he murmured. 'I wanted to test your obedience—for you promised to obey me out of gratitude, but it seems you forgot your promise as soon as it was given.'

'It isn't amusing,' she said, her feathers ruffled by his mockery. 'I—I am sorry, my lord, but I cannot be as submissive as your other women. It is not in my nature. I am too independent.'

'And is it this you fear to lose if you come to my bed, Eleanor?' He nodded as she remained silent. 'Yes, I begin to understand you, my lady—and I find you most amusing. You do not see why, but that is no matter. It is not for you to know everything—you are merely a woman. You should try to remember that and your place in the world. Remember that I am your lord and master—and tell me again why you think you are qualified to be my friend.'

He was provoking her, trying to make her lose her temper! She was beginning to know him now, to understand the quixotic nature of this man who called himself her master.

'You are a wicked, teasing man!' Eleanor cried. 'No one has ever mocked at me before.'

'Have they not?' Now she could see the laughter in his face. 'Then perhaps it is time they did. Now, tell me—what would I enjoy if I made you my counsellor and friend?'

'I have read much of ancient histories and the secrets of the art of astrology are known to me. I know how to cast a chart and how to read it—I could draw yours if it pleased you.'

'Indeed?' Suleiman looked at her, amusement dying to be replaced by a new interest. 'Can you use the instruments you saw in my hall?'

'Yes, my lord—at least, some of them. Some are new to me, but I know how to take the angles of the stars and to interpret what is meant by the alignment of one to another.'

'Then I might find a use for you...' The laughter was back in his eyes again. 'I agree that you would probably be poor sport in bed, Eleanor. You do not have the arts and skills a woman should properly have. It is Karin's duty to teach you these things, but I think in your case it would be a waste of her valuable time. There are other women for pleasure, but I doubt that any of them could cast a horoscope for me.' He nodded, seeming highly pleased with something. 'I shall send for you again tomorrow afternoon. Be ready to come to me every day, Eleanor—and make sure you read the books I send you. I shall expect you to be able to discuss the work I have set you.'

'Oh, yes, my lord,' she agreed eagerly. 'You will not find me lacking in diligence, I promise you. I shall

try to please you—and I do thank you for your for-
bearance in the matter of my brother.'

'I have behaved well for a savage, have I not,
Eleanor?'

Her cheeks flamed as she caught the mockery in
his voice once more. 'I beg you will forgive me for
my ignorance in so naming you, my lord. You are
more intelligent and better educated than most men I
have met in my life. Indeed, I think you the equal of
my father.'

'Then I am truly honoured,' Suleiman replied,
bowing his head. 'For I believe that you could not
give a higher compliment, Eleanor. Go now—I have
important business awaiting me and I have wasted too
much time on a mere woman already.'

Eleanor's temper sparked, then she caught the
flicker in his eyes and knew that once more he was
baiting her—deliberately emphasising a woman's
lowly state to make her fly into a rage. He could read
her far too easily! But he should not have best of her.
She smiled and curtsied to him in the manner she
would employ at an English court.

'I am sure that a man of your rank must always
have important business, my lord. Forgive me for
having given you so much trouble by my foolish
thoughtlessness—but as a woman I must be forgiven
for such lapses. I can know no better.'

Suleiman chuckled deep in his throat and she
sensed that she had pleased him. 'That is very much
better, Eleanor. If you continue to improve your temper, we may yet reach this state of friendship on
which you set so much store. Go now—before you
push me too far. Remember always that though I may
choose to assume the manners of a civilized man—

the savage lies just beneath the surface. Rouse him at
your peril.'

Eleanor left, her heart racing madly. This new
mood of the lord Suleiman was very odd and yet it
pleased her—it pleased her very much. She had begun
by fearing and hating him, had learned to respect him
for his generosity and had now begun to like him.

The women gathered round Eleanor as she returned
to the harem. From their faces it was easy to see that
they were amazed she had returned, apparently untouched and none the worse for her adventure.

'What happened?' Anastasia cried. 'I was so afraid
for you, Eleanor. I thought you would be beaten—or
put to death. You were so foolish. Kissing and hugging that man in full view of our lord's window. Did
you not know what might happen to you if Suleiman
saw you?'

'He did—he witnessed everything,' Eleanor replied. 'But, you see, the youth I kissed was my
brother Richard. He was taken when our ship was
attacked and I thought never to see him again. I did
not think of what I was doing when I hugged and
kissed him. When I saw him bending down to fasten
the cage I simply felt such joy and relief that I ran to
him without considering the consequences of my actions.'

'Were you taken to our lord?' Anastasia asked,
looking at her curiously. 'Did he not punish you?'

'Oh, yes, he punished me in his way,' Eleanor said
ruefully remembering his teasing. 'But I have discovered that the lord Suleiman is not by nature a cruel
man, though his position in this place may lead him

to be so at times—he was just to both me and my brother.'

Anastasia stared at her in awe. No other women would dare to say such things. 'But what did he do to your brother? It is forbidden for a woman of the harem to embrace any man other than her lord—even a brother.'

'Yes, our lord explained that to me,' Eleanor said. She was determined not to disclose Richard's fate, for she believed that Suleiman would not wish it commonly known that he had been lenient. Some might think it weakness on his part and try to abuse his generosity. 'He has done what he thought right and it is not for us to question that. I am to be given more scholarly work to do and I shall be sent for each afternoon to perform those tasks our lord requires.'

Anastasia was stunned into silence. Suleiman was not known for his cruelty, but other women had been punished in the past for less than Eleanor had done. It was clear that she had special influence with him, and that meant the other women must look up to her.

'Fatima has been eagerly anticipating news of your demise,' she said after a moment or two of reflection. 'She will be disappointed to learn that you have not been punished.'

'Yes—but I do not think our lord intends to take me as his wife. It may be that he will send for her again soon. For your own sake, you must do nothing to antagonise her, Anastasia. She is still his favourite.'

'Perhaps...' The other girl looked at her doubtfully. 'Has...has he not taken you to his bed?'

'I think that our lord requires other things of me,' Eleanor replied, though in her heart she knew it was not quite the truth. Suleiman was playing a game with her, but in the end he would win and then she would have no choice but to submit. 'We shall see what happens in the future. I cannot tell…'

Nor could she tell her true feelings concerning these matters. She had been so close to succumbing to those odd feelings that had flooded her whole being as she lay beneath him on the divan. For a few minutes she had wanted to please him—had wanted him to pleasure her!

Surely she had not come so far in such a short time? Eleanor knew that she was gradually losing her fear and dislike of the world to which she had been brought forcibly. She quite enjoyed being in the harem with her friends sometimes, and though she also needed her privacy and her work, Suleiman had made both these things possible. Though she fought against the truth, she knew that the time she spent with him was a joy to her.

Why, then, was she fighting what she knew must be inevitable? He could take her whenever he chose and she would be powerless to resist him—and yet he had waited. Why? What more did he want of her?

She had told him she had come to respect and admire him, and she was beginning to like the man she suspected very few others ever saw—but what was this other feeling he had aroused in her?

Chapter Seven

The expression in Suleiman's eyes was harder than granite as he looked at the creature before him, his fury leashed only by the thinnest of threads. His treatment of Eleanor and her brother earlier had been very different from the punishment he intended for Abu now that his inquiries were complete.

'Do you deny that you sent the youth to the harem gardens?'

Abu looked into the unforgiving eyes of his half-brother and trembled inwardly as he saw the contempt there. 'No, I do not deny it,' he said. There was little point in lying for his plan had somehow gone wrong, and the woman went unpunished despite her crime. 'I saw no harm in it—he was but a youth and I wanted to show you that the infidel woman would betray you given the chance.'

'So it was done for my benefit?' Suleiman's gaze narrowed in contempt. Did the eunuch think he was so easily deceived? Well, he was about to discover his mistake. 'I am not such a fool as to believe that, Abu. You did it because you blamed her for your removal from the harem. You should know that she had nothing to do with that—I have had it in mind to remove you for some time. Rumours have come to my ears...tales that, if true, would mean your death.'

'You may do with me as you will,' Abu muttered sullenly. 'You have the power. Our father gave you everything—while I was given the choice of remaining here as half a man or being sent to work in the galleys. I know that you have always despised me— and now you have your chance to kill me. So be it— my life is worthless to me anyway. I shall not beg you for mercy.'

'Had I been given your choice I would have gone to the galleys,' Suleiman replied harshly. 'You would have had your chance to earn your freedom after five years and could have perhaps become master of a ship yourself. Better to risk death in the galleys than live as you do now.'

'I have not your strength. I should have died chained like a dog,' Abu said and looked at his half-brother with hatred. 'You do not know what it is like to be a slave—you have always been the favourite son...'

'But you knew that before you made your choice. You stayed and you abused your position of trust. And now I may punish you as I see fit. Our father has left the choice to me—what shall I do with you, Abu? What would be a just punishment—not only for the folly you committed in giving the key to the harem gardens to that youth—but for your other crimes?' He saw a flicker of fear in Abu's eyes. 'Did you really imagine that I would not discover what you did, my brother? Did you believe that you could dispose of your master's property without being discovered? You might have succeeded had you been content to indulge in your sly little deals once or twice, but like all thieves you became greedy. You were noticed coming from the slave merchant's house and it was reported to me some months ago. I did nothing for a time, waiting to see if it was just a single mistake—but I know all now. I know that six women and two youths have disappeared without trace from the palace.'

'Then kill me...' Abu's eyes flared with defiance. 'Do it yourself, Suleiman. Give me the honour of death by your scimitar—or have you no stomach for it?'

Suleiman looked at him consideringly for a moment, then he walked over to a little cabinet, opened a drawer and took out a wicked-looking knife with a long curved blade. He removed its sheath and walked back to Abu, the blade revealed in all its deadly beauty. Then he threw the knife to the floor about three feet from Abu's feet, which was an equal distance from his own.

'Pick it up and try to kill me,' he said. 'You complain that I have all the advantages—now I am offering you the chance to live. Kill me and you will be granted your freedom.'

Abu's eyes narrowed in suspicion. 'You lie to trick me,' he cried. 'The moment I move towards the knife your guards will rush in and kill me.'

'No, they have orders not to interfere,' Suleiman said. 'But they are aware of what we are saying, make no mistake. I, Suleiman Bakhar, grant you your life if you can kill me.'

'It's a trick...' Abu shook his head. 'No, you cannot force me to fight you. I should lose anyway. I have no chance of winning against you. Everyone knows you are skilled in these arts. It is a sham and I shall die whatever I do.'

'So you are still a coward?' Suleiman's mouth curved in a sneer of contempt. 'You are brave when you hold the whip and the woman is defenceless, but when it comes to fighting a man you have milk in your veins. You are not worthy to be my brother and I shall not treat you as one. You will be sent to the galleys for five years, and you may earn your freedom by the sweat of your back—it is more than you granted to those women you sold into a life of misery in the lowest brothels.'

Suleiman turned away to pick up a bell that would summon the guard, and in that moment Abu sprang for the knife. He had it in his hand and was aiming for his half-brother's back when Suleiman turned, grabbing Abu's forearm and jerking him so that he went flying over his shoulder. The movement was so fast and so unexpected that the eunuch lay winded and bewildered wondering what had happened, the knife now in his half-brother's possession.

'Kill me, then,' he cried. 'Kill me now. You intended it all the time.'

'I do not lie or cheat,' Suleiman said. 'You had your chance to fight me fairly. Had you done so, I would have spared you and set you free even had I won—but now your punishment is set. Take him away…'

Three guards had come into the room as they spoke, and they laid rough hands on Abu, dragging him to his feet and carrying him off as he screamed abuse at Suleiman's back, which was now turned against him.

'May Allah curse you…may you never reach paradise…may your entrails be eaten by wild dogs.'

Suleiman ignored Abu's curses as he was taken away. A swift death by beheading would perhaps have been kinder than five years in the galleys, but Abu deserved his punishment. Yet even so the whole incident left a sour taste in Suleiman's mouth. Had there been another way…but to have simply banished Abu would have been considered weakness in the eyes of others.

Suleiman understood the nature of the world in which he lived; it was often cruel and even savage as Eleanor had claimed, but a firm hand was needed to keep order. Caliph Bakhar had told him that it was not always easy to hand out the harsh punishments necessary, but it had to be done if the order of the empire was to stand.

For how long would such an empire continue to flourish? Suleiman Bakhar had pondered it often, for although Suleiman the Magnificent was a just and wise ruler he was no longer young—and after him, what? The Ottoman Empire had ruled by blood and fear, and when weakness was added to that it could become corrupt and brutal.

The Caliph's son might never have left his father's palace, but he knew that there was hatred between the outside world and the empire. This hatred was grounded in differences of religion and culture, but it had been compounded by the many victories of Suleiman the Magnificent over his rivals and enemies—yet one day he would be gone and then the empire would begin to crumble. It had been predicted by astrologers and it would come to pass if no lessons were learned from the past.

It was Suleiman Bakhar's opinion that the time had come to try and make peace with the Christian world. If this were not attempted, one day the forces of Christendom would unite to drive their enemies from the sea. Perhaps not while the Sultan lived, but after his death. The Sultan's son Selim was rumoured to be weak and marred with the cruelty of his kind, and if he were to rule in his father's place it could lead only to the gradual downfall of the empire.

Yet there was nothing to be done, for Suleiman Bakhar was tied to his father's palace, kept from any valuable work he might have done for his country by his father's fear of losing him. Besides, his opinion counted for less than a single grain of sand and there was none to heed it.

'May it be as Allah wills it,' he murmured to himself and dismissed the problem from his mind. There were far more pressing problems to be solved for the moment…not least the delicious one of how best to tempt Eleanor to his bed.

Eleanor pored over the book Suleiman had sent her. It had come from the great Venetian printing presses and concerned the benefits of mixing astrology with medicine. Certain remedies were said to be more effective if used when the stars were in a particular conjunction, and although she did not really see how this could be so, it made fascinating reading. How she wished that she might consult her father, for he had known far more on the subject than she. She wished that Sir William could have talked to Suleiman, and believed the two men would have found pleasure in each other.

Once again her thoughts returned to her brother. Richard hated Suleiman and all he stood for.

Knowing her brother was in the palace and attending the school was both a pleasure and a torment to her. As children they had spent much of their time together, and even when they were older they had shared the same delights and pastimes. Richard had often come to seek her out when she was at some female duty and coaxed her into going out with him.

How it must irk him now that he had no freedom to do as he pleased. Like her, Richard would find life very different here to the one they had known at home. They had been fortunate in their father, their lives rich and fulfilling…but at least they were luckier than many who had suffered a fate similar to their own.

Eleanor was growing more content with her lot, though her defiant spirit still struggled against the fact that she was a slave, the property of her master. Yet she knew that she must make the best of things and count her blessings.

Besides the book, Suleiman had also sent her a new journal to replace the one she had almost filled with his own work, and she had transcribed passages of the book she thought might interest him. She thought that he was still concerned about his friend in the Janissaries who had developed a lump in his side, for he had marked one section and she paid particular attention to this so that she could discuss it with him when he sent for her as he had promised.

She could hardly wait for the afternoon to come, and was conscious of excitement when Karin told her that she had at last been sent for.

'You are to take the book you have been studying.'

Karin looked at her in a slightly puzzled way. 'All this is most strange, Eleanor. I have never heard of it happening before—older women are sometimes asked to become an adviser in domestic matters, but never a woman of your age and beauty.'

'I think the lord Suleiman likes to talk to me,' Eleanor said. 'Besides, I have been able to help him with some texts he found difficult to read.'

Karin nodded. 'Yes, I see that, but it is still a little strange.' She frowned and looked thoughtful. 'I tell you this in confidence, Eleanor—and beg that you will speak of it to no one else. It is my lord's wish that none of the concubines should know this... I have been told that Abu has been sent to the galleys as a punishment for what he did—and they also whisper that he tried to kill the lord Suleiman.'

'No!' Eleanor felt a sudden shaft of fear. 'Was he hurt—the lord Suleiman?'

'No, not at all. He disarmed Abu instantly.' Karin smiled at her. 'You have never seen your lord fight, have you? He is both clever and strong, and he always wins in the arena.'

Eleanor nodded, her cheeks warm. She had heard this from others, and found herself thinking that she would enjoy watching such a test of skill. 'Does he often fight?'

'It is one of his main pleasures to train and fight with the Janissaries,' Karin told her.

Eleanor made no reply. It seemed to her that Suleiman Bakhar was a man of extreme contrasts— the fierce competitor who delighted in the arts of war and the clever, studious man who had made his eyes ache looking for a cure for a sick friend.

She knew that this man interested her as no man

ever had before, and the thought of seeing him, of being with him, made her heart beat faster so that she walked more quickly. By the time she arrived at his apartments she was flushed and a little out of breath.

'You look warm, my lady,' Suleiman said, offering her his hand. 'Come, we shall walk in the shade of the garden for a while before we begin our studies. If you would like it, I shall show you my hawks.'

'Do you go hawking, my lord?' Eleanor asked. 'It is a pastime my father greatly enjoyed when in the north of our country. We did not live there, for as I have told you our estates were in the west—but my father had a sister he dearly loved and her husband had a great estate in the north. My uncle had a wonderful falconry, and sometimes he would let me stroke the birds.'

'Did you fly the hawks, Eleanor?'

'Once,' she replied, smiling at the memory. 'My cousin was training a new bird and he showed me how it was done. I was thrilled when the bird came to my lure.'

'It is truly a magnificent sight to see the hawk fly free and then have it return to your hand,' Suleiman said. 'Perhaps one day we shall ride out into the countryside together, Eleanor. You might like to hunt with me when I fly my birds?'

'It would be a pleasure and an honour, my lord.'

Suleiman had been leading her towards a door that opened out into an enclosed garden. She caught a glimpse of shaded walks and fountains playing into little pools, very much as in the gardens of the harem. But now he stopped and glanced at her, a flicker of amusement in his eyes.

'What has caused this transformation, my lady?

Have you no objections to my plans today? No obstinacy?'

'Why should I object when you suggest only that which would give me pleasure, my lord?'

'I am glad that you share my pleasure in the hawks, Eleanor.' He smiled at her, and they continued on in silence until they came to the falconry at the end of a shaded walk. This was a magnificent structure with both open and closed areas, so that the birds might fly free as well as perch inside when night fell.

Suleiman took a key on a chain he wore on his person and unlocked the door, going inside to bring out a fine peregrine falcon. 'How do you like my darling?' he asked in soft husky tones, stroking the head of the bird with his finger. 'Is she not beautiful?'

Eleanor looked at the glossy feathers and dark, glittering eyes of the female falcon, and knew that she was perhaps the most magnificent she had ever seen. Female peregrines were faster and stronger than the male of the species and much prized for their strength in hunting.

'Very beautiful, my lord. What is her name?'

'Scheherazade,' he replied and looked at her expectantly.

Eleanor laughed and met his look with a sparkling one of her own. 'I have heard the name,' she said. 'It is a legend long told amongst the peoples of Arabia, is it not?'

'It has been told for centuries past, and I believe was Persian in origin, though the story is set in India. As perhaps you know, it is the story of the betrayed Sultan who vowed to cut off his wife's head at dawn and take a new one every day,' Suleiman said. 'By her cleverness in telling stories Scheherazade was able to prolong the day of her execution for one hundred and one days, by which time the Sultan had fallen in love with this clever woman and could not bear to be parted from her.'

Eleanor nodded, recognising the humour and wit shown by his choice of the name for the bird. 'Is your peregrine so clever that you could not bear to part with her?'

'She is both brave and clever,' Suleiman replied, 'and yet she has learned to love her master. She will fly free and return to me without a lure.'

'Then she is an exceptional bird,' Eleanor said. 'I do not think my uncle had such a hawk in his aviary.'

'It is very rare to find such loyalty, such devotion— in any female,' Suleiman replied. 'That is what makes her beyond price.'

He lifted his wrist suddenly, giving the peregrine her freedom to circle the gardens. She flew high and circled several times before settling in a tree high above them, but when Suleiman held out his arm and called to her in the soft husky voice that held such fascination for both the bird and the woman who watched, Scheherazade flew back to him.

'I have never seen that before,' Eleanor said and there was a kind of awe in her words. 'Always, the birds come for the lure, for food—but she came to the sound of your voice.'

'She knows that I love her,' Suleiman said softly. 'And she has learned to love her master—though at first she longed to be free. Now she rejects freedom for love.'

Eleanor felt her spine tingle as she met the dark intensity of his eyes. What was he telling her? That she too would have a certain freedom if she gave herself to him in love? To be truly loved would be a wondrous thing. Her heart seemed to catch with an odd pain, and she knew a deep longing within her, but she suppressed it fiercely. She was a woman, not a bird of prey!

She turned away to inhale the perfume of a musk rose and Suleiman left her to return the hawk to its perch in the aviary. When he returned to her, it was as if the incident had never happened.

'Well, my lady,' he said in his mocking tone. 'And what have you learned since we met? I hope you have not been idle?'

'No, my lord. I have been translating the work you set me into English and trying to discover exactly what circumstances are necessary for the cure to work.'

'And what have you discovered?'

'It seems that the stars must be in a certain alignment when the powder is applied—but I fear that particular conjunction will not come about for some weeks yet.'

'That is a pity,' Suleiman said, and his expression was grave. 'The surgeons tell me that if they are to cut it must be soon or the sickness will be too advanced. I had hoped to spare my friend the knife, but I fear there is no hope for it. I shall give the order this evening.'

'I am sorry, my lord.'

'Yes, so am I. Too often the knife leads to infection and death—besides the pain of bearing it.'

'But if there is nothing else to be done…' She saw that he was distressed by the idea of his friend's suffering. 'I have copied out a recipe for an ointment that I know to be helpful in the treatment of wounds.

It is made from cobwebs and might prove useful…if your physicians would care to have it made up.'

'Give it to me,' Suleiman replied. 'We shall try everything that may help him—for he is a brave soldier and does not deserve to die in such a way.'

'Surely no one does, my lord. Medical science can do only so much—the rest is in God's hands.'

Suleiman nodded, his expression thoughtful. 'But whose god, Eleanor—yours or mine?'

'Who can know that for certain?' she asked, wondering that he should voice his thoughts so openly to her, for surely it was forbidden to him to think in such a way? And even a powerful man could be brought down by the jealousy and spite of others. To discuss such matters with her was to make himself vulnerable to bigotry and prejudice. 'When the ship I was on almost floundered in a storm I prayed to all the gods for help—yours, mine and the god of the sea.'

'You should not say such things,' Suleiman warned her, though he himself had begun the discussion. 'Do you not know that you could be put to death for such wickedness?'

'But not by you, my lord,' she replied, her eyes meeting his steadily. 'I believe you have thought more on these matters than most.'

'I am one of the Faithful,' Suleiman answered. 'But it is correct that I have considered other religions to discover what is truth. I remain loyal to my father's faith for it is the basis for my life and any other would make it impossible for me to live here. If I believed in your god and accepted the teachings of your faith I should have to leave—and that would break my fa-

ther's heart. He is a good man, Eleanor, and I would
rather die than bring harm to him.'

'Yes, of course. I knew it must be so.'

Suleiman frowned. 'I think you see too much, my
lady. Be warned—a still tongue makes a wise head.
There are those who would use what you say to destroy you.'

'Yes, my lord. But I have been used to speaking
my mind with my father who, like you, was a man
of vision, with the understanding to question and not
accept blindly all he was taught. It is pleasant sometimes to open your heart and mind to the one person
who will understand.'

'And you believe you can open your mind to me,
Eleanor?' His eyes danced with amusement. 'What is
this? It is not many days since you thought me beyond
any feeling or decency.'

'My lord is pleased to mock me,' she said and
blushed. The look in his eyes was making her heart
race like the wind and she found herself longing to
be held in his arms, her lips parting as if in invitation
of his kiss. 'We have reached a new plane of understanding.'

'Have we, my lady?' Suleiman smiled. 'That is
good…I think. Now, are you prepared to cast my
chart? Think you, you can do it accurately?'

'I can draw up your chart and explain what is the
meaning of the angles and alignments,' Eleanor said.
'But I am not sure that it is always easy to interpret
their precise meaning—but I will willingly show you
how it is done.'

'Then we shall begin at once. I was born on the
fifteenth of August at the hour of midnight…'

'Then you are a Leo,' Eleanor said and smiled. 'I

might have known it would be so—for the lion is king
of the heavens, is he not? He has the power of the
sun and was born to be a leader of men.'

Suleiman's eyes gleamed as he caught the hint of
mockery in her voice. 'I have been told this many
times, my lady. Now tell me, under which sign were
you born?'

'I was born under the sign of Sagittarius,' Eleanor
replied, 'I believe that is the sign of the archer or
hunter.'

'And does the hunter capture and kill the lion?'
Suleiman asked with a lift of his fine dark brows.

'I am told that the two are perfect partners,'
Eleanor replied, but would not meet the gleam in his
eyes.

'Indeed,' Suleiman said. 'I shall test your skill with
the art of astrology, my lady—but I warn you that I
shall know if you seek to flatter or deceive me. Give
me only a true reading, for I value honesty above all
things.'

'Then I shall not seek to deceive you, whether the
readings be good or bad, my lord.'

Suleiman frowned over the chart Eleanor had
drawn for him. His own skill in the art was sufficient
for him to know that she had been as accurate as most
who called themselves astrologers, and that her reading was very similar to that of the last man he had
summoned to cast his horoscope.

She had not mentioned the flame that would burn
him, or that he had lessons to learn, but she had told
him that the stars seemed to forecast change for him.

'This alignment of Jupiter with your star seems to
indicate that there will be a struggle, my lord. I

see…some danger for you in the near future, but after this you will gain something you have long desired.'

'I have been given a similar prediction before this,' he replied. 'I was inclined to doubt the astrologer's words for many have tried to lie to me in the hope of gaining favour. The trouble is, no one can explain exactly what the signs mean. A man may desire many things…'

'Indeed, that is true, but I do not think it is in the power of any man to predict the future exactly, my lord—though I think trends are often very accurate. I believe that your life may be going to change in some fundamental way.'

'Thank you,' Suleiman said and smiled at her. 'You have done well, Eleanor. You may return to your apartments now.'

'Will my lord send for me tomorrow?'

'I shall send you more books,' he replied. 'But I am leaving on a hunting trip with my father in the morning. When I return I shall send for you and we shall discuss what you have learned.'

'Yes, my lord.' She turned to go, feeling a sense of loss though she did not understand why. 'Take care on your trip…'

'Stay a moment.' He caught her arm as she turned away, swinging her round to face him. 'You sounded as if you cared what happened to me. Would it distress you if I did not return, Eleanor?'

'Yes, my lord…' She hung her head and would not look at him for fear that he should gaze into her eyes and read too much. 'And—and I shall miss our talks while you are away.'

'Then perhaps I should take you with me?'

'Take me with you?' She stared up at him, startled

by his suggestion and her heart began to pound with excitement. 'Do you mean that, my lord?'

'It would mean that you have to wear the veil and the casacche you hate so much. You would also have to be carried in a horse-drawn litter—my father would be outraged if I threw you across my saddle, Eleanor. There must be no attempts at escape, no wilfulness. If I took you with me on this outing, I would expect you to behave with all the respect due to the Caliph.'

'Oh yes, yes,' she breathed, her eyes lighting with excitement. 'I promise to behave just as you would wish, my lord.'

'Not as I would wish,' he replied in the soft husky voice that he had used when handling Scheherazade. 'I would let you fly high like my hawks, my lady, trusting you to return to my hand—but my father expects certain behaviour of a woman. It is for his sake that I ask your promise not to try to escape.'

'I give you my word,' Eleanor said, looking into his eyes. 'I shall not abuse your trust, my lord. I swear it on my father's honour.'

'Then I accept your good faith,' he said and reached out his hand to trace the line of her cheek and then the smooth arch of her throat. 'I believe we begin to know one another, my lady. It is good.'

'Yes,' she replied, her throat tight with emotion. She could scarcely breathe and her senses swam as she felt the warmth spread through her whole body. 'It is good, my lord.'

Her heart was singing as she retraced her steps towards the harem. For some reason she was feeling happy—happier than she had ever felt in her life before. She could not believe that her feelings had

changed so soon. Was she a fool to let herself like
Suleiman so much?

Was his kindness to her merely a honeyed trap?
She knew that he was playing her, drawing her to him
on a gossamer-fine thread, and that eventually she
would be bound by it like a fly in a spider's web.
What she did not know was how she would feel then.
Would she struggle against it and regret her lost freedom—or would she fly back to the hand of the man
who had tamed her spirit like the peregrine?

Her thoughts were rudely interrupted by Fatima,
who grabbed her arm as soon as she entered the
harem. It was clear that Suleiman's ex-favourite was
in a temper, her dark eyes flashing as she glared at
Eleanor.

'You lied to me,' she cried viciously. 'You swore
that you did not wish to become Suleiman's wife—
and yet you go to him every day. He has not sent for
me in over a week. It is because of you—because you
have turned him against me as you did against Abu.'

'I have said nothing against you,' Eleanor said. 'I
do not know why Suleiman has not…'

She broke off as Karin came up to them. The older
woman was looking thoughtful and a little anxious.

'Suleiman has asked for you, Fatima,' she said.
'You are to go to him at once.'

'At once?' Fatima looked surprised. 'But I have not
bathed or perfumed myself. Surely you have got the
message wrong?'

'His order was that you should go at once,' Karin
replied. 'I should obey him if I were you, Fatima. He
did not seem best pleased.'

'But he was in such a good mood when I left…'
Eleanor said and then bit back the words as she saw

the flash of anger in Fatima's eyes. 'At least, he seemed to be…'

'Word has come that Abu has escaped his guards,' Karin said as Fatima flounced away, clearly annoyed by the preemptory order from her master. 'Suleiman was very angry. It is said that someone within the palace must have bribed them…'

'But surely…the lord Suleiman's guards are loyal to him, are they not?' Eleanor looked at her anxiously. 'Could this mean danger for our lord? He—he is to leave on a hunting trip with the Caliph tomorrow and…and I am to go with him.'

'Yes, I know. He had sent for me to tell me—that is how I knew about Abu's escape. I was there when the news came.'

'It is very strange that he should be allowed to escape,' Eleanor said. 'Has the lord Suleiman enemies in the palace?'

'There are always intrigues and petty jealousies in a place like this,' Karin told her. 'Suleiman is his father's favourite son—but he is not his only son. Abu is his half-brother and there are others.'

'Abu was my lord's brother?'

'Yes—though because his mother was never a favourite of the Caliph he's been treated no better than any other slave, and I believed he deeply resented this. There are others who have been favoured more than Abu—but given lowly positions within the Caliph's household. Suleiman can do no wrong in his father's eyes, but if he should die the Caliph would have to appoint another son as his heir.'

'It would not be Abu…for the Caliph would want grandsons to carry on his line…'

'No, it would not be Abu—but he could have been

promised his freedom and wealth if he brought about the death of the lord Suleiman.'

Eleanor shivered as the fear trickled like ice down her spine. 'I saw danger for him in the charts,' she whispered. 'And tomorrow he leaves on a hunting trip. Many things may happen at such a time.'

'Yes, that is true,' Karin said. 'You must watch and listen, Eleanor. Suleiman is a worthy successor to his father—but there are others who are not…some who would not hesitate to have all his concubines strangled if they took over his place in the Caliph's household.'

'You do not mean it?' Eleanor was horrified.

'Yes, I do,' Karin said. 'It is often done when a man dies. Sometimes the new master takes pity on the women and allows them to return to their homes—but that is not always the case.'

Eleanor's face went white as she saw the expression in the older woman's eyes. 'That is a terrible custom. I cannot believe anyone could be so cruel.'

'You have been fortunate,' Karin said. 'You were bought by a good master—had you been less fortunate you could have been treated very differently. Your stubbornness would have brought you a beating in many households.'

'Yes, I see that…' She looked at Karin with dark, anxious eyes. 'It would be best not to speak of this to anyone else. I would not have my friends upset by what you have told me.'

'I shall tell no one else what I have told you,' Karin agreed. 'But as Suleiman's intended bride I thought that you should be aware of what had happened. For if your lord is in danger, then so too are you. I fear

that Abu would reserve your punishment to himself…'

Eleanor felt sick as she thought of the cruel eunuch
who believed her responsible for his downfall. She
could not begin to imagine her fate if he were to be
in a position of power once more.

Suleiman cursed himself for a fool. He ought to
have killed Abu when he had the chance. It was what
his father would have done. Their overlord the Sultan
Suleiman the Magnificent had put his own sons to
death for less than the crimes Abu had committed. It
had been a weak moment to spare him, and Suleiman
knew that he might rue the day he had allowed himself to be swayed by the tie of blood.

He had felt guilt because he had been favoured so
much while Abu had been forced to give up so
much—though he knew that, presented with the same
choice, he would have taken the galleys. He would
rather have died than become a eunuch. It was a bar-
barous practice to maim a man in that way, to take
his manhood from him and strip him of a man's natural pride—but it was necessary to their way of life.
A necessary evil to uphold the system.

The eunuchs were thought to be more docile than
true men, and they could not defile the women in their
charge. It was common enough amongst the children
of concubines, for without some form of control there
would be constant fighting amongst the sons of important men. Suleiman's own father had had a favourite wife, whose son he had raised up above all
others, but there were other sons who had not been
dealt with in this way—and Suleiman was aware that
some of them would be only too willing to take his

place. Some would be willing to kill both him and his father to gain power for themselves.

It was because of this that Suleiman could not defy his father's wish to keep him close. The Caliph was still a strong man, but growing older—one day his other sons might try to wrest power and wealth from him, but not while Suleiman had the loyalty of the Janissaries. He knew that he was both feared and respected, and while this was so the elite guard remained faithful to their master.

Now it seemed that at least one or two of the men he had counted as friends had turned against him— who had bribed them and in what coin had they been paid?

Suleiman had heard whispers concerning Fatima. He had been told that she had been in league with Abu in the matter of the women who were spirited away from the harem in the night—and of cruel punishments meted out at her command. There were also other tales, which were even more damning, and made him wonder just how far her betrayal had gone. Had she also been responsible for bribing the Janissaries?

He turned as she entered, throwing herself to her knees before him in her customary way, waiting for him to raise her up. She was smiling as he bid her rise, a confident smile on her lips as if she believed he had sent for her to pleasure him. Did she not yet realise that he no longer wanted her—or did she believe she could continue to deceive him?

As he saw the secret satisfaction in her eyes, Suleiman wondered what he had seen in her for so many months. She was sly and vain, and he must control his sudden dislike of her or he might judge her unfairly. Fatima was not liked by others in the harem and these rumours might be malicious and untrue. He would talk to her and discover what he could—but he would not punish her yet. He must be sure of the truth before he did anything for which he might afterwards be sorry...

Chapter Eight

'Suleiman and the Caliph must both die,' Abu said, eyes glowing like black diamonds. 'For, if one lived, retribution would be swift. Our only hope is to take them by surprise—and by taking this hunting trip together they play into our hands.'

He glanced round at the faces of the men who had been bribed to join him—the Caliph's second son Hasan, four of Hasan's guards and two of Suleiman's own men. Abu was not entirely certain of these two, though they were afraid of him. Both had lain with Fatima, which meant they would be put to death if their crime were discovered. She was insatiable, and even when she had been Suleiman's favourite, she had craved sexual pleasure with others. Abu had arranged for her to lie with these two in return for help with the disappearance of a woman from the harem.

'We shall kill them both—and when they are dead I shall rule in my father's place,' Hasan said, his cruel mouth narrowed in a sneer. 'And you shall be my chief adviser, Abu. You may have a free hand in disposing of Suleiman's concubines.'

Abu inclined his head, his features expressionless.

He knew he could not hope to become Caliph himself, but he could control this weak fool and rule through him. He moistened his lips with the tip of his tongue at the thought of the power he would hold.

'I shall make you more powerful than your father,' he promised. 'Only play your part, Hasan, and within two days you shall be Caliph…'

'Yes, yes…' Hasan's weak face glowed with the thought of his triumph over the brother who had always taken precedence over him in their father's favour. 'And then I shall dispose of all my enemies…'

'Why do you come to me with this tale, Bayezid?' Suleiman's eyes narrowed as they fixed on his younger brother. 'I know well that you do not like Hasan—why should I believe your story? It might be that you wish to make trouble for him.'

'I cannot make you believe my story,' Bayezid said. 'I can only tell you that I have seen Hasan and Abu together. They thought they had concealed their meeting, but I came upon them behind the stables of the Janissaries, and I heard something. I do not know what it means, but I believe they intend to kill you during the hunting trip with our father.'

'And you do not wish to see me killed?'

'They would also need to kill our father, and I respect the Caliph because he is a good and just man—and I would like to be as he is one day if I can earn the respect of others and be given a position of trust.'

Suleiman nodded. Bayezid was young and studious and, although he knew there was envy and hatred between Hasan and Bayezid, he was inclined to believe his story—especially as he had known Abu must have had help from inside the palace to make his escape.

He had thought Abu must have gone long ago, but now he realised the renegade was hiding somewhere within the palace grounds. Clearly he was waiting his chance to do more mischief.

Suleiman could instigate a thorough search, root out the culprits and punish them—or he could allow the conspirators to go ahead with their treachery and have them taken in the act. Perhaps this was the best course, since he would then catch all the birds in one throw.

'Thank you for your warning, brother.' He smiled at Bayezid. 'I believe it took courage to come and tell me—is there some way in which I might reward you?'

Bayezid shook his head. 'I have all that I need, brother. I want only a quiet life and to be left in peace to study. May Allah protect and guide your hand tomorrow.'

'Allah be with you.'

Left alone, Suleiman walked to the window that looked out on the harem gardens. They were deserted at this time of night, for his brother had waited until after dark to come to him in secret.

Suleiman was wrestling with his problem and frowned as he came to his decision. He had given his word to Eleanor that she might accompany them on their hunting trip, but it must be broken. Her presence in the camp would hamper him, for she would be vulnerable and he had no time to watch over her. He would need all his wits about him if he were to defeat his enemies.

Eleanor would be disappointed to be left behind. If it were not so late he would send for her and explain, but the women would be sleeping and anything out of the ordinary might alert the conspirators.

No, he must act as usual, but Eleanor must stay behind tomorrow.

'What do you mean—I am not to accompany the lord Suleiman?' Eleanor stared at Karin in dismay. She had looked forward to this trip outside the confines of the palace and to be denied at the last moment was a terrible disappointment. 'Why? What have I done to displease my lord?'

'I do not know,' Karin replied, frowning. 'He sent word early this morning that you were not to go after all. I am sorry, Eleanor. I suppose that he must have changed his mind.'

'He changed his mind…' Eleanor nodded, her eyes sparking with anger. Suleiman had changed his mind and so she was not to go. Her feelings on the matter were of no importance. He had not even bothered to send for her to tell her himself, merely sending a message at the last moment. It seemed he broke his promises as easily as he made them. 'Yes, I see—I see that he is faithless and cares little for his word.'

'You should not speak so of the lord Suleiman,' Karin said giving her a severe look. 'If it were reported to him, you could be beaten. I am sure he has his reasons for disappointing you.'

Eleanor's temper was at bursting point, but she held it inside. Her anger was almost as much against herself as Suleiman. She had begun to believe in him, to trust him—and now he had done this! It made her realise that he could not be trusted…ever. She would be a fool to let herself be swayed by his soft words and his promises. He was, after all, nothing but a barbarian—and next time they met she would keep her distance.

Her mood was not improved as she saw Fatima preening herself in the harem gardens that morning. She was wearing a satisfied expression that seemed to say *she* was back in Suleiman's favour, and the news that Eleanor was not after all to be taken on the hunting trip made an interesting piece of gossip for the ladies of the harem.

Some of the women cast her pitying glances, others made a fuss of Fatima as if wanting to assure her that they had never even for one moment thought that she had truly been set aside for this new woman.

Anastasia, Elizabetta and Rosamunde were sympathetic towards Eleanor, telling her that Suleiman must have good reason not to take her with him. She smiled and pretended to agree with them, but her heart had begun to ache and it was difficult for her not to creep away and weep. But she would not let Fatima see that it mattered, and so she stayed with the others throughout the day, playing with the monkey and talking to the parrot, which she was trying to teach to say a few polite words in French.

It was not until the evening that she retired to her own room to study and transcribe some of the latest work that Suleiman had sent her—and then the heaviness of her heart was indeed hard to bear. She was a fool to have let down her guard even for a moment; if she once let herself truly care for him, she would be the same as all the other women who sighed and waited for him to notice them.

The attack came on the first night at the camp. During the day the hunting had gone well and they had killed a wolf in the forest above the plains, which was better sport than the wild boar which was seldom hunted by Muslims. It had been decided they would make deer their sport on the next day.

Suleiman had set his spies to watch Hasan and his guards, and he was warned long before the thin blade of a knife began to slit the side of his pavilion. He watched from the shadows in the far corner as the stealthy figure crept towards the sleeping pallet where he ought to have been lying asleep, and as the dagger was brought down into the bundle he had arranged to resemble a man beneath the blanket.

'Die, you dog!'

The voice proclaimed the identity of the assassin had Suleiman needed proof. 'Unfortunately for you, Abu—that was not me.'

The cloaked figure gave a startled oath, the knife still in his hand as he swung round, gasping his dismay. Suleiman moved forward out of the shadows so that the assassin could see his face. Abu cursed. He lunged wildly at his half-brother, the certainty of what would happen when the discovery of his full treachery was known making him lose his fear.

'So you live still!' he yelled. 'Yet I shall kill you— guards, to me! To me!'

His cry to the men who stood on guard outside the tent went unheeded. He had chosen the men who had once served Suleiman, but they had already sensed his plans had gone awry, hesitating about following him inside and slipped away into the night rather than face the fury of the master they had foolishly betrayed. Somehow the lord Suleiman had learned of the treachery planned this night, and their only chance now was to flee.

Suleiman met his half-brother's attack without hesitation, striking a blow at his arm, and then twisting it so that Abu cried out in pain as a bone cracked and his weapon fell uselessly to the ground. He swayed on his feet, half-fainting in his agony, his eyes sullen and disbelieving as he looked at Suleiman. He had known he was strong, but his skill was even more awesome than Abu had imagined. The cowardly dogs he had paid to help him had refused to enter the tent, saying that they would watch over him and he suspected them of betraying him.

'So now you will kill me,' he said as he looked into Suleiman's cold eyes. 'You will not be foolish enough to spare me again.'

'You made a mistake by throwing in your lot with Hasan,' Suleiman replied, his features set like iron. 'Had your attack been just against me I might have kept to my original plans for you, Abu—but you dared to lift your hand against my father and for that there can be only one punishment.' He raised his voice to summon his trusted guards. 'Take him away!'

Three guards entered the pavilion and laid hands on Abu, dragging him away as he cursed and screamed, for they did not and would not spare him. He would suffer horribly, for he had dared to plot against the life of the Caliph, and such a crime must be punished in a way that would deter others. Even Suleiman could not spare him what was to come—nor would he have considered it.

'My father?' Suleiman asked as a fourth man entered the pavilion after the others had gone. 'The Caliph is unharmed?'

'Your instructions were followed to the letter, my

lord,' the captain of the Janissaries replied. 'I took your father's place and when they came to kill him my men were waiting—the traitors have been taken and will be punished in accordance with their crimes.'

'Good—I leave justice in your hands, Omar. And I thank you and your men for their loyalty.'

'The two who betrayed you with Fatima have been arrested—what would you have me do with them, my lord?'

'They may go to the galleys for two years and then be free to go whither they will,' Suleiman said. 'They confessed their crimes and told of the plot against me—and for that I shall spare their lives.'

'You are just, my lord,' Omar said. 'Allah be praised that this night went well—but what of your brother Hasan?'

'Has my father spoken?'

'He says that Hasan may be spared only if you grant him his life.'

'I do not,' Suleiman said, his eyes as cold as deep water ice. 'If he is spared he will plot against us again, and others will be foolish enough to follow. In order that no more lives may be lost, his is forfeit. However, he is not to be tortured and he is to be given a clean death by the sword. I trust you to see that my order is carried out as I have given it, Omar.'

'Again your justice is good, my lord. It is how it should be.'

Suleiman inclined his head, but did not speak as the captain of the guard bowed and left him. A deep shudder went through him as he thought of the fate of the traitors, and he knew that he had never felt so alone—so desperately alone.

The Caliph had felt incapable of ordering the execution of his second son, even though he knew it must be and so he had left it to Suleiman, who had not shrunk from his duty—but it was a hard duty, the hardest thing he had ever done. To condemn his half-brothers to death... Abu he had never liked or trusted, but as a small boy Hasan had been a delightful companion and they had spent much time together. He was sorry that Hasan's life had come to this sorry end.

Yet it had to be, there was no other way open to Suleiman. This world in which they lived was a harsh one and justice must be seen to be done or the fragile order would crumble about their ears. He had been weak in allowing Abu to escape death the first time, but he would not escape this time—and nor would poor foolish Hasan.

And yet Suleiman felt as if it were he who was being punished. He shivered again, feeling the darkness descend on him as he went to open the flap of the pavilion and look out at the stars.

Did those same stars shine in the sky above England? The land of his mother's birth, of which she and Eleanor had told him—and would life be less harsh in such a place?

He doubted it, for had not Eleanor been forced to flee her home in fear of retribution from a harsh regime? Why did human beings do so much harm to each other and themselves?

Suleiman gave himself a mental shake. To dream of a civilisation where people could exist in harmony without spite or cruelty was to live in a fool's paradise. Perhaps one day people would learn a new way, but it would not come in his lifetime.

He smiled wryly at his own thoughts. Saidi Kasim had taught him too well. He was beset with the doubts that would best become a philosopher and were not for the son of Caliph Bakhar, who must be strong and just. He would do better to think of something more pleasant…of a woman's soft limbs and a smile that made him want to drown in her arms.

'Oh, my lady,' he murmured. 'Would that you were here to lie beside me and drive away the demons this night.'

The hunting trip was due to continue for another day, but after that he would send for Eleanor and tell her what he had decided for her future.

Elizabetta was teaching Eleanor to dance, showing her how to sway her hips alluringly. Anastasia was playing music for them, and Rosamunde was standing by to comment and encourage. Some of the other women had also come to watch.

'Yes, you are beginning to get the idea now,' Elizabetta said 'you just need to put a little more feeling into it. Imagine that you are reaching out to your lover, begging him to take you in his arms and caress you…'

Eleanor shook her head, throwing herself down on the cushions and laughing. 'It is no good. I shall never be able to dance the way you do, Elizabetta.'

'That is because you have never learned,' her friend replied. 'It will come if you practise.'

'I will show you how to dance—how it should properly be done.'

Eleanor looked up in surprise as she saw Fatima, wondering how long the other woman had been watching them.

'I have heard that you dance more gracefully than

anyone,' she said. 'Please dance for us, Fatima. I should enjoy it.'

'I need no music,' Fatima said. 'The music is in my head.'

She stood poised for a moment, her eyes closed, head down. Then her head came up, eyes open, a smile on her lips. Eleanor was fascinated by the graceful, sensuous swaying of the other woman's body. She had seen the other women dancing, but none of them had Fatima's magic or mystery. It was little wonder that Suleiman had found so much to please him in his beautiful favourite.

Eleanor clapped her hands when the dance ended with Fatima lying on the floor, her arms outstretched. 'That was beautiful,' she said sincerely. 'I have never seen anyone put so much into their dancing, Fatima. I could never dance half as well as you though I practised for years.'

Fatima looked up and her dark eyes were dark with spite. 'That is why you will never keep the favour of the lord Suleiman,' she said. 'He may find you amusing for a while—but then he will send for me again when he tires of you.'

Eleanor did not answer her. In her heart she feared that Fatima was right. Suleiman had seemed pleased with her, but how could she hope to hold him when he could summon any woman he chose? Fatima was beautiful, but so was Rosamunde, and the others were also extremely lovely in their own way. Why should Suleiman prefer Eleanor to his other women?

There was no reason she could see why he should want her more than half a dozen others, and since Fatima was his favourite it was natural that he would continue to send for her. Eleanor felt the sting of jealousy, though she tried hard to suppress it. She had no right to feel jealous! Had she not declared that she had no wish to be his concubine—and indeed she did not wish for it. But she did wish that she might be his love.

There was so much difference between the two things, but she knew that she was asking for the impossible. In Suleiman's world there was no such thing as love, and though he demanded complete faithfulness from his women, he did not give as much in return. Eleanor would be a fool if she allowed herself to care.

She looked up as Karin approached her. 'Your lord has sent for you, Eleanor,' she said. 'You are to go to him at once.'

Eleanor was about to obey, and then something snapped in her head. She was not his slave, even though he had paid gold coin for her, and she would not be sent for.

'Thank my lord for his attention, Karin, but pray tell him I cannot answer his summons for the moment—because I am not well.'

Karin stared at her. 'Are you refusing an order from your master?'

'Was it an order or a request?'

'He asked that you would go to him at once.'

'Then it was a request,' Eleanor said. 'Pray give him my regrets and tell him I am lying on my bed with a headache.'

'But you were dancing a few moments ago…'

'And that is why I now have a terrible headache. Excuse me, please, I must lie down. I am sure that my lord will understand if you explain why I cannot answer his request.'

She got up from her cushion and walked into her own apartments, leaving the other women to stare after her in awe. How dare she refuse to go to Suleiman? He would be furious with her and was sure to order that she be beaten this time.

'Forgive me, my lord,' Karin said, hardly daring to speak the words. 'Eleanor is lying down with the headache. She begged your pardon for not obeying your summons, and asked that she be excused for the moment.'

Suleiman stared at her. She was clearly ill at ease at bringing such a message, and he saw the reason for her nervousness very plainly. Eleanor was not ill, she was merely being stubborn.

'I trust she is not very ill?' he asked. 'Should I send my physician to her do you think?'

'I—I do not think that necessary,' Karin said. 'I believe it is merely a headache and will pass.'

'But I would leave nothing to chance,' Suleiman replied, a little smile flickering across his mouth. 'Yes, I believe I shall send the physician to her—I would not have my lady languish for want of attention. Go to her now and tell her the physician will see her immediately—for she may need to be bled or perhaps a blister may be more helpful in this case...'

'Yes, my lord. I shall go at once.'

Suleiman nodded and turned away to glance at a trinket he had recently purchased; it was a table clock with pierced sides and fashioned of silver gilt. He had it mind to present it as a gift to his intended bride, but for the moment it would remain a secret since it seemed that Eleanor was sulking.

Suleiman had little doubt of what had brought on

her sudden headache. She was angry because he had broken his promise to her, and as he had not spoken of what had occurred during the hunting trip to Karin, Eleanor would know nothing of it.

Her refusal to come to him would have made him angry had he not understood her better than she guessed. It amused him to play her little games, and he wondered what she would do when she received his message.

As it happened, he did not have long to wait. He was standing at the trestle table examining some manuscripts with the help of a long-handled glass when she came in softly. She made no sound nor did she speak but he knew she was there, for her perfume betrayed her. No other woman smelled quite as she did, for she used few of the heavy oils that were so popular in the harem and her scent was her own.

'I am glad your headache is better,' he said as he turned. 'It would have been a pity to apply the leeches. I think them most unpleasant, but I understand their use to be quite efficacious in the treatment of heated blood.'

'I had no need of leeches or blisters, my lord.'

'No, Eleanor, I did not think you did—your headache was a fit of temper, because I was forced to break my word to you.'

Her cheeks were hot as she looked at him, for he made her seem like a temperamental child. 'I would not have minded if you had told me yourself, my lord—but it seemed so careless to send word like that.'

'As if I did not know or care that you would be disappointed?' Suleiman nodded. 'Yes, I understand that, my lady—and I ask you to forgive me. I would have acted differently if I could. It was not my intention to slight you, believe me.'

Eleanor stared at him, torn between wanting to believe and trust him and the fear that if she gave her heart to him he would abuse her love.

'I know that I am merely a woman and that women are inferior in your eyes…'

'Why do you think that of me, Eleanor? Have I given you cause to believe I consider you inferior? Have I not shown that I respect and admire your intelligence and your bravery—for there are few who would dare to defy the laws as you have, my lady.'

'No…' Eleanor was forced to be truthful as she gazed into his eyes. What she saw there gave her a jolt of surprise. There was such a haunted, unhappy look that it made her want to reach out and comfort him. 'No, you have not, my lord. It is my own fear that makes me say such things to you—because I am afraid of giving too much of myself.'

'Yes, I have realised this,' he said. 'Have you been hurt, my lady?'

'No…not in the way you mean,' she said. 'But I had a cousin I loved who was married against her will. She wept in my arms the night before her wedding, and I have never forgot it. But it was not only Mary's unhappy marriage, my lord. I see women in your harem who sigh and languish for one glance from you—and I would not be like them.'

'If I took a wife I might grant freedom to the concubines,' Suleiman said, surprising her. 'I have come to see that what you say concerning them is true. It is unkind to force so many women to live useless, empty lives when I shall never send for them.'

'You would set them free?' Eleanor's spine tingled.

'But it is your custom…would it not seem strange to others if…?'

'Perhaps.' Suleiman shrugged. 'I care little for the opinion of others, Eleanor. Would you think it a good thing if they were to be returned to their homes?'

'Some of the women have no home, my lord. If you send them away, they will only have to sell themselves back into slavery.'

'Perhaps marriages could be arranged for some of the women. I shall speak to Karin, to discover her thoughts concerning this—but some must remain, of course, as friends and ladies-in-waiting to my wife.'

'Yes, my lord. She would otherwise spend many hours alone.'

'Who should remain, Eleanor? Pray advise me in this matter—who amongst the women are most fitted to be my wife's attendants?'

Eleanor's heart was beating very fast, so fast that she found it difficult to answer immediately. 'Surely it should be for your wife to choose, my lord?' She dared not look at him lest she betray herself. He must not guess how much her heart had softened towards him.

'What—would you play games with me even yet, Eleanor?' He sounded stern, and yet she thought she detected a note of disappointment.

Her gaze lifted to his uncertainly. 'My lord spoke of—of such an honour, but I was not sure…I thought that perhaps I had made you angry? That you might have changed your mind as you did about the hunting trip.' Her head went up, challenging him.

'You have made me angry many times,' he agreed, his expression giving nothing away. 'However, I have decided that you are most fitted to become my wife.

The mother of my sons must have both spirit and intelligence. I have overlooked your faults—and they are many—but I shall expect an improvement in your manners, my lady.'

'Indeed, sir?' Eleanor's head went up, her eyes sparking with indignation. 'In my country it is not the custom for a gentleman to summon the lady he is courting.'

'Courting?' Suleiman's mouth curved in gentle mockery. 'You expect the son of Caliph Bakhar to court you? What would you have me do, Eleanor? Must I go down on my knees and beg you to be my wife?'

'No—no, of course not. But it is the custom to ask rather than instruct in such matters, my lord. You might at least ask me if I would like to marry you.'

'If I asked, you might refuse.' His gaze narrowed as if he tried to read her mind.

'I should certainly refuse,' Eleanor replied, knowing that she lied. Her heart was thumping wildly and she could scarcely breathe.

'Then it is as well for both of us that I give you no choice,' Suleiman replied still inscrutable. 'Now, my lady, go into the bedchamber and change into the clothes you will find lying on the divan.'

Eleanor stared at him in alarm. 'Why? What are you—I mean, what kind of clothes?'

'Do you wish me to assist you to disrobe?'

Suleiman's eyes gleamed and she gave a little yelp and backed away, her face flushed as she saw his amusement. What was he up to now? Some mischief if she had judged that look correctly!

When she saw the robes lying on the silken covers of the divan, Eleanor was even more puzzled. She had expected to see thin, gauzy garments that would show every line of her body through the flimsy material. Instead, she found the costume a youth or small man might wear for riding or working, plain and drab in colour. She glanced over her shoulder, still expecting some hidden meaning and half imagining that Suleiman would pounce on her when she was naked, but he did not come and she donned the trousers, tunic and caftan that a simple country youth might wear. She was trying to work out how to arrange the headdress, which was a plain white turban with a scarf that wrapped about the neck, when Suleiman entered.

He looked at her with approving eyes. 'You make a handsome boy, Eleanor. Let me help you with your headdress—we must make sure that your hair cannot escape and betray you.'

'Why are you dressing me as a youth, my lord?'

'You wished to ride with me, did you not? I thought we would take Scheherazade for a little hunting trip. Come, my lady. My most trusted men await us. We shall leave through my private gardens. No one will notice us go or see us return. This shall remain our secret.'

Eleanor saw his indulgent smile and her heart turned over. 'Oh, this is a wonderful surprise, my lord. Much better than the other hunting trip you promised me.'

'I am glad that you are pleased,' he said. 'Believe me when I tell you that it was as much a disappointment to me that you could not accompany us as it was to you.'

Eleanor wanted to ask him why he had changed his mind, for there was obviously some reason and it had not been a mere whim as she had imagined. However, there was no time; he was urging her on, his mood one of excitement as they slipped away into the gardens and out through a gate Suleiman unlocked to a small courtyard where three guards waited with horses.

Suleiman himself helped Eleanor to mount the pretty white mare provided for her use. Dressed as a youth, she was forced to ride astride, but fortunately her father's indulgence to her as a child meant that she was no stranger to this mode of travel, and Suleiman smiled as he saw how confidently she took her reins.

'Now we shall go,' he said, and mounted his own horse. A servant held up Scheherazade's cage, and the bird took its place on Suleiman's wrist. 'I believe we shall have good sport this afternoon, Eleanor, for my darling is restive. She has not been out of the gardens for some days and longs to try her wings.'

'As I do, my lord.'

Eleanor's eyes were bright with excitement as she looked at him. She had wrapped the two ends of the scarf about her face so that little but her eyes showed above it, but her feelings were plain for Suleiman to see and he smiled at her pleasure.

She had demanded that he court her in the manner of her own people. He could not go so far, but he could give her much that she desired and this hunting trip was only the beginning.

Eleanor watched as the hawk circled and then swooped, its wings closed as it dived upon its prey. Long, cruel talons extended as it clutched its quarry in flight, binding it and swooping lower as it bore the prey to the ground.

'Is she not a fine hunter?' Suleiman asked Eleanor as he recalled the falcon to his hand, holding the jesses securely with his fingers and replacing the leather rufter over Scheherazade's head. 'We have had fine sport with her this afternoon, have we not, my lady?'

'Yes, indeed, my lord,' Eleanor agreed, for the peregrine had successfully taken several birds. However, for Eleanor the pleasure had come as much from riding in the open air with the breeze in her face as from the sport—though it was a fine sight to watch the falcon. 'It is a lovely afternoon, and wonderful to be riding here with you, my lord. I feel so alive and free…'

Riding in the hills above the ancient Byzantine city, which had for so long been a Christian stronghold, the view of the Bosphorus Straits was magnificent, and the sense of almost being able to fly made Eleanor feel as if the past weeks had never happened. She had ridden out with her father often at home, and she had missed the exercise and the exhilaration of being on horseback.

'I am glad that you have enjoyed the outing,' Suleiman replied. 'We should return to the palace now, my lady, for it wants but an hour to sunset and there are still bandits roaming these hills.'

'Yes…yes, I suppose we must, my lord,' Eleanor replied with a stifled sigh. 'I wish we could just go on riding forever.'

Suleiman nodded, and there was a thoughtful, regretful expression in his eyes as though he too felt as she did—but surely that was merely her imagination?

Yet Eleanor was beginning to know him, to sense his moods, and she knew that there were many facets to this man's character.

They rode back to the Caliph's palace side by side as the sun began to sink over the hills and darkness fell. It came quickly at this time of year and by the time they regained the safety of the palace gardens it was almost dark. Suleiman led the way back to his apartments.

'You must change now and return to the harem,' he told Eleanor. 'Say nothing of what we did this afternoon, my lady. We shall keep such outings a secret known only to a trusted few.'

'It shall be as you wish, my lord,' Eleanor replied. 'But may I ask my lord why? Surely you are free to do as you please?'

'I have enemies within the palace,' Suleiman replied gravely. 'It was because of one such that I was not able to take you on our hunting trip.'

'Will my lord not tell me more?' Eleanor had sensed a darkness in his mind all the time they were out with the hawk. He had enjoyed the outing, but she knew that something was troubling him. His dark eyes seemed to reflect pain—and a deeper distress as if he questioned his very existence. 'What has brought those shadows to your eyes?'

'I was forced to order the execution of my half-brother Hasan during the hunting trip,' Suleiman replied, his eyes intent on her face as if he wished to see her reaction. 'Abu and he plotted to kill both the Caliph and myself by stealth as we slept. Hasan planned to rule in my father's stead, but he was weak and Abu would have had the real power. I was warned of the plot only hours before we were due to leave the palace. I could not take you with me once I knew, Eleanor, for your presence would have made me more vulnerable—yet had I told you of my reasons for leaving you behind the traitors might have learned of it and taken flight.'

Eleanor understood how he was feeling; it was evident to her that he had found it difficult to order the death of a brother. She knew that Abu must also have been executed. Suleiman had spared Abu's life once, but he could not do so a second time, because the attack had been against his father and must be punished.

'I am sorry, my lord,' she said softly, and then without thinking she moved towards him, reaching up to kiss his cheek. Her action was one of sympathy, but when Suleiman caught her to him, he kissed her fiercely with a hunger that stirred strange longings deep within her.

His eyes sparked with mockery as he released her. 'You play with fire, Eleanor. Do not tempt me too far or you may discover you have lit a flame that cannot be controlled.'

Eleanor's cheeks flamed, for she had been foolish to imagine he would want her sympathy or understanding. He desired her, but he did not love her—he did not understand the quiet moments lovers shared, or that she had meant only to comfort him.

'Forgive me, my lord. It was an impulse—and kindly meant.'

His eyes glowed like hot coals. 'Do not offer me kindness, my lady. I want much more than that from you—and you should be prepared for your fate. This evening I shall send for Karin and set the preparations in train for our wedding. You shall be my wife, Eleanor.'

She moved away from him, her heart racing wildly as fear returned. 'Do not force me to this, my lord. I pray you wait a while longer. Give me more time to become accustomed to you.'

'No, there is to be no more time,' Suleiman replied, his eyes sparking with anger. 'I have been patient with you long enough, Eleanor. I will have no more of this nonsense. I have shown you that you need not fear your life here. You will be almost as free as I am myself, and that is all I can offer you.'

'Please, I beg you—do not...'

'Go before I lose my temper,' Suleiman said and now he was angry. 'I have given you more than any other woman, Eleanor. I would that you would give me a little in return—but if you are stubborn in your refusal you shall discover that I am not to be denied. If you will not give, I shall take. You are mine, and if you would but look into your foolish heart, you would glory in what you find there. Together we shall find that paradise known only to a few—but there is no escaping your destiny. It is bound with mine.'

Eleanor's cheeks burned as she turned away, and she knew that she was foolish to resist him still. He spoke only the truth when he said they were bound together, for she had cast her own chart as well as his and the stars showed that they were inextricably linked one to the other.

As she returned to the harem, Eleanor looked into her heart as Suleiman had bid her and discovered that it was no longer her own. She loved him despite herself; though a part of her still fought against the inevitable, it was already too late.

Eleanor shook her head in denial as she struggled to come to terms with her own thoughts. No, no, it was not possible! She respected Suleiman, liked him despite her resentment at being made his slave—but love? She could not love him! He was the very symbol of all that she had disliked in men of her own race: arrogance and the assumption that men should always rule, that women were somehow inferior. Yet Suleiman never made her feel inferior, even when he was at his most lordly. Indeed, he seemed at times to treat her as though she was the most special of beings. Her mind raced as she tried to rationalise her feelings, but her heart told her there could be no other reason for the emotions that were raging through her.

She *was* in love with this fierce, strange man of contrasts, and she could find no happiness in anything that was not shared with him—so why had she not told him that? Why must she struggle and fight against her own desires and needs?

If it was a matter of religion and custom—she knew Suleiman well enough to know that they could reach some compromise. It would mean spending her life in this palace except for the times when her lord took her on some expedition, but something he had said to her had made her think that he was no freer than she.

Surely that was not the case? And yet she knew that he held his father in great respect, and the Caliph needed him—he needed Suleiman's strength and cleverness to outwit the enemies that surrounded them.

Chapter Nine

Eleanor spent what was left of the evening talking with her friends in the harem. She braided Elizabetta's hair, and Anastasia painted her toenails for her with a red dye. They laughed and talked together, but no one asked Eleanor what she had been doing, though Anastasia did mention that she had a fresh colour in her cheeks.

Fatima was holding court in another part of the hall, but she did not speak to them or they to her. Most of the other women still seemed to follow the favourite, though Suleiman had not sent for her since before his hunting trip.

No word of the plot to kill the Caliph and Suleiman, or of the subsequent executions, seemed to have filtered through to the harem, and Eleanor felt it best to keep her knowledge to herself. If Suleiman and the Caliph wished it known, Karin would be informed and she would tell the other women.

Karin did not come to the harem that evening, and Eleanor wondered if Suleiman had, after all, decided to wait before announcing his intention to take Eleanor as his wife. She was not sure whether she wanted the announcement to come or not, and spent a restless night going over all the reasons why she should not wish for this wedding.

She was a Christian and he was a Muslim, and she had a right to be free. As Suleiman's wife she would spend the rest of her life in this palace—but what was the alternative? There was no possibility of her being rescued, which meant that she was never going to leave the palace anyway. Surely it was better to live as the favoured wife than as one of the concubines?

She slept fitfully at last, having reached no sensible conclusion. It did not matter what she thought, for Suleiman had made up his mind and she had no choice in the matter of her future.

Yet there was no word from Karin, nor did Suleiman send for her that afternoon, though towards evening one of the eunuchs came to tell her she was needed. She followed him through the passages to a part of the palace she had never been before, and was ushered inside an apartment that she believed must belong to the Caliph's own harem.

Karin was lying on a bed, her face white and beaded with sweat. She looked terrible and as Eleanor came to her, she reached out her hand to her. Eleanor took her hand, holding it and looking at her anxiously.

'You are ill, Karin?'

'Yes. I have been very sick during the night, Eleanor. And the pain in my stomach has been terrible.'

'Has the physician been to see you?'

'Yes, several times. He says I must have eaten something that did not agree with me.' Karin gasped and bit her lip. 'I think someone has tried to poison me.'

'Oh, no, surely not! Who would want to do such a wicked thing?'

'I think…I think it may have been Fatima,' Karin replied. 'I spent some time in the harem when you were with Suleiman yesterday, Eleanor. Dinazade offered me fruit and I ate a little of a peach she gave me. Had I eaten all of it I might have been dead by now.'

'Oh, Karin, this is terrible. Have you told anyone what you suspect?'

'No…I wanted to warn you, because I believe I was meant to die first so that you could be killed without fear of discovery.'

'But why…?' Eleanor looked at her sadly. 'I am sorry that you have suffered, Karin. I can understand why Fatima wants me dead, but that you should have been harmed! I am distressed and angry that this has been done.'

'Fatima knew that I favoured you, and hoped to see you as Suleiman's wife. Perhaps I was wrong to think that…'

'No, you were not wrong,' Eleanor replied, and stroked the damp hair back from Karin's brow. 'This is my fault. Had I not resisted, Suleiman would have made his intentions known before this—and Fatima's anger would have turned against me, not you.'

'If this is true, you must be very careful,' Karin warned. 'She will stop at nothing to be rid of you and regain her lord's favour.'

'Fatima is a foolish woman, but I understand her fear,' Eleanor said. 'She will not be a danger to either of us for much longer, Karin. My lord wishes to know

which women I would keep as my friends and attendants, and which I would have sent away. He was to
have asked your opinion on whether marriages might
be arranged for those who cannot return to their
homes.'

Karin nodded weakly. 'Suleiman sent word that he
would like to see me last evening, but I was already
unwell, and when he knew that I was ill, he sent his
own physicians to me. Had they not treated me I
might have died.'

'I am very glad that you did not,' Eleanor said. 'Is
there anything I may do for you, my friend?'

'No, nothing—except come to visit me again tomorrow. I shall send word to Suleiman and he will
arrange it.'

'He has not sent for me today…'

'I think he is waiting to see what happens to me,'
Karin replied. 'I have not told the lord Suleiman of
my suspicions concerning Fatima, but he must have
some inkling himself.'

'Why do you say that?'

'I have heard stories concerning Fatima,' Karin
said. 'If they are true…any other master would have
dealt with her by now, but he is waiting for her to
betray herself.'

'Of what is she accused?'

'That I may not reveal, even to you,' Karin replied
and sighed. 'She is a foolish woman, but I would have
no ill come to her through me. I could have gone to
Suleiman long ago, but had I done so she would have
been severely punished. That is not my wish—merely
that she is banished so that she can do no harm to
others. I wish that I was not laid in my bed. I fear

what she may do while I am not there to restrain her.'
She gave a little moan of pain.

'May I not bathe your face and hands?' Eleanor
said, looking at her in concern. 'I would make you
more comfortable, Karin.'

'Thank you, Eleanor. My own women will attend
me. I am comfortable enough—but I cannot rest…'

'You must rest,' Eleanor replied. 'Fatima will not
harm anyone else but me. It is me she is jealous of—
and I am warned. Please do not worry for me, Karin.
I do not think she will dare to harm me once it is
known that I am to be my lord's wife.'

'But he has made no announcement…'

'He will once I have spoken to him,' Eleanor said
confidently. 'He waits to please me—but I shall ask
to see him, and I shall tell him that my doubts have
been put aside. I see what I must do now, Karin, and
I shall accept my duty.'

Karin took her hand and squeezed it gently. 'Ask
him to banish Fatima,' she advised. 'He must send
her away before she does more harm.'

'Yes,' Eleanor promised. 'As soon as I see the lord
Suleiman I shall ask that she be sent back to her
homeland.'

'She will see to it that I am sent away!' Fatima
screamed in rage and struck the servant across the
face viciously. 'How dare she presume to think I can
be got rid of so easily?'

Dinazade stared at her resentfully. 'You bid me follow and listen, my lady. I can only tell you what I
heard. The lord Suleiman intends to take the
Englishwoman as his wife. She is to have her choice

of the women she desires about her—and she intends
to ask that you be sent away immediately.'

'Get out!' Fatima threw a cushion at the servant.
'Get out! I shall punish you for telling me lies. It
cannot be that my lord would send me away.'

After the servant had gone, Fatima began to pace
the floor of her apartment, her feet bare against the
coolness of the marble tiles. She was angry and frustrated that the poison she had rubbed into the skin of
the peach had merely made Karin sick and not killed
her. She had hoped that with the older woman out of
the way, she would have complete control over the
harem. While Suleiman continued to favour Eleanor
she would find it difficult to dispose of her—especially now that Abu had been moved from his position in the harem.

Fatima had sent word that she wished to speak with
him, but he had not answered her summons. She was
angry that he should ignore her, for she believed that
he still had access to the harem if he chose to come.
Had he done so, she would have asked him to smug-
gle Eleanor out of the harem. He could then have
disposed of her as he wished, and Fatima believed
she knew what he would do to the upstart
Englishwoman.

With her gone, Suleiman would send for Fatima
again. The last interview she'd had with him had been
very strange, for he had asked her curious questions,
which she had pretended not to understand—questions about women who had disappeared and others
who had lain with two of the Janissaries. Since
Suleiman had neither accused nor punished her,
merely sending her back to the harem, she believed
that he knew nothing of her treachery.

She had been told nothing of Abu having been condemned to the galleys, nor of his escape and subsequent treachery—nor of his death. Had Fatima been aware of these things, she might have feared for her own life, but on Suleiman's orders no one had told her. No whispers had reached her ears concerning these matters. In her vanity and ignorance, she still believed that she had only to be patient and her lord would turn to her again—once Eleanor had been disposed of.

But how was she to achieve this desirable end? Poisons were uncertain, and did not always bring death; besides, without Abu's help they were difficult to come by. Fatima wanted another way, one that would make certain Eleanor died.

She must act soon, while Karin was still tied to her bed. Karin suspected her; Fatima knew that the older woman had heard the inevitable whispers concerning her. She had no proof, of course. Had the proof been there, Karin would surely have taken her suspicions to Suleiman.

She must kill Eleanor herself. It was a risk because she would surely be put to death herself if her crime were discovered. Fatima would have hesitated to take such a step if Dinazade had not brought the news that Eleanor was to become the lord Suleiman's wife. Always before, she had watched as Abu punished the women who displeased her—and she had smiled at her own power. She had not needed to soil her own hands, but things had changed.

She did not know why Abu had not come to her in the gardens as she had asked. They had plotted the meeting between Eleanor and her brother together and their plan had failed, for the Englishwoman went unpunished. It was very odd that she had heard no word of Abu since then...a little tingle of fear went down Fatima's spine.

Had Abu been punished for the part he played in that masquerade—and had he betrayed Fatima? She knew that there were fearful tortures that might cause a man to reveal anything in his agony, but if that were so something would have happened before this. She would surely have been punished if Suleiman suspected her of betraying him.

She must make him want her again. He was bewitched by that golden-haired sorceress! Once she was dead, Suleiman would turn to her again. Fatima would wait no longer. Tonight, Eleanor must die!

Suleiman was studying his manuscripts when the eunuch approached. He turned to look at him, his gaze narrowed, his thoughts with the friend who now lay at death's door after a festering lump had been removed from his side by the surgeon's knife. It seemed that all their efforts to save him might be in vain, though the physicians, at first reluctant to try the poultice Eleanor had written of, were about to apply it that night. Suleiman prayed that this last might be effective.

'Yes?' he asked, brows raised at this intrusion by the eunuch. 'Does the Caliph send for me?'

'No, my lord. The Englishwoman asks if she might speak with you.'

'Eleanor?' Suleiman frowned. It was unusual for such a request to be brought to him by the eunuch. 'Ah, yes, I remember that Karin is ill. You may bring my lady to me.'

He turned back to his manuscripts as the eunuch

left, and then he felt the touch of a hand on his arm and he swung round to look at Eleanor, his eyes going over her hungrily.

'Forgive me for the intrusion, my lord. I have been to visit Karin, and I asked if I might see you for a moment before returning to the harem.'

'Yes, I understand. You are worried for her. The physicians tell me she may have eaten something that was poisonous—but fortunately the dose was not lethal. They tell me she will live.'

'Yes, my lord, thanks to your prompt action in sending your physician to her.'

'Of course it was done. Karin is a good woman, I respect her and would not wish her to die from any neglect.'

'I realise that, my lord.' Eleanor took a deep breath. 'I wished to tell you…to tell you that I have come to realise many things.'

'Have you, my lady?' Suleiman took her hand and led her to one of the divans, indicating that she should sit beside him. 'And they are so important that they could not wait a few days?' His eyes reflected amusement. 'This interest me greatly, Eleanor. Pray continue.'

'My lord chooses to mock me,' Eleanor said and blushed. 'And perhaps I deserve that—for I have been foolish.'

'You admit your folly?'

Her blush deepened to a fiery red. 'It is difficult for me to admit, my lord, but I do. I was wrong to resist my destiny. We are bound together—the stars have foretold it and I know it in my heart. My lord told me to look into my heart and I have done so. I know that it is my destiny and my duty to be your wife.'

Suleiman frowned. 'Why your duty, Eleanor?'

'Karin told me she believed I could bring change to the harem, my lord. She said that it would be for good or evil and that it lay in my hands—and I fear that it may be because of me that—'

'You think that someone may deliberately have tried to kill her?'

Eleanor remembered Karin's warning and her eyes fell before his piercing gaze. 'I do not know how that may be, my lord. It may be that she ate something that she ought not by accident. I did not come here to accuse anyone.'

'But you came with some purpose in mind?'

'Yes, my lord.' Eleanor looked up, her eyes meeting his steadily. 'I came to beg your pardon for being so foolish when you told me of your intention to make me your wife. And to tell you that I should be honoured if that was still in your mind.'

'Did you think I had forgotten?' Suleiman's mouth curved in amusement. 'I could do nothing until Karin is better. She has charge of the women and it is for her to break the news and make the arrangements for the wedding. Customs must be observed, however impatient we may be, my lady. A wedding cannot be arranged overnight—there are many things needful to be done.'

'Yes, my lord.' Eleanor took a deep breath. 'I understand that we must talk of these things—matters of religion and custom. But my lord asked me which of the other women I would like to keep with me— and therefore who should be sent away. I shall consult with the others once the announcement is made as to who would be happy to stay—but I have a request...'

'You want one of the women sent away?' Suleiman raised his brows, guessing her intent.

'Yes, my lord. I bear her no ill will, nor do I want her to suffer—but I think it would be more comfortable for everyone if Fatima were to be sent to her home.'

'Fatima?' Suleiman looked at her, eyes narrowed. 'Will you tell me the reason for your request?'

'I have no reason, my lord—other than that she does not like me.'

Suleiman nodded. 'Yes, I see. It shall be done once the announcement has been made. Do you think you can be patient until then?'

Eleanor hesitated, but if she told Suleiman the whole truth he might punish Fatima, and neither she nor Karin wanted that.

'Yes, my lord. I am content that she should remain for the moment.'

'And is there any other request you would make of me, my lady?'

'None, my lord. I believe we must speak of other things—but I did not come to ask favours of you other than this.'

'And you are content that we are to be married— because you think it your duty to care for the women of the harem?'

She met the quizzing stare of his dark eyes and blushed. 'I—it is a part of my content, my lord.'

'And what of this, Eleanor?'

Suleiman reached out, drawing her to him, crushing her against him as his lips sought and found hers. She felt the heady sensations swirl within her and allowed herself to melt into the heat of his embrace, her lips parting in welcome of his mastery. She felt that she wanted to stay with him like this for always and keened for the loss as he released her.

'You tempt me, my little bird,' he said. 'But I have sworn to keep this night and two more in fasting for the sake of my friend who lies close to death. Since I hunger for you more than food, I should break my vow if I took you to my bed this night. Do not look for me to send for you for two days, Eleanor. I shall be keeping a vigil by his bed.'

'I am very sorry he is so ill,' Eleanor said. 'I wish that I might help him—but I have no skill in these things. I told you of a poultice I know from my studies, but I have never nursed anyone, though I believe Anastasia has. If my lord required her services for his friend, I am sure she would be glad to give them—or perhaps that is forbidden?'

'She shall be sent for,' Suleiman said. 'If she can save him, she shall be given her freedom—that is my promise to you and her.'

Eleanor nodded; she smiled at him as she left, and knew that he was watching her until the last. Her thoughts as she returned to the harem were a mixture of pleasure in the new understanding she had reached with her lord, and anxiety for her friend and his.

Several of the women came to her anxiously as she entered the communal hall. They had heard whispers of Karin's sickness, and they begged her to tell them what was the matter with their friend and comforter.

'She has been very sick,' Eleanor replied, careful to give nothing away. 'The physicians have given her something to make her easier and they say she will recover—but she may need to rest for several days. I shall visit her tomorrow and every day, and bring you news of her.'

'May we see her?' Anastasia asked. 'I might be able to help her—I have some skills with fevers.'

'You are wanted to nurse my lord's friend,' Eleanor told her. 'The eunuchs will take you to him—it is on the orders of the lord Suleiman, so you need not fear that you are to leave the harem quarters. You will not be punished whatever happens—but should your skills save my lord's friend, he will grant you your freedom.'

Anastasia stared at her. 'But I do not wish to leave the harem—or you, Eleanor.'

'Then you will not be forced to do so,' Eleanor replied and smiled at her. 'I shall request some other favour of my lord for you. Indeed, I should be sorry to part from you, Anastasia. I had hoped you might choose to remain with me.'

Anastasia stared at her, then she too began to smile. 'Then the rumours we have heard are true,' she said. 'You are to be the lord Suleiman's wife.'

'We must not speak of this yet,' Eleanor replied. 'Karin will make all clear when she returns to us. My lord has other things on his mind at the moment. He is sorely troubled by his friend's sickness, Anastasia. Please go at once and do what you can for him.'

'Yes, my lady.' Anastasia's manner had altered subtly. She bowed her head submissively, as if acknowledging Eleanor's superior standing in the harem, but Eleanor shook her head at her.

'No, Anastasia. We are friends—it shall always be so as long as you remain here.'

Eleanor noticed that some of the other ladies were staring at her a little oddly. As Anastasia went off to join the eunuch who was waiting to take her to the bedside of the sick Janissary, Eleanor took her customary seat on one of the divans. Immediately, one of the women brought her a dish of fruit, offering it respectfully.

'Would my lady care for something else?' she asked as Eleanor shook her head. 'May I send for food from the kitchens?'

'No, thank you. I am not hungry,' Eleanor said. 'We have not spoken much before—but I believe your name is Marisa. How long have you been here—and where did you live before you were captured?'

'I came from a Greek island called Kos,' the woman replied. 'My family lived close to the sea for they were fishermen. One day I was walking on the beach when the Corsairs took me. I did not see them until they fell upon me and carried me away with them.'

'How long have you been here, Marisa?'

'Three years, my lady. The lord Suleiman has never sent for me in all that time. I think I am not beautiful enough…'

'I think you are pretty,' Eleanor replied. 'And young. Tell me, Marisa—if you had the chance, would you marry or would you prefer to return to your family?'

Marisa blushed. 'It is forbidden to think of such things,' she said, glancing over her shoulder as if she feared that they would be heard and immediately punished. 'But I saw the lord Suleiman fighting with one of the Janissaries…a handsome young man who I think they call Ahmed… He saw me watching him, though I was veiled, of course—but our eyes met…'

Eleanor nodded. 'If Karin asks you this same question, you must answer truthfully, Marisa—will you

promise to do that? I give you my word you will not
be punished.'

'Yes, my lady.' Marisa hesitated, then, greatly daring, 'I know that sometimes when an important man
takes a bride some of the concubines are returned to
their homes or given in marriage to another man.'

'Yes, well, we shall see,' Eleanor said and smiled
at her. 'I want everyone to have what they themselves
want most…and I know that some will want to stay
while others would prefer to leave. But we shall say
no more of this until Karin is better and returns to us.
I should not have spoken so openly. Please do not
repeat what I have said, Marisa.'

'Oh, I give you my word, my lady,' Marisa replied.
'And I am sorry I have not spent more time talking
to you—but I was afraid of offending Fatima.'

'Yes, I understand,' Eleanor replied. 'I have not
taken offence—and you may repeat that to anyone
who feels nervous of change in the harem.'

'Yes, my lady.' Marisa smiled and went off as
Elizabetta brought the monkey to sit beside them.
'Thank you for your confidence.'

'What was all that about?' Elizabetta asked. She
allowed the monkey to climb over her shoulder and
investigate the bowl of fruit on the divan beside them.
'You should know that Marisa is one of Fatima's
most intimate friends, Eleanor. Do not trust her.'

'Yes, I know that,' Eleanor replied. 'I am aware
that I need to be careful…' She broke off as Elizabetta
gave a little cry and looked at the monkey, who had
keeled over and was obviously in pain. He had been
eating a grape, and now his mouth was frothed with
blood as he twitched horribly and then lay still. 'Oh,
no…the poor little fellow. I think he is dead,

Elizabetta. The grape…it must have been poisoned.'
She stared at her friend in horror. 'Marisa brought the
bowl to me…'

'It was meant for you,' Elizabetta said. 'You were
meant to die…'

'Say nothing,' Eleanor warned as the other ladies
began to gather round, their cries of distress shrill at
the sudden death of their pet. 'Give this bowl to
Morna and tell her to guard it well, but on no account
to eat any of the fruit.'

Elizabetta took the bowl and left immediately.
Marisa came hurrying back to see what all the commotion was about. She looked at Eleanor and her eyes
were dark with fear.

'I was told to offer you the fruit,' she said, her
voice a harsh whisper. 'Fatima made me bring it to
you.'

'Would you repeat that to the lord Suleiman if you
were asked?'

Marisa looked into Eleanor's eyes for a moment,
and then nodded. 'Forgive me, my lady. I did not
know that the fruit was…' She could not bring herself
to say the word. 'I ate one of the grapes myself as
we talked…' Her face was ashen. 'I might have died
instead of that poor creature.'

'You should send to the lord Suleiman,' Elizabetta
said. 'Fatima is evil, Eleanor, and she ought to be
punished.'

'Yes, yes, she should be punished,' several voices
were suddenly raised against the woman many of the
others had feared and secretly hated. 'We should tell
Karin.'

'Karin is ill,' Eleanor said. 'And my lord cannot be
disturbed at this time. I shall deal with this myself.'

'Be careful,' Elizabetta warned. 'If you challenge her, she will turn on you like a wounded beast.'

'Yes, I know she may be dangerous,' Eleanor replied. 'But I cannot let this terrible thing she has done go unchallenged. Fatima must be brought to understand that her rule has ended.'

She got up and walked purposefully from the room, leaving the other women staring after her in dismay. Eleanor did not realise how cruel and ruthless Fatima could be. *She* had never been dragged from sleep by Abu and whipped until she begged for mercy.

'We should do something to help her,' Elizabetta said.

'But what can we do?' the others asked and looked at each other helplessly. None of them had ever dared to stand up to the favourite, and they were afraid of her. 'If only Karin were here to guide us.'

'That is why she was poisoned first,' Elizabetta said. 'Fatima is hoping that none of us will be brave enough to stand up to her—but we cannot let her kill Eleanor. She is our salvation.'

'Yes, yes, we must help her,' Marisa agreed, remembering the promise Eleanor had made her. 'We must all help her. Fatima cannot subdue us all if we are of one mind.'

Eleanor was unaware of the debate she had left behind her. She was not afraid of Fatima. She had guessed that poisoned fruit might be offered her by one of the women, and that the women would know nothing of what was planned. She had therefore warned Morna that she must prepare all their food herself, and let no one else touch anything. Yet the ploy had been so obvious that Eleanor suspected the plot went deeper.

Surely Fatima could not have hoped that Eleanor would eat the poisoned grape? Especially since she must know that Karin would have told her of her own suspicions concerning Fatima.

As she approached, she saw Dinazade about to leave her mistress's rooms. When the servant caught sight of Eleanor, she ran back inside to warn her mistress.

Fatima was waiting as Eleanor entered. Her dark eyes flashed with temper and her hatred was almost tangible.

'I did not send for you,' she said. 'How dare you come here without being sent for?'

'I need no invitation,' Eleanor replied quietly. 'We both know why I have come here, Fatima. You ordered Marisa to bring me that bowl of fruit. Why? Only some of the fruit was poisoned—how could you be sure I would eat it?'

'I do not know of what you speak,' Fatima said haughtily. 'I sent you no fruit. If Marisa says otherwise she lies.'

'I refused it,' Eleanor told her, her eyes never leaving the other woman's face for an instant. 'Marisa ate one of the grapes and the monkey ate another. That poor creature died horribly, but Marisa is alive and able to tell her story to the lord Suleiman.'

'He will not believe her,' Fatima said and smiled smugly. 'He knows that the other women are jealous and tell lies about me. Why should I try to kill you? He does not take you to his bed. You are merely his scribe.'

'I have used my skills with the Latin to assist my lord,' Eleanor agreed. 'But I am soon to be his wife—

and when that happens you will be a long way from here, Fatima. You are to be sent back to Algiers.'

'You lie!' Fatima's lovely face was twisted and made ugly by anger. 'My lord will not send me away for your sake. You are merely a passing fancy. When he is tired of you, he will want me again.'

'If Karin were not ill it would already have been done.'

'No!' Fatima suddenly snatched up a knife she had been using to peel a peach and sprang at Eleanor with the blade. 'I shall kill you. When you are dead, my lord will send for me again.'

Eleanor ducked as the other woman stabbed at her viciously. She looked about for something with which to protect herself and caught up a plump cushion, holding it in front of her face. Fatima's knife tore through the silk, rendering it useless.

'Help me!' Fatima demanded of her servant as Eleanor continued to duck and weave, avoiding her slashing blade as the woman lunged at her again and again. 'Catch her and hold her while I teach her who is mistress here. I shall destroy her beauty. My lord will not want her then.'

'Do nothing, Dinazade,' Elizabetta commanded from the doorway. 'Put the knife down, Fatima. We have sent for the eunuchs and they will punish you if you injure…'

Eleanor had been momentarily distracted by the sound of Elizabetta's voice. She took her eyes from Fatima, and in that instant the other woman gave a cry of triumph as her knife struck home, slashing across Eleanor's upper arm. Eleanor gave a cry of pain, stumbled back and fell into Elizabetta's arms.

'You have killed her!' Marisa cried, helping

Elizabetta to support Eleanor. 'You tried to poison her and now you have killed her!'

'She attacked me.' Fatima felt a flicker of fear as she saw accusation in the faces of the other women. They had massed together in the doorway and were staring at her in anger and disgust. 'She was mad! She came here to kill me. You saw her, Dinazade! You saw her attack me. I wrested the knife from her to protect myself from her attack. Tell them! Tell them what you saw!'

Dinazade stared at her mistress in silence. She had hated and feared her for years; now at last she saw the way to be revenged for all the beatings she had suffered at Fatima's hands. Glancing over her shoulder, she saw that the eunuchs were pushing their way past the women.

'I saw you poison the grape,' she said clearly. 'I heard you order Marisa to take the bowl of fruit to the Englishwoman—and I saw you take up the knife. It was your intention to kill her. You wanted her dead because you knew that you had lost the lord Suleiman's favour. You knew that she would have you banished…'

'You traitor!' Fatima had lost all control as she screamed and flew at the servant. She stabbed her twice in the chest before Dinazade fell to the floor at her feet, the blood pouring from her wounds.

A silence had fallen over the women. The chief eunuch Hasar had been kneeling beside Eleanor. He glanced at two others who had followed him in and then pointed at Fatima.

'Take her,' he said harshly. 'She is to be imprisoned in the punishment cells and held there until the lord Suleiman decides her fate.'

'No!' Fatima screamed and struggled as the eunuchs approached her. Her eyes were wild and she still held the bloodied knife that had killed her servant and wounded Eleanor. 'Do not touch me or my lord will have you punished. He wants only me…only me…'

Even as she screamed the words, one of the eunuchs hit her at the base of the neck with the side of his hand, and she collapsed, not dead but rendered unconscious by the disabling blow. He hoisted her over his shoulder and the women parted to let him through, some of them spitting at Fatima's unconscious face as she was taken away. They had hated her with good reason, and not one of them was sorry for her. She deserved her punishment.

'Dinazade is dead,' one of the women said. 'Poor woman, Fatima killed her.'

'Eleanor is alive,' Elizabetta told them. 'She fainted from the pain, but she is alive.'

'I shall send the physician to her,' Hasar said. He bent down and lifted Eleanor in his arms, the other women fluttering behind him as he carried her to her room and laid her gently down on her divan. She was moaning slightly, barely conscious.

'Take care of her,' he instructed Elizabetta. 'The physician will come soon. But you may try to staunch the blood in the meantime.'

'She must not die,' Elizabetta said.

'Pray that Allah grants her life,' Hasar replied harshly. 'The lord Suleiman is at prayer and cannot be disturbed—but should this woman die, his anger will not be contained.'

'We shall care for her,' Elizabetta promised. 'She is our friend. It was only Fatima who hated her.'

'Others were present when this happened and did

nothing to help her,' the eunuch replied severely. 'My master may choose to punish everyone if she dies. My own life is forfeit. I was told to protect her with my life, and I have failed.'

Elizabetta looked at Marisa and the others as he went out. 'We must pray that Eleanor lives—for we may all suffer if she dies.'

'If only Anastasia or Karin were here.'

'We must do what we can,' Marisa said, looking at her fearfully.

'Leave her to me,' Morna said, pushing them aside. 'Bring me clean water and cloths. I shall be the one to tend her, though you must all help to watch over her—but only I shall touch her. My life means little to me. If she dies, I shall take the blame.'

'I shall help you,' Elizabetta said.

'And I—only tell me what to do,' Marisa insisted. 'You cannot bear all the nursing alone, or all the blame.'

'I, too, shall help,' Rosamunde said, coming forward. 'I was in the garden while all this was going on and knew nothing until this moment. Why do you waste time in chatter? Eleanor will bleed to death if you do nothing to staunch the wound. Bring clean cloths and help me. I have seen such wounds before and know what must be done to stop the bleeding.'

Rosamunde's manner of calm authority brought instant response from the others. Elizabetta had been filling a basin with water, and Morna had produced a shift of clean white cloth, which she proceeded to tear into strips.

The other women stood just outside the door watching until Marisa shooed them away.

* * *

'She will sleep now,' the physician told
Rosamunde as Eleanor's eyes closed and he laid her
gently back against the cushions. He glanced at
Rosamunde with approval. 'You did well to staunch
the wound, lady. But she has lost too much blood and
the wound is deep. She will need careful nursing if
she is not to die of the putrid infection.'

'Tell me what I must do,' Rosamunde begged. 'She
is my friend. I love her and would not have her die.'

The physician nodded. He had been robbed of his
manhood long years ago, and no longer felt the desires of a natural man—but even he could appreciate
the beauty of his patient. And he had been told that
she was the intended bride of the Caliph's son.

'You must keep her drugged for at least two days,'
he replied. 'Otherwise she will not bear the pain. Her
bandages must be changed frequently. And if the fever strikes…' He shook his head sorrowfully. 'I shall
bring you a mixture of herbs for her to drink, but in
that case it will be as Allah wills it.'

Rosamunde nodded. She knew that the physician
had done his best for Eleanor, repairing the deep slash
in her arm skilfully. There was no doubt that his work
would leave a scar, but that could not be helped. All
that mattered now was that Eleanor should live.

Rosamunde wished that Anastasia was with them,
for they sorely needed her skills, but somehow, she
and the others must make Eleanor well. Rosamunde
had not heard Hasar's warning herself, but Elizabetta
and Marisa had told her that all their lives might be
forfeit if Eleanor died.

Rosamunde had been sent for a few times by the
lord Suleiman during her first year or two in the
harem. She had found him a stern, passionate man,

though he had asked her only to sing for him. She was not sure what he might be capable of if his anger were aroused.

Everyone said he loved Eleanor. If that were so, he might go mad with grief if she should die of her wound.

Rosamunde glanced at Elizabetta as she came to take her turn at sitting beside their patient.

'Do you think he knows?' she asked. 'Do you suppose that anyone has told the lord Suleiman what has happened to Eleanor?'

'I do not know,' Elizabetta replied. 'I believe he keeps a vigil for his sick friend. I do not think anyone would dare to approach him with such news at this time.'

Rosamunde frowned. 'I have never said it—but I find him intimidating. I thank God that I am not the one who has to tell him.'

'Our lord can be fierce,' Elizabetta said thoughtfully. 'But he was always kind to me, though he sent for me only a few times—and not at all once Fatima came, for her dancing pleased him more than mine. Yet I do not believe that he would punish us all for something that was not our fault.'

'A man may do anything when half out of his mind with grief,' Rosamunde replied. 'We must pray that Eleanor recovers—for her sake and our own.

Chapter Ten

'I thank you for your care of my friend,' Suleiman said. 'Your nursing has done what all my wise physicians could not.' He smiled at Anastasia. 'I would grant you any boon that you ask—including your freedom and a pension to keep you from the need to return to slavery.'

'All I would ask is to be allowed to stay here, my lord. I would like to serve the lady Eleanor—and to be given freedom to nurse the sick. I believe there are many within the palace that would benefit from my help. If there could be a room somewhere within the palace grounds where I might tend any who need me...' She looked at him anxiously. 'And I must tell you, my lord, that the poultice the lady Eleanor recommended was a part of the cure. I have used it before and I know its healing properties.'

'You shall have all that you have asked and more,' Suleiman promised. 'I have been aware that too many die for lack of care—we shall see what can be done to remedy this, lady. From now on you are no longer bound by the rules of the harem. You may come and

go as you please within the palace—and to the city
with an escort to protect you.'

'You are generous, my lord.'

Suleiman shook his head. 'It is I who have much
to thank you for, lady. You may return to the harem
if you wish. I hope that the lady Karin will be well
enough to resume her duties soon. I shall send her to
you with news I believe you may already have
guessed.'

Anastasia smiled and bowed her head as she left
him. He was staring at his manuscripts through the
long-handled glasses he had adopted for studying
when the eunuch approached. At once, Suleiman realised that something was wrong—the man looked terrified!

'Yes, what is it, Hasar?'

The eunuch fell to his knees before him. 'Forgive
me, my lord. I bring bad news...'

Suleiman felt chilled. He had spent two days fasting and praying, but since the remarkable recovery of
the friend his physicians had given up as lost, his
thoughts had been uneasy, though he did not know
why.

'Tell me at once!'

'The concubine Fatima tried to poison the lady
Eleanor,' Hasar said. 'The concubines' pet monkey
ate the poisoned fruit and died—but Lady Eleanor
challenged Fatima and the concubine attacked your
lady and wounded her with a knife.'

'Eleanor has been wounded—badly?' Ice was
creeping through Suleiman's veins as he saw the answer in the eunuch's eyes. 'What has been done for
her—where is the wound?'

'In her upper arm,' Hasar replied. 'The physician

visits her every day and the women tend her—but she has a fever and…'

'Go on,' Suleiman said fiercely as the eunuch faltered. 'Has the wound become infected?'

'They say it is gathering putrid flesh…' Hasar gasped as he saw the flash of anger mixed with pain in his master's eyes. 'I know nothing of these things, my lord. I thought you should know…'

'When did this happen?'

'Two days ago…'

'For two days no one told me?'

'You were at prayer, my lord. We dared not intrude upon your vigil.'

Suleiman raised his clenched fist as if he would strike the eunuch, then turned away with a gasp of anguish and frustration. What good would it do to take his anger out on the unfortunate messenger? It could not change what had happened—and the man had done only as he had been told. Suleiman had left orders that he was not to be disturbed for anything—but he had not expected this!

Yet he should have done. What a blind, stupid fool he was! Eleanor had come to him straight from Karin's bedside with a request that Fatima should be sent away. He ought to have known that something lay behind such a request. Eleanor was not jealous of the other woman, she had no need to be. He should have realised that she was trying to protect herself and the others from Fatima's spite.

Had he not been so concerned for his friend, he might have realised her request was urgent. But his mind had been attuned to the vigil he had vowed to keep—and because he had done nothing, she was like to die of her wounds. His grief tore through him, striking him to the heart so that he was gripped with a terrible agony and hardly knew how to stand upright. Had he been alone, he might have given way to his grief, but pride kept him from shedding unmanly tears. Instead, his heart shed tears of blood.

'I shall come to her at once,' he said to Hasar. He glanced at the eunuch who was shivering, clearly expecting to be punished. 'You are not to blame. What has been done with Fatima?'

'She is in the punishment cells—awaiting your order, my lord.'

'Leave her for the moment,' Suleiman said. 'Give her only bread and water—and she is to see no one until I decide what to do with her.'

Fatima's punishment could wait—for the moment all he could think of was Eleanor. That she should have been harmed—and by a woman he ought to have sent away days ago—festered in Suleiman's mind like a poisoned thorn. It was his fault, his stupidity in being lenient towards the beautiful woman who had once pleased him, that had brought Eleanor to this!

If she should die! Suleiman hardly dared to allow the thought into his mind. She had been like a bright flame in the sky, bringing him closer to happiness than he had ever been in his life. He had thought to find content with her in this palace that had seemed like a prison before her coming; her smiles had soothed his restless nature; her anger had amused and sometimes burned him—and her spirit had delighted him.

As he walked towards the halls of the harem, a place that he had seldom visited, preferring to have his women brought to him, Suleiman's thoughts were gathering darkness. Until Eleanor's coming, he had

sought a woman's company only for sensual pleasure—but she had changed him, teaching him the joy
of companionship with a woman…something he had
never expected to know after his mother's death.

To find such treasure only to lose it was to taste
paradise only to be cast back into the fires of hell. He
felt as if a thousand demons tore at his flesh, their
talons piercing him until his agony was like to drive
him mad. How could he bear it if she should die?

He heard the startled gasps as he strode into the
harem unannounced, the women fluttering like jewel-
bright birds as if a cat had got amongst them. He was
annoyed that his presence should cause such a fluster,
yet dismissed it in an instant. Why should they not
fear him when they knew only that he was their master and could punish them for the slightest misde-
meanour? He had never troubled himself to make
them like or understand him, never spent time in dis-
covering what made them happy. It had been enough
that they were kept in comfort, awaiting his pleasure.

One of the women came to meet him. She seemed
not to fear him, for she looked him in the eyes. 'You
have come to see the lady Eleanor, my lord. Anastasia
is with her now and is about to change her bandages.
If you will wait but a moment…'

'And you are?'

'Elizabetta, my lord. I have danced and sung for
you.'

'Yes, I remember,' Suleiman said. 'You have been
nursing my lady?'

'Yes, with others—but we have not Anastasia's
skill. She was angry when she came back and found
Eleanor so ill. She is making changes and I am sure
my lady will soon be much recovered.'

'Pray do not delay me,' Suleiman said. 'I must see her.'

He walked past Elizabetta, the other women watching him fearfully from a distance as he entered Eleanor's apartments.

Suleiman was shocked as he saw Eleanor's hair damp with sweat, her face flushed and heated from the fever that had her in its grip. Anastasia had just finished sponging her body with cool water, and, after covering her with a sheet, turned to look at him. He stood staring at Eleanor, his dark eyes tormented by fear.

'She will be more comfortable in a moment, my lord,' Anastasia comforted him. They have kept her too warm—but they did not know what they did was wrong. You must not punish them. We all love Eleanor, because she has been so kind to us. No one else would seek to harm her.'

'What makes any of you think I blame you for this?'

'We have been told that we may all be punished if she dies,' Rosamunde said from behind him. 'We have done our best for her, my lord—but none of us had any true skill in nursing.'

Suleiman nodded, eyes narrowing. This was yet another of his harem he hardly recognised. A lovely woman, but one that left him untouched—what was she doing here, wasting her youth?

'How is my lady?' he asked as he turned back to Anastasia. 'Can you save her? Will she die of her wounds?'

Anastasia smiled and shook her head. 'She is nowhere near as ill as the Janissary you summoned me to nurse—she has a fever and her wound must be lanced again to let out a little pus, but she will live, my lord. Had I been here sooner, she would not have been drugged—it is the drugs that have robbed her of her senses and frightened everyone else. Once they are no longer holding her mind prisoner, she will know us again.'

Suleiman controlled his desire to shout his relief aloud. 'Why have you so much knowledge when the physicians seem to have so little?'

Anastasia smiled and shook her head. 'That is not true, my lord. The physician has closed the wound more skilfully than I could—but he was not wise to keep her so heavily drugged. And the others did not understand the importance of making sure she was cool. Now that I am here we shall soon reduce the fever.'

'How can I repay you for all that you have done?'

'You have already repaid me by giving me the freedom to serve others. I am a simple woman, my lord. I was born to serve and I have all that I need.'

'You have not been unhappy here?'

'Only a little, sometimes—when Fatima was unkind to one of us.'

'Yes, Fatima.' Suleiman nodded, his expression hardening as he recalled that she was responsible for Eleanor lying here injured. 'You will send me word of my lady—good or bad?'

'Do not fear, my lord. Eleanor will soon recover her health. She is young and strong and the fever will soon pass.'

Suleiman nodded, and then he walked to the bed and bent to kiss Eleanor's brow. She stirred, moaned a little and whispered something he could not quite catch.

'Rest, my darling,' he said in a voice so low that no one else could hear. 'I—I need you.'

Suleiman's shoulders squared as he left the bedside. He had work to do—things that had been neglected these past two days. As he emerged from Eleanor's apartment, the other women fell back and looked at him uncertainly. He lifted his hand to gain their attention, and then spoke to them in a voice devoid of emotion.

'You have none of you anything to fear from me,' he said. 'Only those who have harmed my lady shall be punished. Karin will come to you soon. She will ask you for the truth of this affair. When I have all the facts before me, the guilty shall be punished as the law demands. I shall take no petty revenge. Karin will discuss other things with you—you may speak to her freely without fear. That is my sworn word.'

The silence continued for several minutes after he had left, until curiosity at last forced them to ask, 'What did he mean? What must we confess to Karin?'

Only Marisa held her silence. She remembered what Eleanor had told her and kept her promise not to reveal anything until Karin was well enough to give them the news herself.

Eleanor's eyelids fluttered. She was aware of feeling very tired, and her arm was painful. She moaned and opened her eyes, looking up into Karin's anxious face.

'So at last you are come to yourself again. You foolish, foolish child,' Karin said, her tone sounding relieved rather than scolding. 'Did I not warn you to be careful?'

'Water...' Eleanor pleaded. She was becoming

more conscious of the pain in her arm and her mouth felt dry. 'What happened to me?'

'Fatima sent you poisoned fruit. You challenged her and she stabbed you in the arm. Thankfully, you must have taken her by surprise for the knife was not contaminated with poison—as it well might have been.'

'Oh, yes…' Eleanor sighed. She vaguely remembered something but her mind was still hazy. Rosamunde brought her water and she sipped it gratefully. 'Thank you. What time is it?'

'It is morning,' Karin replied. 'You have had a fever, Eleanor. It is five days now since this happened.'

'Five days…' She struggled to sit up, but found she was too weak and fell back against the pillows. 'What of my lord's friend…he was near to dying?'

'He is much better,' Anastasia said, bending over her to lay a hand on her forehead. 'Ah, so are you, my lady. The fever has gone and you will mend now.'

'You have been nursing me?'

'Since my return three days ago. My other patient does well; I have but this minute returned from seeing him.'

'Thank you…all of you.' Eleanor sighed and closed her eyes once more.

She woke again that evening, feeling better. Rosamunde was sitting with her now and smiled at her.

'Are you hungry, my lady? Anastasia said that we should give you a little nourishing broth if you woke. Morna will prepare it for you—though none here would seek to harm you now.'

'Fatima?' Eleanor whispered.

'Gone, my lady. We shall not see her again.'

Eleanor nodded, satisfied. Suleiman had sent her home as he'd promised. She need not concern herself further.

'Has Karin gone? She was here earlier. I meant to ask if she had recovered from her sickness?'

'Karin is well,' Rosamunde replied. 'She has spent the last few days talking to everyone. We have been promised nothing yet—but it seems we may be given our freedom should we wish it. Anastasia has already been granted hers, but she chooses to remain here— though she is allowed to go where she pleases within certain areas of the palace. She has not been out yet, but Karin said that a eunuch will take her to the city markets if she desires it.'

Eleanor nodded. It seemed that Suleiman was keeping all his promises. She was too tired to inquire further for the moment. She did not ask and was not told that her lord had come three times to visit her while she was in the grip of the fever.

Rosamunde went on, 'I think I shall stay—if you want me, my lady. I have nothing to return to now. My life is here…'

'Yes, yes, please stay,' Eleanor said and smiled at her. 'If Morna would fetch me something, I think I might try to eat a little…'

'You must eat,' Rosamunde agreed. 'We have all been so worried for you, my lady.'

Eleanor closed her eyes once more as Rosamunde went away to order the food. She still felt desperately tired, but the drugging heaviness was gradually fading. Soon she would begin to feel more like herself.

She ought to ask something, but she could not control her thoughts, could not remember what she wanted to know. All she desired was to rest and be well again and then… She was not sure what would happen then. Suleiman had said that they must observe the customs. Of course she could not expect him to visit her—why should he? A sigh of regret issued from her lips.

If he loved her he would have come—but he merely desired her. He was marrying her because he thought her best fitted from amongst the concubines to bear his sons. She had no choice. She must obey, because he was her master.

'Do you bring me news of my lady?' Suleiman asked eagerly as Karin came in answer to his request. 'You said that she had taken food and was able to sit up and talk to her friends—there has been no relapse?'

'Eleanor improves with every hour,' Karin replied, smiling at the way his eyes seemed to darken and glow at the mention of his intended bride. 'She insisted on getting out of bed, and with help has been sitting in the gardens this morning.'

'Is she well enough to be out of bed so soon? It is barely eight days since I saw her lying in a fever.'

'She is very strong, my lord.' Karin frowned, hesitated, then decided she must speak. 'Her arm is healing well and it seems she will be able to use it normally once the soreness has gone—but I fear there will be a scar.'

Suleiman's eyes narrowed. 'Why do you hesitate to tell me this? Do you imagine that I care for such details? My lady is alive. I thank Allah for her life— a scar means less than nothing.'

'I beg your pardon, my lord. I had not realised…quite what she means to you.'

'And you will keep your new-found knowledge to yourself, Karin,' he replied with a rueful smile. 'I would not have Eleanor know—yet.'

'Ah…' Karin nodded, smiling now herself. 'I believe the lady Eleanor can sometimes be a little headstrong, my lord.'

'Yes.' His mouth quirked at the memory of various instances of her stubbornness. 'That is very true, Karin. Now, to other matters—you have questioned the concubines? They are all innocent of malice against my lady?'

'Most of them admire her for her bravery—some love her.'

'And you have consulted their feelings on the matter of returning to their homes?'

'Yes, my lord.' Karin took out a journal in which she had made notes. 'Ten of them have requested marriages be arranged here—with members of your own guard in most cases. It seems they have watched you at sport with your men—perhaps more often than we knew.' She waited for his reply but he made no comment, seeming indifferent. 'Five have asked to be returned to their families—they are mostly of our own faith and nationality. The others wish to remain here to serve the lady Eleanor, or in Anastasia's case to be allowed to nurse the sick.'

Suleiman nodded. 'Eleanor will make her choice. Those she does not wish to keep may have their wish.'

Karin knew that Eleanor would keep no one who did not wish to remain. Besides, there were more than enough ladies to wait on her, and her three particular friends had all chosen to stay.

'You wish me to speak to her—or shall you see her yourself?'

'My lady must receive instruction in the true religion before the marriage can take place. I believe this news would come best from you, Karin. You must make her aware of her duty—though I do not wish her instructed in the arts of pleasing her husband.'

'I understand, my lord.' Karin hesitated. 'The Caliph has granted me the favour of a visit to my daughters. May I ask when your marriage will take place—so that I may arrange the details of my journey?'

'If Eleanor is well enough—two weeks should suffice. She need only learn sufficient to confirm outwardly to custom.'

'Yes, my lord.' Karin was pleased at the prospect of seeing her daughters so soon. 'I shall convey your message to her—unless you have changed your mind and wish her to come to you?'

'No. I shall not see my bride until the wedding,' Suleiman replied. He did not inform Karin of his reasons, but he was afraid that if he was alone with Eleanor he would not be able to keep from confessing his love—or making love to her. 'Let it all be as we have discussed, Karin. My lady must make her choice, and receive instruction—but she must not tire herself. I do not wish her ill again.'

'Do not fear,' Karin said. 'For the moment she seems content to spend her time sitting quietly with the other ladies. I doubt this mood of tranquillity will last long, but for the moment she takes things easily. If you will excuse me, my lord, I shall go to her now.'

Suleiman nodded. He watched as she left, dark eyes brooding. Would Eleanor accept instruction in the Muslim religion without complaint? He had meant to speak to her himself, to explain that she need pay only lip service—to pacify the feelings of others. In accordance with the law, Suleiman could marry only a woman of his own faith—but he would have no personal objection if she held to her own beliefs in private, as his mother had.

It would have been better to have explained this himself, but she might have lost her temper, and he might have responded in kind—and she was not yet well enough to be thus distressed. She would listen to Karin more easily than to him. If they should both lose control…he could not vouch for what might happen.

He must control his own desires and needs until she was truly healed. He ached for her, longed to hold her in his arms and taste the sweetness of her lips—but he would behave as the civilised gentleman she would have for her husband. If she came to him now he might be tempted beyond bearing, unable to control this raging need inside him, so he would keep his distance until after the marriage ceremony had taken place.

'My lord says he wishes me to study enough of the Qur'an to understand and comply with custom?' Eleanor was aware of a little ache about her heart. Why had he not summoned her to talk of these things as he had promised? 'Please tell my lord that I have studied his religion before I came to this country. I already understand all that he wishes me to—and I shall give the proper responses if I am examined by religious instructors. However, that does not mean I shall believe in them.'

Karin looked at her stubborn face. No wonder Suleiman had left the task of telling Eleanor to her!

'We shall study together for an hour each day—is that so very much to ask?' Karin spoke persuasively. 'Think of the good fortune your...compliance will bring to others. You cannot be wed to the lord Suleiman unless you are believed to have converted to the true faith.'

Eleanor sighed. Karin was telling her it was her duty to marry the lord Suleiman for the sake of the others. She knew that all the women were excited about the wedding. For some it meant freedom, for others a chance to marry—and for those who had chosen to stay with her it meant a life of ease, free from the anxiety of wondering whether they would please their lord when he sent for them. They were to be her companions and friends, but no longer concubines.

Eleanor was already determined that once she was Suleiman's wife, she would ask to be allowed to go shopping in the souks and markets of Constantinople, and some of her ladies would accompany her each time. There would be more freedom for everyone if Eleanor had her way, though she knew that there was no avoiding the customs of the veil and casacche.

'Very well, we shall study together,' Eleanor replied. 'It is no hardship, Karin—and I may learn something new.' She laughed, a teasing look in her eyes. 'Did my lord send you to tell me of my duty lest I fly into a temper with him?'

Karin was tempted to tell her the truth, but held her tongue in check. Suleiman was being generous;

there was no point in provoking his anger by betraying his trust.

She smiled. 'So I may tell him that you agree?'

'Yes—but I want something in return.'

'What is your request?'

'I have been told that my lord likes to wrestle and fight with the Janissaries. I would like to watch such a tournament—and the ladies who are to marry must be allowed to watch with me.'

'I shall ask my lord if he feels inclined to oblige you.'

'One more thing—we wish to come out into the courtyard to watch. We do not want to be hidden away out of sight.' Eleanor's eyes sparkled with mischief. 'Pray tell my lord that we shall wear the veil and the casacche as customs dictates.'

Karin frowned. 'You ask a great deal, Eleanor.'

'My lord would have much of me,' she said, her head going up proudly. 'Unless I have some kind of amusement to distract me, I may discover that I feel unwell again. Already my head begins to ache at the thought of all that study my lord would have me do.'

'Eleanor!' Karin shook her head warningly at her. 'If I were your lord I should have you beaten for wilfulness.'

'But you are not my lord,' Eleanor said and laughed huskily. 'My poor friend—are you afraid to carry my message to him?'

'Once I should not have dared...' Karin smiled. 'But I confess I am curious to hear what he will say when he hears your request.'

'The lady Eleanor says that she will study diligently to please you, my lord, but...' Karin hesitated.

'In return she makes a request of you.'

'Ah…' Suleiman's expression became wary. 'And what would my lady have of me? I thought I had granted all she had asked of me.'

'She—she wishes to watch you at sport with the Janissaries, my lord.' Karin saw that the idea pleased him and dared to go on. 'But not from a window overlooking the courtyard. She asks that she and ten of her ladies be allowed to come outside and watch.'

Suleiman stared at her for so long that Karin feared his anger, then his head went back and he laughed in delight. 'I had feared her illness might crush her spirit,' he murmured more to himself than Karin. 'They must be protected from prying eyes—I cannot have them exposed, but providing they wear the proper clothing, I agree.'

'I believe the lady Eleanor understands that, my lord. I shall make certain their modesty is protected— and I shall be with them.' She smiled in relief. 'I, too, would enjoy this spectacle.'

'Then it shall be arranged—the day after tomorrow. You may tell my lady that in return for her obedience I am pleased to grant her request.'

'Obedience?' Eleanor's eyes flashed. 'Ah yes, I see my lord still means to mock me. Well, we shall see…Go once more to the lord Suleiman, Karin. Ask that the ladies who wish to be returned to their homes should be allowed to leave at once.'

'Surely that can wait until after the wedding?' Karin looked at her suspiciously. 'What game are you playing, Eleanor? Are you trying to provoke the lord

Suleiman? Remember that he is still your master. You could be beaten if you try him too far.'

'But then I should be too ill to marry him.'

'You play with fire,' Karin warned.

'I would tell him myself if he sent for me.'

Karin's gaze narrowed thoughtfully. 'Are you piqued because he does not send? Surely…' She was once again tempted to speak of Suleiman's feelings for Eleanor, but held true to her promise. 'Well, on your own head…'

'I have been thinking much the same,' Suleiman agreed when Karin presented Eleanor's latest request. 'Pray ask my lady if there is anything more I may do to please her. She asks so little…'

Karin saw the mocking glint in his eye and smiled inwardly. 'Why do you not send for her and tell her yourself, my lord?'

'Convey my message, Karin.' Suleiman waved her away. 'Tomorrow we shall have our tournament. Afterwards, I may decide to send for Eleanor. For the moment I am too busy. Please make sure she understands that I have important business and cannot make time to talk of trivial things.'

Karin nodded, wondering what game these two played with each other. Whatever it was, it certainly seemed to amuse the lord Suleiman, for she had seldom seen him in such good humour.

Eleanor fretted after Karin had brought the latest word from Suleiman. Why would he not send for her? She longed to see him, but it seemed he was determined not to speak to her until after the marriage ceremony. Why? It could only mean that he did not truly care for her.

He had granted all her requests, and she had no
more outrageous demands to make of him—save one.
And that she could not make through a third party.

She was beginning to be truly well again. Her arm
was still a little sore, but the drugging weariness had
gone. She was waited on hand and foot by the other
women, who could not do enough to please her, and
spent most of her time talking to them and getting to
know those she had hardly spoken to before her illness. They were all willing and eager to be her
friends, though she still enjoyed most the company of
those she had known first. All three had chosen to
stay with her, and she had promised she would win
favours for them all.

'We shall ask my lord to let us go shopping one
day soon,' she said. 'But first the tournament.' She
smiled wickedly at the ladies who were to accompany
her into the courtyard. 'This time it will be for you
to do the choosing—and what better opportunity? I
think we shall have as good sport as the men.'

The ladies giggled and looked at her excitedly.
Several of them already knew which of the men they
would choose, and could not wait for the tournament
to begin.

Eleanor too was looking forward to the outing. She
had heard much about the lord Suleiman's skill and
now she wanted to see for herself.

Karin came to inspect them before they were conducted through the endless passages of the harem and
then a part of the palace that was normally forbidden
to them, unless special permission had been given. It
was quite a procession, and made Eleanor laugh at all
the fuss. Two eunuchs walked before them, thrusting

aside any servant who dared to glance at them, and two behind.

She felt a shiver of excitement as they emerged into the palace courtyard, remembering the night she had been brought here and unceremoniously dumped while the lord Suleiman rode back to help his men defeat the bandits who had dared to attack them. So much had changed since then that she felt as if she were someone else and not the frightened girl who had been brought to this place against her will.

Screens had been placed at one end of the arena, and stools were placed beneath a silken awning to protect the ladies from the fierce heat of the afternoon sun. They were to see, but not be seen or approached by any who might wish to stare at them. The men taking part in the tournament could of course see them seated at the far end—but woe betide any man foolish enough to let his eyes stray from his opponent!

It was to be a contest of skill and strength, and no sacrifice of life would be demanded. Yet in the matched pairs the weapons were real and wounds could be inflicted, which might become infected—so the combatants would have no time to stare at the ladies!

The first contest was between a giant with coal-black skin and a man of equal size, but with fair skin and hair the colour of sunlight.

'The Nubian is called Mosra,' Marisa whispered in Eleanor's ear. 'And his opponent is Ahmed…'

Eleanor saw her smile and knew that this was the man she wished to marry. The contestants saluted the ladies, but their faces were expressionless. Did they know that they were performing to please their future brides?

The women were whispering to each other. Hidden behind their veils and enveloping cloaks, there was little to be seen of them except their eyes. But what messages might pass with a flash of sparkling eyes!

The contest was with the short sword, and fiercely fought. The two men pressed hard, seeming equally matched, but Ahmed eventually succeeded in overcoming his opponent. He came to salute the ladies as the victor, and Eleanor noted the way his eyes searched for and found Marisa's. It seemed that their future had been settled—though how he could know his bride in her casacche was difficult to say. Perhaps the ladies of the harem had had more opportunity to see what went on outside the harem than anyone supposed! Eleanor imagined there was always a way for those with the courage to seek it. It was as well that Suleiman chose not to notice.

After that, there was a succession of fierce fights. Eleanor heard the indrawn breath and little squeals of fright and knew that their chosen partners were not always winners. However, no one was injured apart from a few scratches and bruises, and so no harm was done.

The last contest was a wrestling match between Omar and the lord Suleiman. Eleanor's spine tingled as they came to salute the ladies, her eyes meeting Suleiman's—which seemed to gleam with mockery. He was stripped to the waist and wore only a loincloth to cover his lower body. She had known he was strong and lean when he pressed her in his arms, but she had not guessed how beautiful his body would look when he was all but naked.

His muscles rippled like those of a thoroughbred horse, and the sweat made his olive-toned skin glisten like silk. She swallowed hard as desire gripped her by the throat and she wanted— Oh, damn the wretch! She wanted him to love her.

'Omar is the captain of the palace guard,' Marisa whispered in her ear as the men walked to the centre of the arena. 'They say he is the strongest and most skilled of all—apart from your lord.'

Eleanor nodded but could not speak. Her chest was tight with the mixed emotions raging inside her. She was conscious of an overwhelming excitement, but there was also fear. Supposing her lord was hurt? She had requested this contest, and it had proved entertaining—but now she was tingling from head to toe.

She watched breathlessly as the contest began. The men seemed evenly matched as they circled each other, waiting their time. Omar moved in first, his arms surrounding Suleiman in a huge bear hug, but Suleiman's strength broke that hold easily. Before Eleanor could draw breath, Omar had seized Suleiman's arm and had him flipped over and lying on his back on the ground beneath him.

She gave a little cry of alarm, but the next moment they were on their feet again. 'What is happening?' she asked Marisa.

'The first fall has gone to Omar—there are two more, for it is the best of three.'

Eleanor watched in apprehension. She suddenly wanted Suleiman to win. He must win! She could not bear to see him lose. He was her lord and her love and she wanted to see him triumph.

Seconds later, Suleiman brought Omar down and held him easily. He was laughing as they both regained their feet, and Omar was grinning as if he too enjoyed this test of skill between them. They were the best of friends, yet neither wanted to be bested and it was a true contest.

'One fall each,' Marisa said. 'All depends on the last!'

Eleanor could not speak. She could see that both men were relishing their fight, testing each other to the full. The third fall did not come easily, for both were skilled in the art and both seemed determined to win. The tension was almost unbearable for Eleanor. Her nails curled into the palms of her hands as she watched, on the edge of her seat, breath catching as the advantage swayed one way and then the other—and then quite suddenly it was over. Suleiman had won!

Eleanor jumped to her feet to applaud, then, conscious of all eyes upon her, sat down again. Perhaps she was not supposed to show her approval so openly.

The two men were laughing and hugging each other, still jostling as though they would have liked to continue the contest.

'The tournament is over,' Karin announced and stood up, beckoning to the other ladies. 'We should return to the palace now. Come along, Eleanor. We must not linger. The lord Suleiman will send for you later if he wishes to see you.'

Eleanor was reluctant to leave. She glanced at Suleiman, wanting to catch his eye, but he was still laughing and jesting with his friend. She knew that she must do as Karin told her, for the ladies had become very excited and she had noticed that the men who had taken part and were still in the courtyard arena were looking their way rather too often. It was not seemly, and it would not do to flout the customs too much. Suleiman had been generous to give so much; his trust must not be abused.

'Yes, we shall come,' she said, taking Marisa's arm firmly. The other woman was clearly very reluctant to move and she gave her a little push. 'Be patient, Marisa. Karin will arrange the marriage if Ahmed is willing.'

'I wish that I could speak with him.' Marisa's tone was petulant. The promise of a marriage with a man of her choice had made her impatient.

'I am sorry, but you cannot,' Eleanor said. 'Be grateful that you are to be allowed to marry.'

'Yes—yes, I am grateful to you and the lord Suleiman,' Marisa said with a last wistful look over her shoulder. 'I am so thankful that Fatima did not kill you, Eleanor. She deserved her punishment, awful though it was.'

They were back inside the palace now. Eleanor felt the chill strike her as she stopped walking and turned to look at her companion.

'What do you mean—her punishment? I thought she had been sent back to her home?'

'Oh, my foolish tongue! I am so sorry.' Marisa's eyes darkened with remorse. 'Karin told us we were not to say anything—in case it distressed you. I forgot after all the excitement. She will be so cross with me!'

'And I shall be angry if you do not tell me what happened to Fatima.'

'The lord Suleiman ordered that she be beaten and sent to the slave merchants. She will have been sold by now, but not to the harem of a noble lord. She—she was marked by the whip. Our master ordered it so, because she had misused her beauty and must never be able to do so again.'

'How cruel!' Eleanor cried. Her face was white with shock and she felt sick. 'How could he have done such a wicked thing? I cannot bear to think what will become of her.'

'I should not have told you,' Marisa said, looking guilty. 'It was no more than she deserved, my lady—truly.'

Eleanor did not speak again until they were back in the harem. She went up to Karin as the other woman prepared to leave them.

'Why did you not tell me about Fatima?'

Karin stared at her in silence for a moment, and then sighed. 'Because I knew you would react this way. You do not understand, Eleanor. The lord Suleiman had to make an example of her. She could not simply be banished after all her wickedness. He might have had her put to death for her crimes had he wished.'

'Would not that have been kinder?' Eleanor asked angrily. 'She has been treated worse than a dog. To have her beaten in such a way that she could not hope to be sold into a harem! What will happen to her now? Is she to be sent to a brothel in the back streets of the city, to be used and abused by any man willing to pay a few coins for her? Cruel! Wicked! I cannot believe that my lord would do such a thing.'

Karin hesitated, but it was not for her to tell Eleanor the extent of Fatima's crimes, 'She tried to kill you,' she said. 'You should not blame Suleiman. He had little choice. Fatima knew what she did was punishable by death. She is fortunate to have escaped it.'

'Fortunate?' Eleanor stared at her in disbelief. 'I think what he has done is barbaric—despicable. Suleiman promised me she would be sent home. He promised!'

'That was before she tried to kill you.' Karin gave her a severe look. 'Remember where you are, Eleanor. I warned you that a beast lurks in all men. The lord Suleiman is no different from any other man, though I have always found him just. As he has been this time. He has acted according to the law.'

'A savage, cruel law!' Eleanor retorted.

'But the law by which we all live,' Karin reminded her. 'You have been much indulged—perhaps too much. Our laws are perhaps wiser than you think, though they may seem harsh at times. You must learn to accept that there are some things you cannot change.'

'Never! I shall never accept such brutality.'

'Learn this, then,' Karin said and her tone was harsh. 'You will gain nothing by defiance. The lord Suleiman cares for you and you might make life easier for many in this place—but only if you learn to bend a little, to give as well as take. Tame the beast with tenderness, make him weak with chains of love, Eleanor, and you could bring happiness to many. Do not seek to fight the beast—or it may turn and devour you.'

'I want to see the lord Suleiman!'

Karin looked at her beautiful, tempestuous face, then shook her head. 'No, I shall not request an audience for you. Not while you are in this mood.'

'Then I shall go without permission.' Eleanor cried impetuously. 'I shall demand to see him.'

'You do not yet rule here.' Karin gave her a hard

look. 'If you persist in this folly I shall have you locked in your room and place a guard over you—' She broke off as Hasar approached. 'Yes? You wished to speak with me?'

'The lord Suleiman has sent for the lady Eleanor. He wishes to see her at once.'

'I shall come at once.' Eleanor's eyes were bright with anger. 'I must not keep my lord waiting, Karin.'

Karin caught at her arm as she would have passed. 'Take care, Eleanor,' she warned. 'I am not your enemy. You know that I tried to protect Fatima from herself. I would have had her banished if that were possible—but Suleiman was angry. He came to you when we feared you might die, and he was half out of his mind with grief. I have never seen a man so close to breaking. I do not say that he was kind to have punished Fatima as he did—but he was within the law. He could have punished her a thousand times more harshly. Many men in his position have done far worse things for less reason.'

'But I do not wish to marry those other men,' Eleanor cried. 'I believed I had come to love Suleiman—but he is a barbarian. A cruel savage! And I do not wish to marry such a man.'

She tore herself from Karin's grasp and walked away. Karin stared after her with anxious eyes. Although it was not often allowed to rage out of control, Suleiman did have a fearful temper. And she was very much afraid that this time Eleanor would try his patience too far.

Chapter Eleven

The struggle with Omar had heated Suleiman's blood, leaving him with a sense of exhilaration and triumph. He had won fairly and Eleanor had been watching—that gave him a deep sense of satisfaction. Her request for the tournament had told him that she was far from being indifferent to him, as she had tried to pretend. Indeed, he had sensed the last time he'd held her in his arms that she was close to surrender. He could have taken her then, but he had controlled his desire and let her go.

Suleiman knew that he could possess Eleanor with or without her consent, but the act of possession without love was only a fleeting pleasure that he might have found with any of his concubines. There must be more! He had for some time past been aware of an emptiness within himself, but until he had begun to know and understand Eleanor he had not realised what was lacking in his life.

He loved her—not just with his body, but with his heart and mind. For the first time in his life he had met a woman who could touch the inner man. His loins burned with the need to lie with her, and sometimes at night he had lain restless, unable to sleep for the need inside him, but he had given her the time she had begged for because he wanted her to come to him in love.

'The hawk is made weak by the dove,' he murmured to himself, amused by the discovery within himself that he would once have termed folly in others. 'Yet I would have her come to me...'

His pulses quickened as he heard footsteps and knew that she had answered his call. It was for her sake that he had not sent for her before this, because she had been so ill and he had wanted her to be truly well again. But there must be no more play-acting. It was time that Eleanor understood the true nature of his feelings for her. He caught the scent of her perfume and turned eagerly. His smile faded as he saw the expression on her beautiful face. She had not looked at him this way since that first meeting in the gardens of the Corsair Mohamed Ali ben Ibn!

'Why are you angry?'

'You ask me why—after what you have done?' Her eyes narrowed, her look one of utter contempt. 'No one told me until after the contest. Karin ordered that it should be kept from me...'

'Of what do you speak?' Suleiman felt a sharp searing pain as he saw what he believed to be hatred in her eyes. 'What have I done that has so displeased you?'

'Was it so little to you that you cannot even remember?' Eleanor's eyes flashed in anger. 'You told me that Fatima would be sent back to her home. How could you have had her beaten so cruelly and then—to have condemned her to a life of true slavery! She had been treated almost as a queen in your household…' Her voice broke with emotion. 'I cannot be-lieve that you could have been so savage, so unjust.'

'You think I was unjust?' Suleiman stared at her haughtily. That she should speak to him thus! It was unforgivable. How dare she criticise his judgement? He had allowed her much, but she went too far. A woman might not seek to dictate in such matters. 'Fat-ima was guilty of many crimes—more than you know. I might have ordered a painful death for her—or imprisonment—but I granted her life.'

'Life as a whore to be used and abused by any man who pays for her!'

'She tried to kill you—and she murdered the woman Dinazade.' His expression hardened. 'I was merciful because she had once pleased me—but such crimes must be punished. Even in your own country murder is punishable by death!'

'You are a barbarian!' Eleanor cried, too angry to recognise the justice in what he said. 'I had begun to believe that you were a man of wisdom and justice—but now I see I was wrong. You are as ruthless and cruel as those men who slew my father.'

Suleiman stared at her, his lips white with fury. 'Enough! You are insolent, woman. I have allowed you too much freedom, and now you seek to dictate what I may or may not do. I am the master here. You are a woman and my property.'

'I am well aware that a female slave is less than nothing in your eyes,' Eleanor retorted scornfully. 'I almost believed in you—but now I know you for what you are! Do with me as you please, my master. You are strong and I am weak—but punish me as you will, compel me to your bed, you shall never, never have me.'

'Be careful, Eleanor. You push me too far at your peril.'

'I care for nothing you do or say to me,' she cried. 'I thought I could be happy as your wife—that I could live here content to please you and leave behind all that I had known and loved—but now you make me hate you. You may force me to submit, but I shall never love you.'

She felt a flash of fear as she saw the silver flame leap up in his eyes and knew that she had indeed pushed him too far. He moved towards her purposefully, his intent stamped like a smouldering brand into the iron of his features.

'Then there is no point in waiting...' he muttered fiercely and there was something wild and primitive about him then as he reached out and caught her wrist. 'I had hoped you would come to accept your duty, Eleanor—but as you will not, I must teach you to know your master.'

'No!' Eleanor caught her breath as she gazed up into those dark eyes. 'Please...do not do this, my lord. I—I beg you. Let me go—send me away and let me be free.'

'I wanted your love,' he said in a voice that even in her distress she recognised as tormented. 'But if it is to be denied me even now, I shall glory in your hatred. You belong to me, Eleanor—and I will have you, willingly or no.'

She gave a cry of denial and pulled away as he began to draw her towards the inner chamber, struggling and fighting him every step of the way. He was much too strong for her. His fingers held her in a vice-like grip and she knew that she was helpless against the beast she had aroused in him. His grip bruised her, causing her to whimper with pain.

'Let me go!' she cried, fear sweeping her as she recognised the wisdom of Karin's warning too late. 'Let me go. If you do this I shall not forgive you.'

'You hate me anyway. Why should I not take that which is mine?'

She pulled back sharply and managed to break free of him, but he caught her before she could reach the outer hall, seizing her about the waist and sweeping off her feet. She beat against him with her fists as he carried her to the inner chamber and tossed her down on the silken softness of the divan. She lay gazing up at him as he untied the belt at his waist and threw off his caftan. His plain white tunic followed that to the floor, revealing the rippling muscles and bronzed skin she had found so exciting in the courtyard. He towered above her, magnificent, a pagan god in all his beauty, about to take a human sacrifice.

Eleanor caught her breath. Suleiman's hair was slightly damp as if he had bathed just before she came to him, and there was a clean, fresh scent exuding from his body that she found enticing. His dark eyes sought and held hers as he bent over her and unfastened the jeweled clasp at her waist. Beneath the heavy silk of her waistcoat, the flimsy gauze tunic did nothing to hide the perfection of her breasts, which were peaked by the sudden arousal of desire that had begun to sweep her body like a forest fire.

Suleiman's eyes seemed to devour her as he reached out and ripped away the fine material, exposing her soft, pale flesh to his burning gaze. His hand moved to her face, his fingers stroking her cheek and then down the arch of her slender throat, moving slowly down to caress the dark rose nipples, and then cupping the fullness of her breasts.

'Beautiful,' he murmured huskily. 'Beautiful… I have wanted to touch you this way since I first saw you bathing in that pool. I have burned for you, Eleanor.'

Her throat was tight with emotion; her anger drained away as she recognised the need in him and felt it answered deep within her. She could scarcely breathe for the churning excitement that now possessed her, spirals of desire curling up from the centre of her being. She should beg him to stop! She should fight him tooth and claw, but the will to resist was draining from her as she gazed into his dark eyes. He was savage and wild, an arrogant cruel man who would be her master…yet even as she formed the protest in her mind she denied it.

He could be capable of harshness, of that she had ample proof, but he was not wantonly cruel. The news of Fatima's punishment had shocked her, making her react angrily—but her accusations had not been entirely fair. She knew that Karin had spoken truly, and that many men in his position would have done much worse.

Why had she begun to defend him in her own mind? Why was her body betraying her, yearning to meld with his? Yet she knew all too well. It was because, despite his threats to show her he was the master, he was still hesitating, still careful not to hurt her. She might have expected rape after their fierce quarrel, but this was seduction. He was drawing her to him, coaxing her response with a tender care. His eyes held hers as his hand continued to stroke and explore the softness of her body, his touch beginning to make her flesh tingle with an exquisite pleasure.

'Do not fear me, my love,' he murmured, his voice husky with passion. 'The die is cast and I cannot draw back, but I shall not hurt you. I would never hurt you.'

'I do not fear you,' she whispered breathily. 'I have never feared you—only myself. I feared to give lest I was truly your slave.'

'You are my love,' he said. 'My only love.'

Eleanor moaned with pleasure as he bent his head to kiss her breasts, taking the rosy tips into his mouth one by one to taste and tease them with his tongue. Her breath quickened as he pushed the flimsy drawers down over her hips, tossing them away. Now he was kissing and tasting each inch of her, as if he found her as sweet as honey.

'I feel so strange,' she said, gazing up at him, her eyes wide with wonder. 'I have no will…no thought but you.'

Suleiman raised his head to smile at her. 'I am about to take you into paradise, my houri. We shall find our heaven on this earth, I promise you.'

The feelings his kisses and gentle stroking aroused in her were so unexpected and so sweet. Eleanor discovered that her body was no longer her own; it vibrated like the strings of a musical instrument beneath his hands as she arched and moaned beneath him.

'I think I shall die,' she whispered as his lips followed his stroking fingers to the centre of her femininity, making her gasp and writhe with the pleasure she could not hide. 'Oh…oh, my lord.'

She felt him move so that his body covered hers and knew that he was as naked as she. The heat of his loins burned her, and without needing instruction she opened to receive the sudden thrust of his throbbing manhood. A sharp pain made her cry out and draw back as the hugeness of him filled her, but his lips were on hers, teasing and coaxing her to acceptance once more. And then the pain was over and she could feel the rising tide of her own desire, swelling within her, driving her to meet his urgent thrusting, her hips grinding against him in her own need. Her lips parted in little mewing cries as he swept her on with him to that far place.

She was falling…falling through time and space into something that wrapped her about with warmth and pleasure. Indeed, it was as though she had died and gone to paradise. She moaned a little as she felt Suleiman move and tightened her arms about him, as if to hold her to him a little longer.

'Do not leave me,' she whispered.

'I shall never leave you or put you from me,' he vowed as he raised himself above her on one elbow so that he might look down at her. He wiped a tear from her cheek. 'Forgive me if I hurt you, my darling. It must always be so the first time.'

'You did not hurt me so very much,' she said, looking up at him shyly now as she marvelled in the sense of well being flooding through her. 'I think I cried because I am happy—and because I have been foolish to resist you. I did not know that I could feel like this…'

'You do not hate me now?' His gaze was thoughtful as it rested on her lovely face, flushed and smiling now. 'I meant to wait until you were my wife, Eleanor. I never intended to force you.'

'You did not,' she replied and blushed. 'At first, yes—but that was because I provoked you into losing your temper. I fear that I spoke harshly to you, my lord. I was distressed and hurt that you had punished Fatima—but I did not know that she had killed Dinazade. I thought it was because of what she did to me, that you had taken revenge out of anger.'

Suleiman straightened up. He reached for his robe and pulled it on, before sitting on the edge of the divan beside her. 'I did punish her the way I did because of how she attacked you, Eleanor. I am guilty of harshness towards her. I thought you would die and I hated her. She had committed many crimes, which were punishable by death, yet I stayed my hand against her these many weeks. I would have been content to banish her—until I thought she had robbed me of that which I treasure more than my life. Then indeed I acted with the savage anger my fear aroused. I warned you I was not perfect—though I have strived to be just. Love made me cruel—my love and need for you.'

'Oh, my lord…' Eleanor caught back a sob. 'I—I did know. I have held back, taunted you… Can you forgive me?'

'I shall no doubt think of some suitable punishment,' he said huskily. 'You must learn to know me, my dove.'

'Yes, my lord,' she replied demurely. 'I shall pay heed to your instruction most diligently.'

'So obedient!' Suleiman laughed. 'Why do I suspect you most when you are meek?'

'Perhaps because I have been wilful and impudent in the past?'

'Yes, that may have some bearing on the matter. But know that I would not have you change too much, my love. I think I gain much from battle with you—especially when I win!'

Eleanor's eyes sparked with mischief as she sat up and looked at him. 'You have shown me that I was foolish to fear love, my lord—but what makes you imagine you won the argument?'

'It is an argument neither of us can win,' he said, the laughter dying from his face. 'We do not live in a perfect world, Eleanor—nor am I without my faults.'

'Indeed, you are not, my lord!'

He smiled wryly. 'I have a feeling you will teach me to be more considerate of others, Eleanor. I have perhaps been too much indulged. Everything was always as I ordered it—until one woman refused to obey me when I told her I would dry her hair.'

Eleanor smiled. 'Why did you not drown me as you threatened—or have me beaten for my disobedience?'

'I could not bear to think of you in pain. When they told me you had been so ill...' He touched his fingers to the bandage on her arm. 'Does the wound still pain you?'

'Sometimes it is a little sore, but I do not regard it. I fear it will leave a scar—I am worth less than I was before.'

'You are beyond price to me,' he told her. He cursed suddenly, then stood up and began to pace about the room as if in agitation. She watched, sensing that he was fighting a battle within himself, and then he returned to her. 'I cannot hold you against your will. It would be a mockery of the love I bear you. I grant you your freedom, Eleanor. You may return to your family if that is your wish.'

For a moment Eleanor was stunned. Was he really

offering her freedom? Once it had been all she wanted, a chance to return to her homeland and the life she had known…but now she knew deep in her heart that she could never leave him. Not because he was her master, but because she was bound to him by the ties of love. But supposing he did not truly want her?

She looked at him uncertainly. 'Do you want me to go?'

'You know that I do not. I would keep you with me always as my wife—my only wife, for I vow that I shall take no other.'

'Supposing I cannot give you a son?' She knew that it was very important to him to have a son, and that his religion made it possible for him to take another wife if she was unable to provide him with one.

He had been silent for several seconds now, and her heart caught. She could not expect him to renounce all that he had been born to for her sake, the culture that was so much a part of him, but when he spoke his words were so unexpected and so touching that they brought tears to her eyes.

'Then I shall have no son.'

'Do you love me so much, my lord?' she asked, misty-eyed.

'I have not the words to tell you—only time will show that I speak the truth.'

'Then I shall stay with you, my lord—for I love you. I tried to fight my feelings for you, but you were too strong for me.'

Suleiman sat beside her again. He reached out to trail his fingers down the curve of her cheek. 'If you left me I should be lost. I am trapped in this place, Eleanor. Caught by love and duty—and even my love for you cannot free me from the web that binds me. If you stay, you must live by our customs and religion, though I shall pretend not to notice if you cling to your own in private.'

'I know this, my lord. I have accepted it.'

'I would have you as free as my falcon when she flies, but you will never truly be free in this land. We protect our women from the harshness of a cruel world, Eleanor. I cannot let you go out without the eunuchs to guard you, because you would not be safe. A woman alone would not be considered worthy of respect and therefore vulnerable to abuse. Men are not to be trusted, my love. We are but base creatures, and only love may redeem us.'

'This also I know,' Eleanor assured him and smiled teasingly. 'Karin has done her work well, my lord. I know that I must conform in public, but in private…'

'Ah…in private you may command,' he said and laughed. 'I am your slave here, Eleanor.'

'My lord seeks to mock me,' she replied and shook her head at him, for there was a wildness in him that would never be quite tamed, though like his beloved hawk he could be coaxed. 'But I do have one request…'

'I imagined you might. Ask and it shall be granted—if it is possible.'

'Could you not buy Fatima back and send her home?'

Suleiman looked at her for some seconds in silence.

'It is already done,' he said at last. 'I have told no one in the palace—but the man who sold you to me held her for me at his house in the city. After she had been beaten, I regretted what I had done, Eleanor. Yet to have been seen to do less would have seemed weak. Fatima pleased me once, though she also betrayed me. I have given her into the charge of Mohamed, and he will take her back to Algiers. What she does then will be of her own choosing.'

Eleanor took his hand and held it. 'And I accused you of being unjust. Please forgive me. It is I who have wronged you, my lord.'

'What—am I no longer a savage?' His eyes gleamed with amusement.

'My lord is a most noble savage,' Eleanor replied. She put her hand out to pull his head down so that their lips touched, and then she kissed him...sweetly, slowly and with passion. 'I think that my master should continue my instruction...'

Suleiman's eyes glowed like hot coals, as he bent over her. 'My love...' he murmured. 'It will be my pleasure to meet this latest request of yours...'

They lay close together long into the night, whispering, sharing the secrets that neither had ever confessed to another, kissing, touching...loving as they came to know and enjoy each other's body.

'Should I not return to the harem?' Eleanor asked at one point. 'What will the others think?'

'They will know that their mistress has found her rightful place at last—and that place is here by my side, Eleanor.'

'I cannot stay forever in your bed. We are not yet married.'

'But we soon shall be,' he murmured, holding her fastened against him as if he would never release her. 'It must be soon. Tomorrow your brother shall be brought here to my apartments, Eleanor. I shall make arrangements for him to be returned to your family,

but that will take time and until then you will want
to see him as often as possible.'

'Yes, I should like to see Richard.' Eleanor kissed
his shoulder, tasting the salt of his sweat. 'When did
you decide to give him his freedom?'

'When I realised that I loved you. I could not keep
your brother against his will, but I needed to make
you understand that we were meant for each other.
Had I told you before this, you would have asked to
go with him.'

'Yes, I should,' Eleanor admitted, snuggling
against his hard chest with a sigh. 'I did not know
myself. I think that I began to love you when you
turned your back that day in the gardens...but it took
me a long time to know my own heart.'

Suleiman's arms tightened about her and she felt
the shudder run through him. 'Supposing Mohamed
had not offered you to me—I cannot bear to think of
what might have happened to you.'

'Or if I had managed to escape you!' She gazed up
at him mischievously. 'How much I should have
missed.'

'There was never any chance of you escaping me,
woman!'

Eleanor laughed. He would always be the master
of her heart, no matter what concessions he made to
her—but he loved her and that was all she wanted of
life.

'You look well, sister.' Richard seemed uncomfortable. He had been brought to the lord Suleiman's
apartments wondering what to expect and was con-
fused by what he found. Eleanor was richly dressed
in cloth of gold and wearing jewels fit for a queen.

'Are you better? They told me you were ill for a while.'

'It was nothing much,' Eleanor replied carelessly. 'I had a fever, but I have recovered. Are you content, Richard? They are treating you well at the school?'

'The discipline is harsh,' her brother replied. 'Most of the students are beaten for disobedience every now and then—but it is no more than a tutor would do at home. I enjoy it when they give us training in the courtyard. I saw you at the tournament.'

'I did not notice you. I am sorry.'

'You were watching the lord Suleiman.' Richard frowned at her. 'They say he is to take you as his wife in three days…'

'Yes, that is so…' She hesitated. 'Suleiman has told me that you will be given passage to Cyprus after our wedding. He has been arranging it.'

'So I am to be free…' Richard's eyes narrowed. 'What price have you paid for my freedom, sister? Are you his harlot? Yes, I see it is so—and it will never be any different. This marriage ceremony has no meaning. You are not of his faith. You will still be a whore in the eyes of the true church.'

'Richard…' Eleanor's face had gone white. Richard's scorn hurt her, all the more because she had always loved him dearly. 'You are unfair.'

'He has bewitched you…turned your head with fine gifts,' Richard said sourly. 'You have sold yourself to him, Eleanor. You are his property now—his thing to do with as he will.'

'You do not know of what you speak,' she replied, her lovely eyes mirroring her hurt. 'Suleiman loves me, and I love him. I want to be his wife.'

Richard stared at her, his manner hostile and disbelieving. 'Then you are a fool,' he said. 'He may promise many things now, but wait a while and he will put you aside as any man puts aside his whore when he tires of her.'

'Why do you want to hurt me?' Eleanor cried, tears slipping down her cheeks. 'Why do you say such terrible things to me? Do you hate me?'

Richard's face twisted with anger. 'I hate them, Eleanor. I hate the men who killed our father, and those who sold us—and I hate him. I hate and despise the man who will be your husband.'

'He has not harmed you.'

Richard gave a harsh laugh. 'He bought me as another man might buy a dog. I have been beaten and humiliated in his house, treated like dirt. Do you expect me to love him?'

'No…' Eleanor's heart contracted with pain. 'No, I do not expect you to love him—but you could try to understand his ways, as he does ours.'

Richard scowled. 'It is easy for him to understand. He made me his slave, now he will release me to please his whore. Should I grovel at his feet to thank him?'

'No—but you might respect what he has done. This is his country, Richard, and he lives by his customs. They may seem harsh to us sometimes, but he seeks always to be just.'

'I shall never respect him or his way of life. Nor you if you stay here willingly, Eleanor.'

'Then you must forget me,' she said sadly. 'Please leave, Richard. We have nothing more to say to each other.'

His eyes gleamed, then he turned and left without another word. Eleanor blinked away her tears as

Suleiman came to her and opened his arms to receive her. He had been standing behind the screen, where he had retired to give her privacy with her brother.

'You heard?' She looked at him anxiously as he drew her close to comfort her. 'He is so bitter, my lord. He knows not what he says.'

'Richard hates me and my world,' Suleiman replied. 'He is not alone in this—many of his faith and ours have been sworn enemies for too long. I have often wished that we might begin to build a bridge towards a new understanding and peace, but I fear it may be too great a divide. Men like your brother will never try to understand us.'

'Yes, I know you are right' she said and sighed. 'It makes me sad for him, Suleiman.'

'I had hoped that he might have returned to visit you one day. I could have arranged for him to travel freely in our land and on the seas. It is not as difficult as you might imagine. I had thought it might be the start of understanding…'

'Perhaps he will relent one day,' Eleanor said. 'He is still raw from the grief of his father's death.'

'You have suffered as much as he in this.'

'Perhaps more. I was closer to my father. It may be that he resents that he was never given a chance to know Father better.'

Suleiman nodded agreement. 'Yes, perhaps. The relationship between father and son can be difficult. I have been blessed, but it was not thus for Hasan. Had my father shown him more favour, it might have prevented his treachery—and punishment.'

'That hurt you, my lord.' She moved towards him, reaching out to touch his cheek with the tips of her fingers. 'I saw it in your face when you told me what had happened…'

Suleiman pulled her close, his lips against her hair. 'We have both felt the sting of a brother's scorn, my love—but we have each other.'

'Yes, my lord. We are blessed indeed.'

As he drew her to him, Eleanor closed her eyes, shutting out the grief Richard's rejection had caused her. It would ease in time as did all such pain.

Eleanor sat with the other ladies. For this special occasion all the women had been allowed to mingle in the Caliph's own hall. Some of them were heavily veiled, but most wore a simple headdress with only gossamer of gauze to cover their faces if they so chose.

Several eunuchs were present, also the lord Suleiman, his younger brother Bayezid, who had been persuaded to leave the seclusion of his studies for the evening, and the Caliph himself.

It was the eve of Eleanor's wedding, and in what she believed was a departure from custom, she had been formally presented to her lord's father and brother. She herself wore only a pretty scarf over her hair, for the men present were family, and Suleiman had told her it was permissible to show her face to them if she chose.

'You show favour to those who are to be your family by not wearing the veil,' Suleiman had told her. 'And I am happy for you to do so at a private gathering.'

The Caliph had smiled on her, nodding and welcoming her to his family. 'My son has chosen well,' he told her. 'And though you are yet strange to our ways, I hear good things of you.'

In the strictest adherence to custom, Suleiman would probably not have met his bride or seen her face until the wedding ceremony was over, for often men of his standing married women who had been chosen for their own nobility. However, the Caliph himself had taken a concubine to wife and saw no reason to quarrel with his son's decision.

Caliph Bakhar had long been aware of Suleiman's restlessness, but could not bring himself to give him permission to leave. Perhaps now his son would find content at home.

That evening, Suleiman entertained the court with his singing, while one of the eunuchs accompanied him on a lute. Eleanor listened entranced, for the husky, sensual notes of her lord's song were deeply moving.

He sang of unrequited love and a young man dying of a broken heart because the woman he desired had been given to another man.

Eleanor's eyelashes were wet with tears as the last notes died away. She met his sultry gaze and knew that though he had sung at his father's request, his song had been for her. He was telling her that his heart would break if they were ever parted.

Since the unpleasant, hurtful meeting with Richard, Eleanor's mood had veered between happiness and near despair. She loved Suleiman, but her brother's cruel words had hurt her.

Would she truly be her lord's wife? They were to marry according to his religion, but in her heart she still believed in her own faith. Did that make her the whore her brother had named her?

After Suleiman's song, there was a display of dancing by beautiful girls who wore the scantiest of clothing, which revealed their charms. Then a little later, a eunuch juggled with balls and also ate fire. It was late in the evening when the ladies were escorted back to the harem.

Eleanor said goodnight to Suleiman, but they did not kiss or touch, because it would not be seemly before the court. She was to spend the night with her friends in accordance with custom, and would be heavily veiled when she went to her lord as a bride the next day.

She slept but little that night, wishing that she lay beside her lord so that he could hold her close and banish the doubts that plagued her throughout the dark hours.

Oh, she was foolish to doubt him! Eleanor had proof enough of his love, and he had been more than generous. She knew that she had only to ask for some boon and it would be granted.

She fell asleep just before dawn, but her dreams were unkind and she thought herself at sea again, witnessing the way her beloved father had been struck down.

Eleanor could not blame her brother for his bitterness. She too felt anger when she remembered the way they had been captured. Yet in her heart she knew that her destiny lay with the man she was to marry. And at last she was at peace.

The ceremony of the bath, and the sweet oils that were so gently massaged into her skin, were very soothing. Eleanor's hair was braided like a coronet around her head, and the rest left to fall in shining waves to the small of her back. Then a heavy silk veil was placed over her head; she was just able to see through it, but it would not be possible for others to see her face.

Her robes were of white silk heavily embroidered with gold thread and encrusted with jewels, and she had been told that Suleiman would wear much the same.

Eleanor was trembling inside as her ladies dressed her, fluttering about her like tiny humming birds. Their laughter and happiness for her was easing the knot of anxiety inside her. She laughed and blushed as they teased her, making her promise to have many children so that they could all enjoy looking after them.

Her fear and doubt had dissolved as though it had never been. This was a very different life to the one she had been born to, yet it was a good one. As long as Suleiman loved her she knew that she could be happy here.

The time for the ceremony had arrived, and Karin came to conduct the ladies to the Caliph's hall, where the marriage was to take place. Six eunuchs preceded them, all richly robed, and another six followed behind. The traditional music of the marriage dance sounded strange and slightly discordant to her ears, but also stirring.

Eleanor was showered with rose petals every step of the way, her ladies leading her as though she could not see—which was indeed difficult through the heavy veil. She held out her hand to Karin as they halted outside the hall, while her coming was heralded inside.

'You know your responses,' Karin whispered and

smiled at her encouragingly. 'No one expects more of you.'

Eleanor's heart beat very fast as she saw how handsome Suleiman looked in his ceremonial robes. He usually preferred a simple mode of dress that any man might wear, but today he was clothed richly as befitted the Caliph's son on his wedding day.

The religious chanting had begun. Eleanor moved as if in a dream, following the words and ritual in her head. She had memorised them and was aware of all that was going around her, even though it had an unreal quality. She could scarcely breathe as she was led slowly towards her lord. The time had come for her responses; she made them flawlessly, bowing her head as a ceremonial garland of flowers was placed about her neck. She gave him a garland in return, and then she placed her hand in his as the words that would make them man and wife were intoned. It was as he was about to raise her veil that the interruption came.

'Stop! In the name of the Sultan Suleiman the Magnificent, I forbid this marriage. It is not legal, for the bride is a Christian and was brought here against her will.'

Eleanor was as startled as everyone else present. Surely she had misheard? How could this be? Who would dare to intrude on them at this time?

She peered through the thick veil, trying to discover what was happening and then, as she saw the men coming towards them, a gasp escaped her. The man who had commanded the ceremony to cease was Count Giovani Salvadore. But that was not possible! How could he be here? And how had he gained access to the palace?

'How dare you intrude?' Suleiman started forward angrily but even as he did so, several guards moved to surround him. Eleanor saw that they were wearing different colours to the Caliph's own men. 'Who gave you permission to enter here?'

'We are the Sultan's personal guard,' one of the Janissaries replied harshly. 'It is at our master's command that we prevent this marriage. Suleiman Bakhar, you are under arrest for treachery—and Miss Eleanor Nash is to be taken to the Sultan's palace at once.'

'Suleiman!' Eleanor looked at him, her face white with shock beneath the veil. 'Can they do this?'

'It is a mistake,' Suleiman said. 'I shall speak to the Sultan myself. Do not be frightened, my dove. We shall be together again soon.'

The guards had laid hands on him and were hustling him away from her. Eleanor tried to follow him, but the count took hold of her arm, preventing her.

'There is no need to be afraid,' he said. 'I believe we were in time to halt the ceremony. It took some hours of negotiation or we should have been here yesterday. I have come to take you and Richard to Italy, Eleanor.'

'No! I shall not go with you. I am the lord Suleiman's wife.' She drew herself up haughtily. 'Pray take your hand from my arm, sir. It is forbidden that another man should touch me.'

'This ceremony will not stand,' he said, frowning at her. 'Your father did not consent.'

'My father?' She stared at him, eyes widening in shock. 'But my father is dead…'

'No, lady.' The count smiled. 'He was struck unconscious by those rogues who attacked your ship, but he was alive when the Spanish war galley reached him. Instead of continuing to Cyprus, he was brought back by them to Italy and now awaits you at my home.'

'My father is alive?' Eleanor stared at him. She was conscious of a feeling of joy that her father was not dead, but there was also pain. 'Does Richard know that our father lives?'

'He is being taken to the Sultan's palace under separate escort. We shall see him there. Come, we must go. I do not like the look of things here.'

Eleanor had been too stunned to realise what was going on around her. Now she saw that the eunuchs were muttering angrily amongst themselves at this intrusion—and the Caliph had disappeared. The women who had gathered to witness the ceremony were being quickly ushered from the hall. The atmosphere was tense and uneasy, for an insult had been offered to the Caliph's son and his wife.

She had no choice but to go with Count Salvadore. It was an order from the Sultan himself and must be obeyed. Besides, she needed to know what was happening to Suleiman. He had told her not to be frightened, but she could not help herself. Why had he been arrested? What crime had he committed?

She was surprised as Karin joined her just as they were leaving the hall. 'I have permission,' Karin whispered in the language of the harem. 'The Caliph has sent me to look after his son's wife.'

'I am his wife?'

'Yes, it is done. The Caliph fears for his son—but he will do what he can.'

'What is that woman saying to you?'

'She is my lady in waiting,' Eleanor replied. She

did not wish the count to know that Karin was the Caliph's second wife lest they were separated. 'She comes with me. It is not seemly for me to travel without a female companion.'

'Very well,' the count replied. 'I have a litter waiting to convey you to the Seraglio. It will carry you both.'

Karin was wearing her casacche, and she had brought one for Eleanor, which she donned as she went out into the courtyard. They were just in time to witness a scuffle between some of the Caliph's guards and the Sultan's own elite Janissaries.

It was Suleiman himself who forbade his men to fight, warning them that they could be executed for treachery against their master.

'You must not resist. Fear not, my friends,' he told them. 'I shall return.'

Eleanor watched as he was told to mount a horse. He had not been bound, but he was clearly a prisoner. To resist an order from the Sultan was to invite a painful death.

Suleiman glanced towards Eleanor before he rode away. Since she was still wearing the heavy veil over her head, he could not see her anguished look—but she saw his and her heart wrenched with pain.

Supposing he could not reason with the Grand Turk? In the Ottoman Empire the Sultan's word was law. If he had decided that Eleanor must be returned to her father it would happen. But it must not be! It would break her heart if she were forced to leave Suleiman now.

Eleanor was happy to learn that her father lived, but her pleasure was clouded by the brutal end to her dreams of marrying the man she loved. She feared that she would be parted from Suleiman and never see him again.

'Do not despair,' Karin said when they were together in the litter and the escort had begun to move off. 'The Caliph has influence with the Sultan—and Suleiman has done nothing against the law.'

'Am I truly his wife?' Eleanor asked. 'Were they in time to halt the ceremony?'

'According to our laws, you are bound to him,' Karin assured her. 'As a true believer, you are his legal wife. It is up to you, Eleanor. If you deny your own faith and swear that you are a true convert, the Sultan may decide that you cannot now be returned to your father.'

'Then I shall do whatever I must,' Eleanor replied. 'Oh, Karin! I am so glad you made me study with you. If a religious teacher questions me, I shall be able to give the right responses.'

'It may be that you will be questioned by more than one such man,' Karin said. 'Is there anything that puzzles you? Any question you need to ask me?'

'Only why you chose to come with me? You were to have gone to your daughters tomorrow.'

'You are more important, my dearest Eleanor. Do you not know that you are as a daughter to me?'

Eleanor's eyes were moist with tears as she took the other woman's hand and held it. 'Thank you, Karin. I am not frightened as long as you are with me—not for myself.'

'You fear for your lord?'

'Yes. What will they do to him? Will he be beaten—or tortured?' A shiver ran through her as she thought of what could happen to Suleiman.

'I do not know,' Karin admitted. 'The Caliph and

his son are sparing with punishments, but it is not always so. The law is harsh in this country, Eleanor. I do not understand why Suleiman has been arrested. They could have stopped the wedding—but there was no need for such harshness. Unless Suleiman has displeased the Sultan…'

'Why should he be displeased?' Eleanor asked. 'My lord bought me. I was his property and he chose to marry me. That is not against your laws. We did not flout the customs, Karin. Suleiman was careful to observe them.'

'That is what I do not understand,' Karin replied. 'We must be patient, Eleanor. It may be that the Sultan will send for you—and if he does you must be respectful. Do not imagine that you may speak boldly as you do with your lord. Be very careful. Answer when he questions you—but if you wish to say something more, ask permission to address his Magnificence.'

'Yes, I shall remember,' Eleanor replied. 'I have listened well to your teachings, Karin—though I have not always obeyed them in the past. This time my lord's life may depend on my behaving as you would have had me behave long ago.'

She looked out and saw the old walls of the city, which were remnants of the original settlement built in the year three hundred and twenty four by Constantine I of Rome, and then the building of the magnificent palace of the Ottoman sultans. An icy trickle went down her spine as she was carried towards it, and she remembered that Suleiman had intended her as a gift for the Sultan.

What would have been her fate if she had been brought here then?

'I shall be very careful. And I pray that the Sultan will give me the chance to tell him what I truly desire.'

'You wish to stay here—even though you father lives?'

'Yes, I have no choice,' Eleanor said. 'Suleiman is my husband. I love him, Karin. So much that I would rather die than be sent away from him…'

Chapter Twelve

O nce within the palace, the women were led away by one of the Sultan's Kadins to a part of the harem reserved for visitors. She told them her name was Sonia, and welcomed them in the traditional way, offering refreshment before she left them alone.

'It seems that we are to be treated with respect,' Karin said. 'I wondered what might happen here, Eleanor—but for the moment it seems that we are to be welcomed as honoured guests.'

'How long do you think it will be before the Sultan sends for us?' Eleanor asked. 'How long before I am permitted to see my husband?'

Karin looked at her anxiously. 'You must be patient…' she began. 'These things take their course. There is nothing you can do until you are sent for, Eleanor. You have no power to command here and nor have I. The Caliph has some influence with his royal master. He will do all he can. We must leave the negotiations to him.'

Eleanor nodded. She glanced at the bowls of fruit and sweetmeats that had been provided for them.

'You should eat, Karin. I am sure you must be hungry.'

'Will you not try something yourself? I know that you have eaten little today.'

'I was too excited…' Eleanor caught back a sob. 'When I was first taken to the Caliph's palace I prayed that I might be returned to my family, but now…if they take me away from Suleiman, it will break my heart.'

'You can do nothing but wait,' Karin told her. 'You must accept what happens—it is Allah's will.'

Eleanor was about to deny her angrily, then, remembering all the warnings she had been given, she bent her head submissively. '*Insh'allah*—may it be as Allah wills.'

Karin smiled at her approvingly. 'Just so, Eleanor. Our master the Sultan will decide your fate in his wisdom and greatness. You must accept his judgement for he is just and good.'

'Yes, this I have been told by my husband,' Eleanor replied, following her lead. 'He has often told me how much he admires our overlord.'

'Sit and eat,' Karin bade her again. 'It may be some days before you are sent for.'

'Some days…' Eleanor was about to protest angrily when she remembered that everything they were saying was possibly being listened to by spies, who would carry tales to the Sultan. 'Then I must be patient—there is no more I can do.'

But how was she to be patient when she did not know what was going on elsewhere in the palace? How she wished there was some way she could discover what had happened to Suleiman—and whether

the Count Salvadore had already persuaded the Grand
Turk to let him take her back to Italy.

'I really must protest, your Magnificence,' Count
Salvadore was saying. 'Why has Miss Nash been
taken to the women's quarters? I have been refused
permission to speak to her—and yet I believed you
had given permission for me to take her home to her
family?'

Suleiman the Magnificent, Sultan, Grand Turk, the
giver of laws and absolute ruler of the powerful
Ottoman Empire, met the impatient demands of his
visitor with an inscrutable look. His face was thin and
narrow, and he wore a slight beard and side-whiskers,
his eyes piercing and cold. A huge jewel sparkled in
the folds of his silken turban as he faced the pompous
banking merchant in silence. Such men had their uses,
and Suleiman was not called the Lawgiver for nothing. His victories in other lands had gained him a
reputation as a ruthless destroyer, but in his own
country he was revered because he had revised the
legal system, bringing benefits to many of his sub-
jects. Eleanor's father had told her that the Sultan was
a clever, calculating man who would not hesitate to
use others for his own purpose.

'Please be seated, noble lord,' the Sultan's Vizier
replied for his master. 'His Magnificence wishes to
question you on certain matters.'

'But we have talked,' Count Salvadore blustered.
'All day yesterday. I believed we had reached an understanding—Sir William's son and daughter are to
be returned to him in return for trade and certain
banking arrangements you have named.'

'But circumstances are altered,' the Vizier replied

in a calm even tone. 'Forgive me, noble lord—but it may be that the woman in question is no longer the daughter of her father but the wife of Suleiman Bakhar, and belongs to him under the law.'

'How can this be? I was told that it is impossible for a Christian woman to become the wife of a Muslim.' Salvadore was on the point of losing his temper. All this had been gone through at length before permission to enter the Caliph's palace had been given.

'But it seems that the lady has become a Muslim…' the Vizier replied. 'My master requires to know why you wish to take Miss Nash away from her lawful husband.'

'It cannot be lawful to force a Christian woman to marry against her will.'

'Are you sure it was done against her will?'

'Of course. She could not want to live in a harem!'

The Vizier was about to continue with his questions, when the Sultan beckoned to him. He approached his master, bending to hear the whispered words, and then he nodded and turned to beckon one of the eunuchs.

'What is going on?' Count Salvadore demanded as the eunuch went away. 'What did his Magnificence say?'

'My master commanded that the woman be brought to answer for herself.'

'But…but…' the count faltered uncertainly. 'I do not see that this will serve. She will be afraid to speak her mind for fear of what may happen to her. Besides, only her father can consent to her marriage—and he does not. I have paid the ransom. A very generous ransom…'

The Vizier held up his hand to silence him. 'Your gift gained you an audience with the Sultan, nothing more. Be careful what you demand, infidel. It would not be wise to displease my master.'

Count Salvadore fumed inwardly. It was impossible to treat with these people! They said one thing and did another. He distrusted them and wished that he might conclude his business quickly and leave. There was some mischief going on here—he felt it instinctively.

Yet surely Eleanor would tell them that she desired to be returned to her family? She could not wish to remain here as some kind of a harlot…unless…? He frowned as he recalled her haughty manner the previous day. Perhaps she had already become the Turk's mistress.

The seconds ticked by slowly, and Count Salvadore cursed inwardly. He had a ship waiting, and he wanted to catch the tide. The sooner he left this accursed place the better! He turned as he heard a slight commotion, and then saw that two women had returned with the eunuch. He started to rise, but a sharp gesture from the Vizier made him keep his seat.

Eleanor came forward, her heart beating very fast as she realised she had been brought into the presence of the Sultan and his court, who, Karin had told her, were gathered in the State Audience Chamber. It was here that the Grand Vizier held meetings with foreign ambassadors, and there was a window from which the Sultan could watch unobserved if he chose—but today he was seated on a magnificent throne on a raised dais.

Eleanor was still wearing her wedding veil, for no

other had been given her, and she held tight to Karin's hand as they were told to approach the throne.

'Down on your knees, and keep your head bent until you are spoken to,' Karin whispered as they were told to halt their approach still some little distance from the throne. 'Remember all I have told you, Eleanor.'

Eleanor made no reply. She peered through her veil in an effort to see if Suleiman was also present, but there was no sign of him. Where was he? What was happening to him? She had lain awake most of the night, her heart aching for a sight of him, but other than the Kadin who had brought them more food that evening, they had seen no one.

'You are Miss Eleanor Nash, daughter of the noble lord Sir William?' a voice asked her. Eleanor looked up and saw a man richly dressed in robes of purple and gold. He was stout and his beard was grey, but she looked into his eyes and saw that there was no malice there. He smiled at her reassuringly as she hesitated. 'Speak to me—and then I will question you. You must not speak to the Sultan unless he gives permission.'

'Yes, my lord Vizier,' Eleanor replied. 'I have been taught what is proper by my lord's family.'

'Your lord?' The Vizier looked at her hard, his eyes searching but unable to see through the veil that covered her face. 'Of whom do you speak, lady—your master? The man who bought you from the Corsair Mohamed Ali ben Ibn? Do you wish to remain with him?'

'I have no master, sir. Suleiman Bakhar is my husband. I was married to him within the law yesterday, and I am his true wife. It is both my duty and my wish to remain with him. Under the law I can have no other husband—and must retire from life if we are parted. If I am sent back to Italy, I shall be desolate.'

'Are you then a believer?'

'Yes, my lord. I have studied the Qur'an.' Eleanor lifted her veil, looking into the Vizier's face. 'Forgive me for any immodesty, my lord Vizier, but I wish you to be able to see that I do not lie to you. Long before I came to this country, I knew of your faith and I had studied the Qur'an. When my lord Suleiman did me the honour to ask me to become his wife, I studied diligently to become one of the Faithful. Karin, Caliph Bakhar's wife, taught me. She is with me now and will confirm this if asked.'

'This we have been told of already,' the Vizier replied. 'But if what you say is true about already being a believer before you came here, then there can be no accusations that you have been forced to convert to the true faith. Yet we would have the truth of this matter from you, lady.'

'If you will permit me, I can prove it is the truth, my lord.'

The Vizier's eyes narrowed. He glanced towards the Sultan, who beckoned him forward to whisper in his ear. After a few seconds, he nodded and came back to Eleanor.

'His Magnificence would hear more of this proof.'

'This was given to me by my father,' Eleanor said, reaching beneath her tunic for the treasure of the Far Cross. 'We were researching a legend when this came into our possession—and my father gave it to me to look after for him on our voyage. When we were at sea and our ship was tossed by the winds, it gave me courage—and I prayed to Allah to save me. I believe it was through his goodness that I was saved from the storm and delivered into the hands of a good and just man.'

'What is it?' the Vizier asked as he took the jewelled object from her, turning it over in his hand. 'I do not see the significance of this trinket.'

'If the lord Vizier would undo the stopper, he would see that it contains an ancient manuscript writ very small—and the words inscribed are a part of the Qur'an. It is a part of the treasure of the Abbot of the Far Cross and was stolen many centuries ago by pirates.'

'Bring it to me!'

Eleanor looked at the man who had spoken. The Sultan was clearly interested in her treasure and she thought she saw a gleam of excitement in his eyes as he held out his hand imperiously. She handed the small vial to the Vizier who carried it to his master and offered it to him.

'Open it,' the Sultan commanded, and watched eagerly as his Vizier obeyed. 'Take out what is inside and tell me if she speaks the truth.'

The Vizier did as he was bid, then turned to his master and held it out once more. 'The woman speaks the truth, Magnificence.'

'Give it to me—the manuscript.' The Sultan studied it in silence for a moment, then his dark eyes returned it to his Vizier. 'Ask her why she wore it around her neck?'

Eleanor waited until the Vizier came back to her and asked the question of her before replying. It would be presumptuous of her to speak directly to the Sultan unless invited.

'My master wishes to know why you wear the trinket about your neck?'

'Because it has brought me good fortune,' Eleanor replied. 'I believe it protected me during the storm and afterwards when I was on the pirates' galley. I have not been treated ill—at least since I was brought to this country—and have known only kindness at the hands of Caliph Bakhar and my husband. Therefore, I kept it as a talisman even though my lord gave me finer jewels to wear.'

The Vizier glanced towards the Sultan once more, then back at Eleanor. 'His Magnificence has listened to your explanation. You may return to your apartments and await his judgement.' He did not return either the manuscript or its container to her.

'Thank you.' Eleanor let her veil fall forward to cover her face once more. 'I—I am grateful to you, my lord Vizier—and to his Magnificence for his patience.'

The Vizier waved her away, and she stood up, moving backwards from the hall until Karin touched her arm and told her they could now leave normally without giving offence.

She glanced at her friend when they were outside, but said nothing as they were conducted through the courtyard to the harem, which was a vast labyrinth of halls and rooms. The Royal Palace was the main residence of the Sultans of the Ottoman Empire and had been the headquarters of their seat of government from the year 1465. It was a huge complex of buildings, which was built on the Seraglio Point, overlooking the Mamara and the Bosphorus. The palace itself had been begun in 1459 by order of Sultan Muhammad II, who had conquered the city of Constantinople six years before that date.

It was here that the government and the elite units of the Janissaries lived, its various buildings separated by four large courtyards and many gardens. Karin had told Eleanor of the Divan in which the Grand Vizier and officials worked, and the school for the men who wished to learn about justice and government, besides the huge kitchens, the Imperial wardrobe—which was very large—and the harem baths.

'The Sultanas live in much grander state than we do at home,' she had told Eleanor. 'I have been told that the baths here have a domed roof supported on many pillars and are very beautiful.'

Eleanor was able to see for herself that the palace was richly appointed, and there were many marvels on display. She thought she caught sight of the magnificent clock Suleiman had given to his overlord, but she could not be certain. There were so many treasures, which stood testament to the Sultan's love of beautiful things. Besides those on show, she understood that there were storerooms filled with rare objects, and the armoury contained suits of fabulous armour used by the Sultans for ceremonial occasions.

'What will happen now?' she asked when they were alone again. 'Why did no one say anything about what had been decided? My lord was not there—do you think he has been imprisoned?'

'Patience,' Karin counselled. 'You did well, Eleanor. I do not know what will happen—but you were very convincing. And that trinket you wore—I think the Sultan was very interested in the story you told about that.'

'He did not return it to me,' Eleanor said. 'But I

do not care for such things. All I want is to be able
to go home with Suleiman.'

'It was a mere trinket,' Karin replied. 'I do not
suppose our master will wish to keep it—but it would
be a small price to pay if he let you have your way.'

'He may have it and welcome,' Eleanor replied.
'Though it is more than just a trinket—and part of a
far greater treasure, which may still exist somewhere.
It was discovered on my father's land in Cyprus, and
he had hoped he might find more in time.'

'Then it may please his Magnificence,' Karin said.
'We must hope so, Eleanor—for he will only grant
your wish if he believes your story.'

Eleanor looked at her fearfully. She had hoped that
Suleiman would be waiting for her when she was
taken to the Sultan's halls, but there had been no sign
of him. What had happened to him? She and Karin
had been treated kindly enough, but it might not have
been the same for her husband.

'How much longer do you think we shall be kept
here?' Eleanor asked. 'Oh, how I wish I knew what
was going on! Do you think the Sultan will send me
back with Count Salvadore? I do not like him, Karin,
and I fear what he may do. He wanted me for himself...'

'You must continue to be patient,' Karin warned.
'Remember that we can do nothing...we must await
our master's judgement. As I have told you before,
these things take time and diplomacy—they cannot
be rushed.'

Eleanor turned away, her eyes dark with rebellion.
She was angry at her own powerlessness, but there
was nothing she could do. She had been granted an
audience, which was more than might have been

granted her—and now she must do as Karin bid her and wait patiently. But, oh, how hard that was, when her whole being cried out for the man she loved!

Supposing they had beaten him—or put him to death? What had Suleiman Bakhar done that had so angered the Sultan that he should be arrested?

Was it because he had kept her for himself? Had the Sultan learned that she was to have been a gift to him—but surely the fabulous clock Suleiman had given him would bring a man who loved beautiful things so much more pleasure than any woman? He must have so many women in his harem already!

The thoughts went round and round in Eleanor's mind, torturing her. Yet she knew that she could do nothing to hasten the decision; she could only pray that when it came it would be the right one.

Eleanor looked at Karin and sighed. How much longer could she bear this? They had now been in the Sultan's harem for three days. At some point clothes had been brought for them from the Caliph's palace, so that they had their own things about them, but no one had spoken to them or told them anything.

Eleanor had wondered if a religious teacher would question her, but no one came and she was not sent for again. She had begun to think that she might be kept here for ever, and spent much of the time pacing about the little courtyard garden to which they had been given free access.

It was halfway through the fourth day that the Kadin who had brought them here came to tell them they were wanted.

'Where are you taking us?' Eleanor asked as she

beckoned them to follow. 'Are we to be taken to the Sultan again? What decision has been made?'

The Kadin smiled and shook her head. 'I do not know,' she said in her soft, husky voice. 'I have merely been told to show you the way.'

Eleanor's heart was pounding as they left the harem quarters under the escort of a eunuch. It was a different route to the one they had been taken previously and she thought they could not be going to the Sultan's halls this time. Where then were they being taken?

When at last they emerged into a large courtyard, she saw that it housed most of the service buildings, including the bakery, hospital and what Karin whispered was the mint. It was opened to the public and not the private part of the palace to which she had been taken the first time. Eleanor's heart caught with fright as she saw that two litters were waiting—one with an escort that she recognized as wearing the Caliph's colours of red and gold, and the other with the Sultan's colours.

'You must say goodbye now,' the eunuch told them. 'The lady Karin returns to the Caliph's household—you do not.'

'Where am I going?' Eleanor stared at her friend in horror. 'Karin—where are they taking me?'

'I do not know,' the older woman replied. She reached out to take Eleanor's hand and squeezed it tightly. 'I love you, my dear. Have courage. It is useless to resist—for they will only punish you, and Suleiman. Do as you are told and he may escape further punishment.'

'But he has done nothing,' Eleanor cried, the tears starting to her eyes. 'Oh, Karin! I cannot bear to leave you. I love you as the mother I lost long ago. Forgive me for all the trouble I have caused you...'

'You were never a trouble to me, only a joy and a delight,' Karin said. 'Go in peace, my daughter. I pray that Allah will guide your footsteps and bring you happiness.'

'I shall never be happy without Suleiman,' Eleanor wept, clinging to her hand. 'Oh, why must I go? Why will they send me away when all I want is to stay here?'

'It is the Sultan's will,' Karin replied. 'And he is guided only by Allah.'

Eleanor nodded, but looked at her through tear-misted eyes as they were parted, the eunuch urging them to enter the litters that had been provided for their transport.

Karin let go her hand, and Eleanor was obliged to do as she was told. She looked for Count Salvadore but could not see him—her escort was made up entirely of the Sultan's guard. Glancing back at the palace, she tried to send a message of farewell to her love.

'God bless and keep you,' she whispered. 'They may rend us apart, my darling, but no other man but you shall be my husband. This I swear—to keep faith with our love for my life long.'

Once inside the litter, she could no longer hold back her tears, and wept as all hope left her. She knew that the litter was carrying her towards the harbour and that a ship awaited her. She was being taken back to Italy against her will, and silently she raged against the power of men. Women were mere possessions, at the mercy of their menfolk! It was wrong that she should be treated thus for the second time in her life.

But no one should force her to marry. She would take her own life first. All she could hope for now was that her father would allow her to spend the rest of her life in prayer and study.

Eleanor's heart caught with pain as she saw the ship in the harbour. If she had hoped that she might after all be returned to the Caliph's palace, that hope vanished. It was a merchant ship…but that flag! Had she not sailed beneath such a flag before? It was her uncle's vessel—Sir John Faversham, merchant of Cyprus. She had thought to travel on the count's ship. He had not mentioned that her uncle was also here— though if truth were told she had not given him much encouragement to tell her anything.

A tall gentleman with grey hair and a neat beard was standing on deck, waiting to greet her. He was dressed in the manner of a wealthy Englishman, and was distinguished looking with faded blue eyes that seemed to look at her with understanding. She was, of course, still dressed as a woman of the harem, her face half covered by a fine veil.

'Eleanor—you are Eleanor?' he asked as he came to greet her, hands outstretched in greeting. 'My dear child, how glad I am to meet you at last. There were times when I feared I should never find you.'

'Sir John?' Eleanor looked at him uncertainly. 'You are my uncle?'

'Yes, child. Your mother was my sister and I loved her dearly. I have left no stone unturned to find you…'

'But I thought Count Salvadore… He said he was taking me to Italy—' She halted as her uncle frowned.

'That fellow sought to steal a march on me. He

hoped to find you and also reach a trading agreement with Suleiman the Magnificent. Fortunately, my own agreement was settled some months ago and I was able to reach the Sultan before him.'

'You were here before the count?' She stared at him. 'But it was he who…came to the palace to stop the marriage.'

'I could not prevent that, for he gave the Sultan a magnificent gift and out of politeness had to be given something in return…the customs here adhere to a strict ritual, Eleanor—which was something the count did not understand. He imagined that his gift would buy your freedom. However, that is not the way the Sultan does business—and your father's letter asks that you be given into my care, Eleanor. Sir William was unwell for some weeks, but is better now and on his way to Cyprus. He will be waiting for you when we arrive. I do not think that he quite trusted Count Salvadore—though he was forced to accept his help until he could contact me.'

'Do you know that I am married, Uncle?' Eleanor looked at him anxiously. 'Will you help me? My husband has been arrested and is a prisoner at the Sultan's palace.'

'All in good time,' her uncle said, smiling at her. 'We are about to sail for Cyprus, my child. Go below to your cabin and change into something more suitable—my cabin boy will show you where to go and I shall be with you shortly.'

Eleanor sighed. Once again, it seemed that she must obey. It was no different here than it had been in the palace. Suleiman had been so indulgent towards her, so generous. But at least she would soon see her father, for that at least she must be grateful.

If only she could stop this ache in her chest from threatening to crush the life from her. She wished that she might run back to the Sultan's palace and beg for her husband's release, but such actions would merely cause more trouble. Perhaps when they were back in Cyprus, she might persuade her uncle to make inquires. She might even persuade him to let her return—if Suleiman still lived.

She nodded to the young boy who had stopped outside what was clearly the most important cabin on board ship. Her uncle must have given up his own accommodation for her sake, which was kind of him.

She went inside, and then stopped as she saw someone standing by the porthole, her heart catching as she saw the tall, broad-shouldered man with his back towards her. He was dressed in the simple, traditional style he liked to adopt when private—yet it could not be!

'Suleiman?' she breathed, walking towards him as if she were in a dream. 'Is it really you?'

He turned and smiled at her, opening his arms as she gave a scream of surprise and delight and ran to him. His arms closed about her, crushing her to him as their lips met in a hungry kiss that made her feel like swooning.

'I thought you were still a prisoner,' she cried, the tears running down her cheeks. 'I thought they were sending me away from you—that I should never see you again.'

'Would you have cared so much, my dove?'

'You know I would! I should not want to live if I could not be your wife. I *am* your wife, Suleiman—and can never marry any other man.'

'If you do, I shall kill him!' Suleiman said hoarsely.

'Did you really think I would let you go, Eleanor? I would have fought my way out of the palace if necessary rather than lose you. Better I died than let you go away from me.'

'But what are you doing here on my uncle's ship?' Eleanor looked up at him uncertainly. 'Did you not tell me that you could never leave your father?'

'I do so only on the Sultan's orders,' Suleiman replied, his expression serious. 'I have seen my father and he gave me his blessing—but he knows the time has come for me to leave him. I am to be our master's ambassador, Eleanor. The Sultan wishes for more trade with merchants like your uncle, and he also wishes me to seek out a way of building peace between our empire and its enemies—if one can be found that does not require him to make concessions.'

'Do you think that is possible?' Eleanor asked doubtfully.

'Perhaps there is a chance—I cannot tell,' Suleiman said. 'As you know, there is a wide divide between the Christian and Muslim way of life. Much blood has been spilled, and much hatred exists between our peoples—but the Sultan and I spoke much on this subject privately, and we are agreed that the empire will suffer in time if nothing is done.'

Eleanor stared at him. 'You spoke to the Sultan yourself—directly to him and not the Grand Vizier?'

'Yes.' Suleiman laughed. 'You, of course, were not permitted to address him yourself—but have you forgot, my love—you are merely a woman and I am a man. The case is entirely different.'

'You! You are a wicked tease,' she replied, her eyes flashing at him. 'I should punish you for your arrogance, my lord. Do not forget that we shall not be in your country for much longer!'

'And yet I am your husband—and a woman is the property of her husband wherever she may be in the world, Eleanor. I am sorry, my love, but it is the way of men to be superior.'

'You… Oh, I shall punish you,' she cried and beat against him with her fists until he caught her wrists. Then he drew her to him once more to kiss her lips. She stopped fighting him and clung to him, her body melting into his as the love flowed through her. 'I was so frightened when they arrested you,' she said when he released her lips at last. 'I do not know what I should have done if we had been parted, my lord.'

'Nor I, my darling,' he murmured and touched her cheek with the tips of his fingers. 'I could not bear it any more than you. That is why I told the Sultan of my desire to serve him. It means that we must travel the world in search of treasures, Eleanor—and in doing trade perhaps we shall teach others that we Turks are not all as savage as they think us.'

'But what of your father? Shall you never see him again?'

'From time to time I shall return, to take back the treasures I have found—and to visit my home. My brother Bayezid will do his best to take my place, though I fear he would prefer to spend his time in study—but he will become my father's heir in my stead. It must be so or he would be exposed and vulnerable. Besides, Bayezid is worthy to take my father's place, more fitted for the honour of being Caliph than I could ever be.'

'Do you mind that, Suleiman?' she asked, looking at him anxiously.

'No—for I have used my privileges well, Eleanor. I am a wealthy man through my own endeavours, which is why the Sultan wanted me to become his ambassador. It was the clock I gave him that convinced him I was the man he sought for this task.'

'The clock you gave him instead of me?' Eleanor smiled up at him. 'I was sure he must be better pleased with such a gift than a mere woman.'

Suleiman laughed huskily. 'He told me that when he looked upon your face he was convinced that my taste in all things beautiful was not to be faulted. He said that a man who had the wisdom to choose such a woman over a clock was the man he desired as his representative in the capitals of the Western world.'

Eleanor blushed. 'I revealed my face so that the Vizier would know I did not lie about the fact that I had studied the Qur'an before I ever came to your country. Forgive me, my lord. I know it was immodest of me.'

'It was done for my sake,' Suleiman said. 'Besides, that custom belongs in my father's house—in your father's house you will wear the clothes you were used to before your abduction.'

'Must I?' Eleanor sighed. 'The clothes you gave me were so much more becoming—and so comfortable. May I not at least wear them in private?'

Suleiman laughed down at her. 'So—you have become a convert to our way of life after all.'

'Yes, my lord—though I am not sure what I believe in the matter of religion.'

'In that you are not alone,' Suleiman said and sighed. 'I learned of your faith from my mother, Eleanor—and I have studied the Bible. I do not know where the truth may lie.'

'Perhaps there is only one God,' Eleanor replied, wrinkling her brow in thought. 'He may be called different names and worshipped in different ways—but He remains the same.'

'I think that perhaps to believe something of that sort is the only way we can be at peace within ourselves,' Suleiman said. 'We must live good lives, Eleanor, you and I—and in that way we may achieve the ideal that all the gods tell us is the true way.'

'If only others could be as tolerant as you,' Eleanor said and sighed as she gazed up at him with love in her eyes. 'I am so lucky to have found you, my dearest husband. I do love you so very much.'

'And I love you,' he replied. 'Now you must change into the clothes your uncle has provided, Eleanor. Once we are at sea, he will come for you. For we are to be married by the captain of this ship.'

'Married?' Eleanor stared at him. 'But I am already your wife. Karin said the ceremony was complete.'

'According to Muslim law that is so, but your family will not be happy until we are married in their eyes—and that means under their law. Sir John explained to me that we could be married at sea by the captain of his ship and need not enter a Christian church—and I agreed that I would be happy to take part in such a ceremony for your sake.'

'You would do that for me?' She stared at him in wonder, her heart swelling with love for him.

'It is no more than you have already done for me.'

Suleiman came towards her, drawing her to him once more to kiss her on the lips tenderly. 'Had we never been married according to your law or mine, you would always have been my love—my life. You came to me as a slave, Eleanor—but you have become the queen of my heart. I know that I shall never love another woman.'

'And I shall never want more than your love,' she said. 'For you are all that I want and need...'

Epilogue

Eleanor stood looking out to sea as they left the shores of England far behind. She had thought never to return, but Suleiman had visited the English court as the Grand Turk's ambassador and she had gone with him. Afterwards, they had travelled to her old home in the west of England.

'It is just as you described it to me,' Suleiman had told her one night as they lay together in the huge four-poster bed after they had made love. 'Richard says that he will never return to England—but I think that we may choose to visit your home from time to time, my love.'

'Will my father sell the estate to you?'

Suleiman smiled down at her. Over the past three years he and Sir William had become firm friends, spending time examining many of the treasures Suleiman had discovered on his travels. Their return to Cyprus was always eagerly awaited—and it would be no different this time.

'Your father asked Richard his opinion first, my love—and he said that he had no objection.'

'I still cannot believe that you and my brother are friends.'

'I think that happened after our first child was born,' Suleiman replied. 'How could Richard hate me when he adores little Isabelle?'

Eleanor smiled and leaned against his shoulder as the shores of England faded into the distance. She had already given her lord a daughter and a son, Kasim, both of whom Suleiman spoiled dreadfully—but she was with child again.

They would teach their children to have open minds, to respect others and do what they could to unite the people of their two lands and cultures. And one day their children would live and flourish in the misty, beautiful countryside of her childhood home…

*   *   *   *   *

Modern Romance™
...seduction and
passion guaranteed

Tender Romance™
...love affairs that
last a lifetime

Sensual Romance™
...sassy, sexy and
seductive

Blaze
...sultry days and
steamy nights

Medical Romance™
...medical drama on
the pulse

Historical Romance™
...rich, vivid and
passionate

MILLS & BOON®

Winner at

2001 **IDEA** INTERNATIONAL
DESIGN
EFFECTIVENESS
AWARDS

MAT5

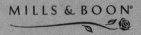

GIVE US YOUR THOUGHTS

Mills & Boon® want to give you the best possible read, so we have put together this short questionnaire to understand exactly what you enjoy reading.

Please tick the box that corresponds to how appealing you find each of the following storylines.

32 Richmond Square

They're fab, fashionable – and for rent. When the apartments in this central London location are let, the occupants find amazing things happen to their love lives. The mysterious landlord always makes sure that there's a happy ending for everyone who comes to live at number 32.

How much do you like this storyline?

❑ Strongly like ❑ Like ❑ Neutral – neither like nor dislike
❑ Dislike ❑ Strongly dislike

Please give reasons for your preference:

_____

_____

The Marriage Broker

This city agency matches marriage partners for practical as well as emotional reasons. Upmarket, discreet and with an international clientele, The Marriage Broker offers a personal service to match clients' needs and situations.

How much do you like this storyline?

❑ Strongly like ❑ Like ❑ Neutral – neither like nor dislike
❑ Dislike ❑ Strongly dislike

Please give reasons for your preference:

_____

_____

A Town Down Under

Meet the men of Paradise Creek, an Australian outback township, where temperatures and passions run high. These guys are rich, rugged and ripe for romance – because Paradise Creek needs eligible young women!

How much do you like this storyline?

❑ Strongly like   ❑ Like   ❑ Neutral – neither like nor dislike
❑ Dislike   ❑ Strongly dislike

Please give reasons for your preference:
_____

_____

The Marriage Treatment

Welcome to Byblis, an exclusive spa resort in the beautiful English countryside. None of the guests have ever found the one person who would make their private lives complete…until the legend of Byblis works its magic – and marriage proves to be the ultimate treatment!

How much do you like this storyline?

❑ Strongly like   ❑ Like   ❑ Neutral – neither like nor dislike
❑ Dislike   ❑ Strongly dislike

Please give reasons for your preference:
_____

_____

Name: _____

Address: _____

_____

Postcode: _____

Thank you for your help. Please return this to:

Mills & Boon (Publishers) Ltd
FREEPOST SEA 12282
RICHMOND, TW9 1BR

NO STAMP NEEDED – postage has been paid.

Coming in July

❧❧❧

The Ultimate
Betty Neels
Collection

❧❧❧

❋ A stunning 12 book collection beautifully
packaged for you to collect each month
from bestselling author Betty Neels.

❋ Loved by millions of women around the
world, this collection of heartwarming
stories will be a joy to treasure forever.

*Available at most branches of WH Smith,
Tesco, Martins, Borders, Eason, Sainsbury's
and most good paperback bookshops.*

2 FREE

books and a surprise gift!

We would like to take this opportunity to thank you for reading this Mills & Boon® book by offering you the chance to take TWO more specially selected titles from the Historical Romance™ series absolutely FREE! We're also making this offer to introduce you to the benefits of the Reader Service™—

- ★ FREE home delivery
- ★ FREE gifts and competitions
- ★ FREE monthly Newsletter
- ★ Exclusive Reader Service discount
- ★ Books available before they're in the shops

Accepting these FREE books and gift places you under no obligation to buy, you may cancel at any time, even after receiving your free shipment. Simply complete your details below and return the entire page to the address below. *You don't even need a stamp!*

YES! Please send me 2 free Historical Romance books and a surprise gift. I understand that unless you hear from me, I will receive 4 superb new titles every month for just £3.49 each, postage and packing free. I am under no obligation to purchase any books and may cancel my subscription at any time. The free books and gift will be mine to keep in any case.

H2ZEA

Ms/Mrs/Miss/Mr ....Initials...
                                                        BLOCK CAPITALS PLEASE

Surname ....

Address ....

....

....Postcode...................................

Send this whole page to:
UK: FREEPOST CN81, Croydon, CR9 3WZ
EIRE: PO Box 4546, Kilcock, County Kildare (stamp required)